Lord Thurston's
Challenge

Lord Thurston's Challenge

Fenella-Jane Miller

ROBERT HALE · LONDON

© Fenella-Jane Miller 2007
First published in Great Britain 2007

ISBN 978-0-7090-8338-2

Robert Hale Limited
Clerkenwell House
Clerkenwell Green
London EC1R 0HT

2 4 6 8 10 9 7 5 3 1

Typeset in 10/14pt Palatino
by Derek Doyle & Associates, Shaw Heath
Printed and bound in Great Britain
by Biddles Limited, King's Lynn

For Dusty – whose love and support has kept the dream alive.

CHAPTER ONE

England 1816

'PROMISE me, Charlotte, you must promise me, that when I am gone you will go to your grandfather; take Beth and Harry with you.'

Charlotte swallowed the lump in her throat. 'Please do not talk about dying, Mama; you have had worse bouts of fever and recovered. I am sure it will be no different this time.'

Mrs Carstairs closed her eyes, trying to marshal her remaining strength to extract a promise from her elder daughter. 'I have very little time; we both know that, my darling. You must give me your word that whatever your feelings on the matter, you will take your brother and sister to Thurston Hall and persuade my father to take you in.'

Charlotte had no choice. Her beloved mother was fading, how could she deny her last wish? Her eyes brimmed as she bent down to kiss her mother's pallid cheek. 'I promise. I shall do as you wish. I am going to call in Beth and Harry to say goodnight.' They both knew she meant goodbye.

She rose gracefully and hurried across the sparsely furnished bedchamber to the door. She opened it softly. 'Beth, Harry, you must come in now.'

At eleven, Beth was almost a replica of her older sister, with russet hair, and a perfect oval face. Her white pinafore was crumpled from her long wait outside the chamber and her faded, blue cambric dress, tight around her chest. The girl scrambled to her feet, green eyes huge in her pale face.

'Is it time? How can I bear it, Lottie?'

'You have to be brave, my love, for Harry's sake.' She knelt down and shook her little brother gently. 'Wake up, Harry. Mama wishes to speak to you.'

The boy yawned sleepily and rubbed his eyes, smiling up at her. Then he remembered and his face crumpled and he buried his face in her skirts.

'Hush now, darling. We must not upset Mama. She will be going to join Papa in Heaven very soon. We do not want her last moments here on earth to be sad, do we?'

Charlotte led the reluctant children back into the room, illuminated by a single candelabra, the three candles scarcely enough to see by. 'Mama, we are here. We love you and you must not worry. I shall take care of all of us. You can go to join Papa; he is waiting for you in Paradise.'

Mrs Carstairs opened her eyes and a faint smile flickered across her wasted features; then,with a barely audible hiss, she breathed her last. For a moment Charlotte did not understand what had happened. It was Beth who whispered to her.

'Lottie – Mama's not breathing anymore.' Then the girl snatched her hand free and ran, sobbing from the room. Before Charlotte could react, Harry vanished also, leaving her alone in the semi-darkness with the body of her mother.

Overwhelmed with grief, forgetting for a moment her promise to be strong, she collapsed across the bed, bathing her mother's rapidly cooling features with her tears. She heard footsteps behind her.

'Oh, miss, you must come away. Let me take care of madam now.' She felt the strong arms of her mother's maid lift her, and she made no protest.

'Thank you, Annie. I have to find the children, offer them what comfort I can.' She hesitated, for once at a loss.

'Go along, Miss Carstairs. Betty and I will take care of everything here. I sent young Bill to fetch the undertaker. Your mother did not wish you to be involved with the laying out.'

Charlotte left; there was nothing there to keep her. She paused in the draughty passageway, scrubbing her cheeks dry with her fists. She must push her own grief aside; she was the only mother Beth and Harry had now.

If only there was more time, but she knew the funds they had relied on for the past two years would cease on her mother's death. They had barely managed these past few months as it was; the medical bills had bitten deeply into their limited resources.

The small house was rented, and was theirs for a few weeks longer, but then they would have to seek alternative accommodation, and it would have to be with Lord Thurston. She shivered at the thought of approaching the man who had cast off her mother when she had refused to marry the suitor he had selected for her and chosen instead to marry her childhood sweetheart, the dashing army captain, who had become her father, Major Charles Carstairs.

Charlotte recalled the terrible time two years ago when Papa had returned from the Battle of Waterloo grievously wounded. He had lingered on, in agony, before finally succumbing to his injuries a year ago. She had had only Annie and Betty to turn to for advice. She had felt it would be unfitting to discuss such matters with the staff so had made the decision to write to Lord Thurston herself. The letter had been returned. It had been opened, but there was no reply. From that moment she had formed an implacable hatred for her grandfather who had rejected his only child for the second time. Now she had promised to take the children to live with him.

This would not do: she had responsibilities. Whatever her own feelings, when matters were concluded here, she had to travel to Thurston Hall. She had given her word.

However, *she* would not stay there; she was determined to find a position as a housekeeper, or maybe a companion. As soon as the children were comfortable she would depart, knowing she had fulfilled her mother's deathbed request. At nineteen she felt she was quite old enough to fend for herself. She was an accomplished seamstress, indeed, made all the family's clothes, and she could cook, clean, and manage a household.

She knew she would be considered too young for employment as a governess but prayed she might find a more menial position some-where in the ranks of the wealthy tradespeople. It was possible that one of them might be glad to employ a gentlewoman such as herself.

Upstairs, she discovered her siblings – Beth cradling her brother, rocking back and forth, as they both cried. 'Come along, Beth, that will do,' Charlotte admonished her gently. 'You are not helping. We must be strong. Harry is too small to understand.'

The small boy raised his tear-streaked face. 'I am not small, I'm a big boy. I'm four years old!'

'You are, my love. And big boys do not cry; they are brave and strong.' She bent down, pulling the children to their feet. 'We must look to the future. Mama is happy now with Papa in Heaven.'

Three weeks later, at seven o'clock, Charlotte closed the door of the house in which she had spent the last five years, and led her small party down the steps to the waiting diligence.

'Mornin', Miss Carstairs. A lovely day for a journey,' Mr Turner, the carter, called as he waited, reins in hand, to depart. 'Your trunks are all safely stowed.'

'Thank you, Mr Turner; I am sorry we have kept you waiting.' Charlotte lifted Harry into the vehicle and offered her hand to Beth, who ignored it and scrambled up unaided. 'Annie, can you and Betty manage the carpetbags, or do you need Mr Turner's assistance?'

'Bless you, we can manage fine, thank you, miss. You get yourselves settled; Betty and I can take care of the bags.'

Glad that both Annie and Betty had decided to take their chances with them at Thurston Hall, Charlotte climbed into the cart. Harry and Beth shifted up the hard wooden seat to make room for her. Once Annie and Betty were safely aboard, seated next to Mr Turner, he slapped the reins and the large brown horse ambled forward.

'Is it far to the White Hart, Lottie?' Harry asked between bounces.

She righted her bonnet before answering. 'A mile, no more. I have allowed ample time to reach our destination. The mail coach does not depart until twelve minutes past nine.'

Beth chimed in. 'Is Thurston Hall a long way from Ipswich, Lottie?

Will Grandfather send a carriage for us, do you think?'

Charlotte hated to lie to them, but she had no choice. 'Thurston Hall is less than five miles from Ipswich, where we alight from the mail coach tomorrow, and I am sure Grandfather will have made some arrangement to transport all of us to our new home.'

She could not tell any of them that Lord Thurston was not even aware of their imminent arrival. She had decided it would be better to give him no opportunity to refuse to take them in. It would be much harder to send them packing if they were already on his doorstep.

By the time they arrived in Ipswich and descended, for the last time, from the mail coach, the children were fractious and the adults exhausted. Charlotte checked the time on the large clock in the vestibule of the inn. 'It is too late to travel to Thurston today. We shall overnight here and set out, refreshed and tidy, tomorrow morning.'

Luckily there was a commodious front room available which housed two tester beds and still had room left over for a table and chairs in the bay window. Trays were sent up, stacked high with cold meats, pickles and pastries, also several slices of a rich plum cake.

'This looks appetizing – as soon as we have eaten I think we must all retire.'

Annie nodded. 'We're all that tired, Miss Carstairs, we've been jolted around in that mail coach for the best part of two days and it's an exhausting business, especially for someone of my age.'

Charlotte attempted to shake out the creases in her travelling dress. 'Annie, if you and Betty will see to the children, I have business to attend to downstairs.'

'Yes, miss.'

Downstairs the vestibule was empty, no one behind the desk. Charlotte rang the bell vigorously. The passengers from the mail coach, who were continuing their journey to Norwich, had long since departed. The landlady bustled through from a back room, wiping her work roughened hands on her apron.

'Miss Carstairs, I hopes as nothing's wrong?'

'No, Mrs Brady, the room is perfect and the food was excellent. It is another matter entirely that I wish to discuss with you.'

'Yes, Miss Carstairs, I'll do what I can to help.'

'I shall require transport of some sort tomorrow morning to convey us to our final destination. Can you arrange that for me?'

Mrs Brady nodded, her many chins wobbling. 'Indeed I can. We have a suitable conveyance here. My son, Ned, can drive you anywhere you wish to go. What time will you be wishing to leave?'

Charlotte thought for a moment. It would not do to arrive too early; Lord Thurston was an elderly gentleman, so he might not rise before noon. She had checked and knew the village of Thurston to be a journey of less than five miles; not much more than an hour or so even on narrow, rutted lanes. 'I do not wish to leave until eleven o'clock. It is my intention to look around the town before we go.'

'Very well, miss. What time shall I have your trays sent up tomorrow morning?'

'Could you send up several jugs of hot water at eight o'clock? Then we shall break our fast at nine.'

The landlady nodded and bobbed a curtsy. She recognized gentry when she saw it, however unfashionably dressed. 'If you require anything else, just ring the bell in your chamber, Miss Carstairs.'

'Goodnight, Mrs Brady. Thank you for your help.'

At eleven o'clock sharp Charlotte escorted her brother and sister downstairs. They were all dressed in their best. Harry, in smart royal-blue velvet britches and jacket, his shirt white and his stockings, pulled up for once, pristine in his black shiny boots. Beth, her hair in one thick braid, with green ribbons threaded through it, was in a dress of moss green cotton, her spencer in a darker shade of that same colour. This had been beautifully embroidered with a riot of flowers and birds by her sister.

'You look very smart, Harry. Please try not to get any grime on your shirt or stockings on the journey,' Charlotte told her little brother.

'Promise, Lottie.' He grinned as he spoke; the excitement of the journey had already overtaken the grief for his mother. Beth reached out and ran her fingers down her sister's skirt of fine French cambric, in a becoming shade of palest gold.

'This gown is so beautiful, Lottie. I wish Mama could see you now.'

Charlotte's eyes filled but she pinned a smile on her face. 'Thank you, darling. I am glad you approve. I am particularly fond of the darker gold material from which I made the spencer, and of my chip-straw bonnet. It took me hours to pleat the matching material that lines it.' She glanced down, confident that they all looked very well turned out. Her brown half boots and York tan gloves, she believed, set off her ensemble perfectly.

'Look, Annie and Betty are waiting by that smart gig. I do believe we are to travel in style today.' She glanced round but could see no sign of the trunks and bags anywhere. 'Annie, where are our things? I do hope they are not to be left behind.'

Annie pointed to a smaller cart. 'They're in that, miss; it is to follow us. Do you wish us to travel with the baggage, or in here with you?'

Beth spoke first. 'In here, Annie. You and Betty are far too finely dressed to travel anywhere else.'

The maid's creased face split into a happy smile. 'Why bless you, Miss Beth. Don't we all look fine as paint this morning?'

Charlotte, meanwhile, had become uncomfortably aware that a huge gentleman, in a many caped riding coat, his face obscured by his turned-up collar, was staring at her most rudely. Perhaps her dress was a trifle low-cut for a country town and exposed more of her creamy bosom than she was accustomed to. She wished she had buttoned up her spencer, but it was too late to repine. Feeling flustered by the unwanted attention, she bundled her charges up the steps of the carriage and jumped in behind them. She tapped loudly with her parasol to indicate that they were ready to depart. When the carriage failed to move she drew breath to protest, but the driver, young Ned Brady, grinned over his shoulder.

'Where to, Miss Carstairs? You never told me ma last night, where you want to go this morning.'

Blushing furiously at her stupidity she spoke rather more loudly than she had intended. 'To Thurston Hall, Thurston village, if you please, Ned.' The carriage bowled out of the yard, closely followed by the pony cart containing their two trunks and four carpetbags.

The tall man, in the drab coat, on overhearing her remarks, swore loudly, deeply shocking two elderly matrons on their way to book seats for the following day's mail coach to Norwich. He vaulted on to his grey stallion and galloped out of the yard moments after Charlotte's party had left.

The gig travelled past pretty villages, the whitewashed cottages well kept, their thatched roofs immaculate. Smiling, well-fed children came out to wave as they passed, much to Harry's delight.

'Why are we not wearing black, again, Lottie?' Beth asked later, as she studied her green dress with interest.

'Mama said we had been in black for far too long already. She made me promise we would not go in to mourning for her, but continue as normal.' She felt as if a stone had lodged in her throat and for a moment she was unable to speak.

Harry, unaware of her distress, piped up. 'Look, Lottie, those cottages have holes in the roof. They are not at all clean and white like the others.'

Charlotte pushed her misery aside to follow his pointing finger. Automatically she corrected his behaviour. 'You must not point, Harry; you know it is impolite.' His hand dropped instantly to his lap. 'You are quite correct, my dear. These dwellings do not appear well maintained. Do you see, there are no hens or hog houses either?'

Annie sniffed loudly. 'An absentee landlord, miss, or an uncaring one. There's some who squeeze their poor tenants dry and never put naught back.'

Beth sank back against the squabs. 'Did you see how those men scowled at us? And they were so thin and raggedy looking.'

'Things are harder in the countryside when the landlord does not look after his own. The price of corn is so high and there is little outside work to be had in areas such as these. In fact—'

Her words were lost in a scream as a stone, hurled by an unseen assailant, struck her on the temple. She slipped into unconsciousness, blood pouring from her forehead, to the floor.

Ned whipped up his horse. 'Hold on, ladies, we're not far from Thurston Hall; you'll be safe there.'

14

CHAPTER TWO

L ORD Thurston stormed into the house, his face a mask of fury. 'Meltham get in here – damn you!' A black-garbed man of indeterminate years scampered across the grimy marble floor and knocked on the drawing-room door.

'You wish to speak to me, my lord?'

Jack's jaw clenched but, for once, he refrained from swearing. 'Yes. I expect a parcel of ladies to arrive later today. Do not let them over the threshold; is that quite clear?'

The butler shook his head. 'Ladies, my lord?'

'God dammit, man, yes; ladies and children! Whatever they say, you will not let them in. Your position here depends on it.'

Meltham blanched. He knew more than likely it was his life depended on it. 'Of course, my lord. I fully understand.'

Jack watched him shuffle backwards reminding him of a black crab and a flicker of amusement crossed his face. He strode down the worn carpet to the walnut sideboard upon which his decanter of brandy was waiting. He poured himself a liberal glass and finished it in one swallow. He waited for the fiery liquid to hit his gut – start its healing work.

Slowly his pulse steadied and he regained his composure. My God, what a lucky escape! If he had not been returning from that overnight cockfight, he would never have seen the girl, and her entourage, emerge from the inn. Nor have heard her instruct the driver to take her to Thurston Hall. If he had not been able to arrive before them, he would have returned to find them ensconced, waiting to speak to him.

He would have been obliged to see a pair of sparkling green eyes round with horror, see that lovely girl turn away in disgust. He snatched at the decanter and refilled his glass and for the second time it disappeared in a single gulp.

He knew he was drinking too much, had become careless of his appearance, took no interest in his estate, but he could not help himself. The day the Frenchie's sabre slashed through his face his life had changed irrevocably. He had lost the sight in his right eye, and his cheek and corner of his mouth were twisted. He was a monster, not fit for female company.

Even discovering on his arrival in England, that he had inherited Thurston Hall from a distant uncle, that he was no longer plain Major Jack Griffin but Lord Thurston of Thurston Hall, a local magistrate, owner of three villages, eight farms and several thousand acres of land, had not made up for his disfigurement. But at least it gave him somewhere to hole up out of sight, so that he did not have to endure the stares of revulsion from strangers and the looks of pity from his friends.

His fists clenched and the glass shattered in his hand. He threw the broken crystal shards into the fire, ignoring the blood that dribbled from his palm. Damn it! He needed another drink to ease the pain – to erase the image of Miss Sophia Owens's gasp of shock when she saw her betrothed for the first time. She had turned her back, holding up a hand as if to ward away a leper. Her words had cut him to the quick: 'You are hideous, Jack. I cannot marry a man so disfigured. I beg you to release me from our arrangement.'

He reached over with his good hand and pulled the bell-strap. Meltham appeared immediately. There were no parlour maids to answer his summons. He kept no female staff at Thurston Hall.

'Bring me another glass. This one is broken.'

He heard the startled gasp from behind him. Then his hand was lifted and a clean white napkin bound around it. He kept his face averted, touched by the small act of kindness.

'My lord, you will require sutures in that cut. If you permit, I shall send for the physician; he lives in nearby Upton Magna.'

Jack shrugged, indifferent. Bleeding to death was as good a way as any to go, and pain free. The butler took his gesture as agreement and hurried off to find a groom to take the message.

The gig thundered through the wrought-iron gates and on to the long drive, Charlotte was still comatose but now her head was cradled in Annie's ample lap. Two strips of torn white petticoat held a makeshift pad across her wound, partially stemming the copious flow of blood.

Beth was gripping the sides of the violently rocking carriage with one hand and holding on to Harry with the other. 'Betty,' she whispered, 'why does God keep hurting the people that I love? How can he be a loving Father if He does that?'

'Hush, Miss Beth, you must not talk like that. We are in His hands and must endure whatever He puts in our way. Say a prayer, miss, it will help you and your sister.'

The drive ran through overhanging trees, the grass verges unscythed, more like a meadow than the entrance to a grand estate. But no one in the swaying carriage noticed this, nor did they see the weeds growing through the gravel, or observe the dilapidation of the massive house. All the occupants cared was that they had arrived and help was at hand.

The vehicle was scarcely stationary before Ned threw down the reins and raced for the front door. He hammered on it. 'Open up! We have an injured lady – she needs assistance. Open up in there.'

The door swung open a fraction and Meltham peered out. 'I am sorry, but I have instructions not to let you in. Lord Thurston does not receive visitors. You will have to go away.'

'We shall do no such thing,' Betty shouted, as she barrelled her way up to the massive access. Without waiting for a second refusal she put her shoulder to the crack and pushed. The butler had no option, he yielded, glad the matter had been taken from his hands. The noise in the hall was heard by Lord Thurston.

The drawing-room door opened and he emerged, his voice dripping ice. 'How dare you intrude in my house? Remove yourself, madam, this instant.' He was so enraged he did not notice that the servant woman appeared unmoved by his disfigurement.

'My lord, my mistress, Miss Carstairs, is grievously injured. Someone threw a stone as we passed through the last village and it struck her on the forehead. She is still unconscious.'

Jack, for the first time since his return from Waterloo, took charge of events. 'Meltham, have a chamber prepared. I shall bring the lady inside.' He covered the distance from the door to the turning circle in three bounds. He bent down and his heart faltered. Was it too late?

'Here, let me take her.' Without waiting for an answer he scooped Charlotte up and, holding her carefully, the injured temple away from his shoulder, strode back inside, leaving Annie to follow on with Beth and Harry. 'Meltham, where shall I take her?' His deep voice ricocheted around the empty hallway.

The butler appeared on the gallery. 'Here, my lord. The green rooms are in reasonable repair. I have two footmen making up the bed and hot water is being fetched from the scullery.'

Jack did not like the way the girl's head lolled on his shoulder, or the darkening red stain on the bandage that covered her wound. Head wounds were the very devil. He had lost good men from apparently trivial injuries to the skull. Carefully, he adjusted his burden and climbed the carved oak stairs, his booted feet loud on the boards. He could hear the maid puffing along behind him and was glad of it.

The butler led him to the rear of the house. He had never bothered to visit this part of the rambling building. The room chosen was large and light, with windows overlooking the unkempt park. The four-poster bed, its hangings dusty and torn, stood isolated in the centre of the room.

'God damn it, man, is there nothing better than this? There is no furniture and the chamber smells musty and damp.'

'It is the best there is, my lord. The previous Lord Thurston sadly neglected this part of the hall. He resided, as you do, downstairs, and never came up here after Miss Emily left.'

Jack scowled. 'If there is nothing else, then this will have to do.' He placed Charlotte gently on the bed then, pushing away the blood-soaked hair from her face, he gazed down at the injured girl. She was so beautiful – even ashen-faced and covered in gore. He studied the perfect oval of her countenance, her finally arched brows, her short nose with its delicate nostrils and her eminently kissable mouth. He felt a hardening in his groin and half smiled – it was certainly a day for firsts.

'Step aside, if you please, sir; I must attend to Miss Carstairs,' Betty said firmly. 'She needs to see a doctor urgently.'

He moved back. 'Fortuitously, a physician has already been sent for as I need sutures in my hand.'

Betty glanced back at the red-stained cloth around his hand. 'That's good news, sir. I shall require our trunks and bags be brought up when they arrive and hot water and clean cloths.'

'My man will see to all that.' He straightened, the habitual sneer back in his voice. 'You are intending to make a long stay then, madam?'

Betty snorted. 'This is to be our home now. I have no inkling who you might be, sir, but Lord Thurston, Miss Carstairs's grandfather, is to be informed at once of our arrival.'

'Christ in His Heaven! What next? The old man has been dead these past two years. I am Lord Thurston. And I can assure you, madam, that as soon as Miss Carstairs is well enough she, and the brats, will be leaving here.'

Betty turned to stare at the formidable man glaring across the bedchamber. 'If you are Lord Thurston then you will be Miss Carstairs, Miss Elizabeth and Master Harry's legal guardian. You cannot evict them, for they are your responsibility.'

The sound of running footsteps in the passageway outside alerted Jack to the arrival of the hated children. They were worse than adults for pointing and staring and asking in loud piercing voices why the gentleman was so hideous.

'I have no intention of discussing the matter with a servant. Get on with your duties.' He spun and left the room his head down, his right-hand obscuring his injury, ignoring the arrival of the nursemaid and her charges.

He headed back to his own domain. The drawing-room, study and morning-room – now serving as his bedchamber – were the only places he felt safe. He needed a drink – badly. What he didn't need was a parcel of brats and their sister foisted on him. They could stay for the moment, a week or so, until the girl was well enough to travel, then he would send them packing.

Charlotte opened her eyes, unsure where she was or why her head hurt so abominably. She was in a strange dark room; it was not the room at the inn for that had contained more furniture. She tried to raise herself and instantly regretted it. A wave of nausea flooded over her and she sank back on the pillows.

'Oh miss, you're awake, I'm so glad. You have given us quite a turn these past few days.' Annie dipped a cloth into a chipped china bowl and carefully wiped Charlotte's face. 'There, is that better?'

'A little.' Her voice was scarcely audible. 'Where am I? Why am I hurt?'

'You're at Thurston Hall, miss – you was struck by a stone. The doctor has visited every day, and very nice soft-spoken man he is too, and he insists that you remain in your bed for a day or two longer, at least.' Annie fussed with the bed covers. 'You have a concussion and a nasty cut, but it has been stitched up a treat.'

'Good. And the children, how are they?'

'They love it here. Betty is taking care of them so you mustn't worry. Just rest and recover yourself, miss.'

Charlotte closed her eyes; even with shutters the sun filtered through and aggravated her headache. Why had Annie not pulled the bed hangings? Feeling too ill to ask, she allowed the welcome blackness to sweep her away once more.

It was early the next morning when she was woken by a shuffling and rustling and muted whispers. Her lips curved in welcome. 'Beth, Harry, come over and speak to me. Do not hide in the shadows like burglars.'

'Lottie, you're well again. We have been so worried, but neither Annie nor Betty would let us in,' Beth said, as she hurried to the bedside.

'And we were ever so quiet – did you really think we were robbers?'
Harry asked.

Charlotte opened her eyes. The room, this time, remained still. She
risked turning her head a few inches – no searing pain. 'Help me to sit
up, both of you. I want to know what Thurston Hall is like and what
you have both been doing these past few days to occupy yourself. And
more importantly, how did Grandfather take to our arrival?'

Beth managed to pull her forward whilst Harry pushed a pile of
wilted pillows behind her.

'There, Lottie, you can lean back, you'll be comfortable now.'

'Thank you, Harry, that is splendid. And thank you, Beth darling.
Now, can you and Harry open the shutters? I would really like to see
exactly how unsatisfactory my chamber is.'

The children ran across and with much banging and muttering
finally achieved their objective. Sunlight flooded the room and
Charlotte glanced around in horror. 'Good heavens! There is no carpet,
no *chaise-longue*, or indeed furniture of any sort in here. It is far worse
than I thought.'

Harry scrambled up beside her on the bed. 'The whole house is like
this, Lottie,' he told her gleefully. 'I can run about where I like and not
break anything and the mud from my boots does not notice on the
floors.'

'Oh dear! Beth? Is it as bad as Harry suggests?'

'It is. Annie and Betty have scrubbed and cleaned the rooms we're
using, but the rest of the Hall is in a dreadful state. Do you know we've
even seen rats running along the nursery floors?'

Charlotte shuddered. What had she brought the children to? Her
mother had always spoken of Thurston Hall as well appointed, well
run and comfortable. Had Grandfather lost his fortune dabbling in the
funds? Or had he gambled it away? A small door, hidden in the dark
panelled wall, flew open and Annie emerged, a tray in her hands.

'You scamps! Poor Betty is searching everywhere for you. Your
breakfast is ready and waiting in your parlour. Off you go now.'

Charlotte watched the children run out, her brow creased. 'Annie,
they have been telling the most dreadful tales. Please assure me they

are exaggerating about the parlous state of this establishment.'

'No, miss, they aren't. This place is a disgrace – falling down almost – and no staff to keep it clean. Only three footmen and the butler, and no outside men at all, apart from a couple of grooms and the coachman.'

Charlotte's head began to thump, her initial optimism fading. 'And Grandfather?'

'That's the worst of it, miss. Your grandpa died two years since. The present Lord Thurston is a madman, begging your pardon, Miss Carstairs.'

'Whatever do you mean?'

'Well, when he isn't hiding away in his rooms drinking brandy, he is galloping all over the neighbourhood on one of his half-broken stallions. He takes no interest in the house, estate, or his own appearance.'

'Go on, Annie, what are you not telling me?'

'Well, miss, he has said as we are to leave here as soon as you are well. I told him that he was now your legal guardian, but he was having none of it. He said as he would discuss the matter with you when you was up to it.'

Charlotte closed her eyes in despair. If Lord Thurston turned them out they would be destitute, taken to the poorhouse, or worse. She could not let it happen. If only her head did not hurt so much, she was sure she would be able to think of a solution. She drew a calming breath and the appetizing smell of chocolate and warm fresh bread wafted across from the tray Annie was holding.

'I believe that I am hungry. Maybe when I have eaten, bathed and dressed I shall feel more ready to face this problem.'

'You mustn't get up, Miss Carstairs, the doctor was adamant. But he'll be calling later today and you can ask him then when it is permissible for you to get dressed.'

She smiled; when had Annie become so determined? 'Very well, but I would really like a bath and fresh nightwear.'

'There's a hip-bath in the dressing-room. I'll have it filled for you whilst you're eating,' Annie told her with a smile.

*

By mid-afternoon, bathed and refreshed, Charlotte sat propped up in a freshly made bed, her young brother and sister beside her. So far she had heard the stables held only two riding horses and four matched bays to pull either a high-perch phaeton or a curricle. There were no cats or dogs to play with, but there was an overgrown maze in the garden. She thought it odd that neither child had mentioned Lord Thurston.

'Beth, what is Lord Thurston like? What manner of man is he?'

'We have only seen him the once, Lottie, when we arrived. He is very tall and he has long dark hair tied at the back with a ribbon.'

Harry joined in. 'He's broad as well; he has dirty boots and he stays in his rooms.'

'Well, I shall just have to wait until I am well enough to get up and meet him for myself.'

'Annie and Betty have spoken with him so they can tell you what he's like,' Beth told her.

'In that case, I shall ask one of them when they return. Do you know exactly where they are, Beth? It seems an age since I saw either one.'

'They are scrubbing out the kitchen because it was full of—'

'Oh pray, do not tell me! I have no desire to know what awful things reside in there.'

Beth grinned. 'Can we go down to the maze? You can see it from your window if you look out, and then we can wave to you.'

'As I am in bed that is of little help. But go – I am sure it is safe. On your way out to the garden please tell Annie to come and speak to me.'

She swung her legs to the floor for the second time that day. Her head remained on her shoulders and her legs did not tremble. She stood, holding on to an oak corner post to steady herself. Should she risk a small walk around the room? She would dearly like to see the maze; she recalled her mother had mentioned it once.

The journey to the window was slow but completed without mishap. She collapsed gratefully on the wooden window seat and rested her face against the leaded panes. Yes, there it was, but where were the smooth lawns and trimmed and cultivated flowerbeds? It was a veritable meadow – long golden grass flecked with late poppies and

23

cornflowers stretched in all directions. The yew maze was discernible, but so dense she wondered how the children were managing to negotiate it.

The stone mullion was cool beneath her fingertips and she was glad she had on her thick wrapper. She heard heavy footsteps approaching and smiled. At last; Annie was coming up to answer her questions. It did not occur to her to question why her maidservant was not using the servant's passage.

The knock on the door was loud, startling her. 'Come in.'

The bedchamber door swung open and a man in his shirt sleeves and stockings, burst in. Her mouth rounded in shock. His eyes narrowed in appreciation.

'I beg your pardon for intruding, Miss Carstairs, but I need to talk to you.'

She shrunk back into the embrasure, her hands clenched in her lap. He looked so big, so tough and so very angry. It was only then she noticed the vicious scar that ran from the right side of his temple, down across the corner of his eye to his mouth. He was a soldier, no wonder he appeared formidable.

'Excuse me, my lord, but I must ask you to leave my room, this instant.'

His mouth curled with contempt. These words had an all too familiar ring. 'I shall do as you bid. But speak to you I shall. And sooner, rather than later.'

She watched him straighten his shoulders and turn. He swayed, and for a moment she thought he would fall, but he regained control of his limbs and left the chamber as abruptly as he had entered. She felt strangely stimulated by the unexpected encounter. She scrambled to her feet and walked across to the bell rope by the mantelshelf.

She tugged it hard. There was a rattle, a cloud of plaster and dust, and it came free from the ceiling leaving a gaping hole in its place. Coughing and spluttering, she stepped away from the debris.

'Good lord, miss, whatever next?' Annie bustled in, her round features creased with concern.

'I am unhurt, but I now have a large hole in my ceiling.' She grinned.

'I have just received a visit from Lord Thurston. I know, do not poker up, Annie, I sent him out immediately.'

'I should hope so too. Whatever was Lord Thurston thinking of, to visit you here, like that?'

'I do not believe he was thinking at all; I believe he was a trifle bosky. Imagine coming to see me in his shirt sleeves and stockings!'

'And you should not be out of bed; remember what Dr Andrews said?'

Charlotte shrugged. 'I have no recollection of any doctor saying anything. However, I intend to get up, with or without your assistance.'

'If you insist, Miss Carstairs. You sit down on the bed whilst I fetch your garments. Is there anything particular you wish to wear?'

There was not a great deal of choice in her limited wardrobe. 'I should like to wear my green afternoon dress. The one with the long sleeves and high neckline.' She had no intention of exposing her bosom to Lord Thurston twice in one day.

It took longer than usual for Charlotte to be dressed to her satisfaction. 'I think that will suffice, Annie, thank you. It is too painful to have my hair up. I shall have to leave it in a braid down my back, like Beth.' She stood up, surprised to find her legs unsteady. Furtively, she gripped the bed post. It would never do to betray her weakness, or her maid might insist that she accompanied her downstairs.

'The children are outside in the garden and I am going to join them, but first I shall sit down for a while, and enjoy the view from the window. I am sure you have duties to perform elsewhere, Annie. Beth was telling me about the kitchen.'

'Indeed I do, miss. The house is a disgrace. I must go down right away and find someone to repair the ceiling. You cannot sleep in this room until it is done.'

Charlotte shivered. 'Rats?'

Annie nodded. 'What we need here are a couple of cats and a terrier or two; they would soon rid the place of vermin.'

Charlotte waited until Annie had vanished through the servant's door. Then she stood up, shook out her skirts, checked her appearance for the last time and left the comparative safety of her chamber to seek an audience with Lord Thurston.

CHAPTER THREE

CHARLOTTE paused; the passage stretched in both directions, the sunlight highlighting the cobwebs that festooned the ceilings and walls. She smiled as she realized that all she had to do was follow Lord Thurston's footprints in the dust, for they were clearly discernible on the floor. She didn't attempt to look through the grimy windows; she could guess what scenes of neglect would meet her eye.

The long corridor became lighter as she approached the gallery that overlooked the entrance hall. She glanced down not surprised to see that the hem of her gown was already blackened. Her mouth curled ruefully; she doubted Lord Thurston would notice in his inebriated state. She admired the ornately carved banisters, noticing the heraldic animals and flowers but, like the rest of the house, they were sadly in need of a good polish.

The entrance hall was deserted – no sign of the butler or any footmen. She stopped, unsure which of the many closed doors was the one she sought. It was impossible to follow the footprints down here; there were too many other marks obscuring them.

'Can I help you, Miss Carstairs?' The voice came from behind her and Charlotte exclaimed in shock.

'Good heavens! You startled me.' She glared at the elderly man in faded black tailcoat. 'I presume you are the butler?'

'Yes, miss.' He bowed. 'I am Meltham, at your service.'

'In which room shall I discover Lord Thurston? I wish to speak to him urgently.' She saw the shocked expression on the butler's face.

'Lord Thurston had the temerity to visit me in my chambers. I agreed to come down directly and speak to him in more suitable surroundings.' This was a half-truth but it served.

Meltham relaxed. 'In that case, Miss Carstairs, I shall announce you.' He frowned. 'I must inform you, miss, that his lordship is not quite himself this afternoon.'

'If you are trying to tell me in a roundabout way that he is in his cups, then I am well aware of that, I can assure you.' She smiled and, decrepit as he was, the butler felt his heart skip a beat or two.

'I shall remain in the vicinity, Miss Carstairs, in case you should have need of me.' She understood his message.

'Thank you. That is kind of you.'

The butler led her across the dark empty space which even the glass set into the high vaulted ceiling failed to illuminate, for these panes were so obscured by dirt that they failed to let in sufficient sunlight. Charlotte fixed her eyes ahead, resolutely ignoring the signs of decay all around her.

The butler halted in front of dark panelled doors, almost indistinguishable in a wall of the same material. He knocked, then paused, waiting to hear the reply.

'Come in, damn you, Meltham.'

Charlotte stood behind him, her fingers clenched into fists and her pulse racing.

'Are you quite sure you wish to see Lord Thurston? Perhaps it would be better to leave it until another time, Miss Carstairs?'

'No, announce me, please. I shall see him.' Her voice did not reflect her nervousness.

The doors were opened and the butler stepped aside. A wave of alcoholic fumes and the stench of unwashed humanity engulfed her and for an instant she recoiled. Forcing down her distaste she tried to see past Meltham into the gloom beyond.

'Miss Carstairs wishes to speak to you, my lord. Are you receiving visitors this afternoon?'

There was a pause, as if he was considering his response. Then a deep baritone replied, 'Then send her in, man, send her in.'

The room was dark, the shutters closed blocking out the autumn sunlight. A huge fire burned brightly in the cavernous fireplace making the room not only foul smelling but uncomfortably hot. She took a few tentative steps forward but was still unable to see her quarry. Where was he? Slowly her eyes adjusted and a slight movement from the depths of a battered leather armchair, facing the fire, attracted her attention.

She moved further into the room. Yes – it was he! Lord Thurston had not bothered to stand up to greet her and this omission annoyed her. He sprawled, glass in hand, his face hidden by the wings of the chair. This was outrageous! How dare he treat her so uncivilly? First he had barged into her bedchamber, now he remained seated in her presence. The man was a disgrace to his title. Grandfather must be turning in his grave.

Fuelled by her righteous indignation at his unmannerly behaviour, she sailed across the room to halt a few feet from him. 'Lord Thurston, you are no gentleman.'

His harsh laugh made her regret her rash decision to enter his domain. 'I do not profess to be one. I am as you see me; either accept, or depart, the choice is yours.'

She was tempted to retreat, leaving him to his brandy and self-pity, but this matter must be settled. She was fighting for the survival of her family.

'May I be seated, Lord Thurston?' Her voice dripped scorn. He waved a hand in the direction of a second leather chair placed far too close to his. Charlotte swallowed her fear and took the indicated seat. A smell of stale feet rose to greet her and she gagged; for an awful moment she thought she would cast up her accounts.

She closed her eyes as a wave of dizziness engulfed her. She felt cold perspiration prickle her forehead and desperately she clutched her handkerchief to her mouth. To her astonishment she felt herself being lifted and carried to the locked French doors. She heard him release the catches and she was outside, and fresh clean air filled her lungs.

'Hold still. Here is a bench, I shall place you on it.' The tenderness in his voice sent a different kind of tremor down her spine. 'There, you can open your eyes now, Miss Carstairs, and breathe freely without fear of inhaling my stench.'

She opened her eyes and carefully avoided looking in his direction whilst she drew in a lungful of sweet air. 'I must apologize for my indisposition, Lord Thurston. I am obviously not as fully recovered as I had hoped.'

'It is I who must apologize.' His voice was sincere, all traces of roughness gone. She risked a glance and her involuntary smile surprised them both.

'Good heavens, my lord, you are in no state to have been carrying me. You are swaying like a reed in the wind. Please seat yourself before it is I who must assist you.'

He folded his length on to the far end of the stone bench, the undamaged side of his face towards her.

'Lord Thurston, my maid tells me that you wish us to leave here?' When he didn't answer she half turned to face him. He was staring at his feet. 'This has to be our home now; we have nowhere else to go. You are our only living relative, however remote the connection, and it is your duty to provide for us.'

Still she received no answer. She watched him flex his toes, clearly visible through the holes in his stockings, and her temper flared. 'For heaven's sake, what ails you? My father *died* from his wounds. You are lucky, you have your life. You must put aside your self-pity and take charge of your responsibilities.'

She saw his shoulders stiffen and the muscles in his neck contract, but he did not answer or look her way. Unwisely she decided to continue her attack. 'Why should so many others have to suffer because you have been disfigured? Have you no compassion? Your tenants and villagers are starving because of your neglect, they—' Her words ended on a squeak as his arm shot out and his hand clamped, vice-like, around her arm.

Finally he turned. 'Enough! You forget yourself, Miss Carstairs, it is I who am master here.' His slate-grey eye bored into her, daring her to reply.

She dropped her head, defeated by his rage. 'I beg your pardon, my lord. I spoke out of turn. I had no right to criticize you.' The hand around her arm was removed and she heard him stand up. Dare she risk a glance? Or would she be impaled by that dagger stare again?

She looked up and to her astonishment he was smiling, his anger gone as quickly as it had come. She smiled back and when he held out his hand she took it, allowing him to pull her to her feet. He released his hold once she was upright.

'Well, that was invigorating! You are the first person to have the courage to tell me what I already know.'

'My lord, if you know you are . . . you are neglecting your duties, why do you do so?'

He shook his head and was forced to brace himself against the wall as he swayed dangerously. 'I lost the only thing I cared for when this happened.' He ran strong fingers down his scar. 'It is not my fault the estate is in decay: it was this way when I arrived. It was your precious grandfather who let it go.' Having recovered his equilibrium he straightened. 'I merely exist here. I am a tenant at Thurston Hall as much as anyone else.'

Her jaw dropped. She had never heard such fustian. 'Lord Thurston. . . .' She hesitated, unwilling to antagonize him a second time. 'May I speak freely?'

He half bowed, his expression guarded, his tone chilly. 'Pray continue, Miss Carstairs. I cannot wait to hear what else you have to tell me.'

'If you wish to . . .' She paused, perhaps, 'wallow' was not a good choice. She racked her brain for a more suitable word. 'If you wish to remain in your chambers – umm – repining on your fate – then so be it, but that is no reason why someone else should not run the estate for you. I presume that there are still sufficient funds to do this?'

He shrugged. 'I have no idea how matters stand. I never bothered to enquire. But please feel free to interfere as much as you wish, my dear. If you can persuade the lawyers to speak to you, find the funds to run the estate, then go ahead, you have my full permission to do so.'

'You are jesting, my lord! How can I run the estate? I have not yet

31

reached my majority and even when I do, women have no rights under the law.'

His smile was not friendly. 'Exactly! However, I shall have a document drawn up giving you permission to spend funds and order things as you wish.'

'Let me understand you, my lord. You are willing to allow us to stay here; you are not going to send us away?'

'Ah – yes! But, my dear, Miss Carstairs, there is a proviso. You and those brats can remain at Thurston Hall only if you can show demonstrable improvements to the estate at the end of a specified time.'

'But that is impossible. It is an outrageous suggestion – how can I act as your bailiff?'

'That is my stipulation, however. I shall give you . . . let me see . . . two months from today. If you fail to improve the estate in any significant way then you shall all leave here, never to return. Is that clear?'

She glared at the hateful man staring down at her. 'You have given me no alternative. I accept your challenge. But my two months cannot start until the necessary documents have been drawn up by the lawyers.'

He nodded. 'Very well. I will do that much. After that, the matter shall rest entirely on your shoulders. Do not think to come to me every five minutes for assistance.'

She leapt to her feet, her anger giving her the courage she required to answer him. 'You are despicable. As I have said before, you are a disgrace to your name. But, do not worry, I shall be more than happy to allow you to wallow in your filth and drink yourself to death whilst *I* am the one to save Thurston from ruin.'

She saw his fingers turn into fists and wondered, for a moment, if he would strike her, but she stood her ground. He did not answer her, taunts. Then, unexpectedly, his shoulders slumped and he retreated back into his lair and she heard the click as he locked the doors behind him.

Her anger dissipated but so did her confidence. With a sigh of despair she slumped back on to the stone bench. They were both insane! He to offer her such a challenge and she to accept it. But at least she had gained them two months' respite, and a lot could happen in that time.

She considered the irascible Lord Thurston. Perhaps he was not all bad – after all he had taken care of her, twice, in the past few days. He just had to be shown that his injuries were superficial, that he was the same man on the inside as he had always been. Her lips parted and she felt an interesting heat suffuse her limbs. In spite of his scar he was still a fine-looking man. He stood well over six feet in his stockings and, as Harry had said, his shoulders were broad. That his arms were strong she could vouch for herself. How could he have given up so completely? What was it he had said? That he had lost the only thing he cared for – that had to mean a woman had rejected him. She could understand this, for after all, grief at losing the man she loved, had eventually killed her own mother.

She strolled along the terrace, making sure she did not trip on the broken edges of the flagstones. She went to the far edge of the paved expanse and stared up at the massive edifice. She was delighted to note that most of the many dozen windows were intact – a good clean with vinegar and paper should soon get them pristine again.

The roof appeared sound; it had no sagging gutters and none of the orange peg-tiles was missing. Well, at least she would not have to deal with leaks as well as a vermin-infested interior.

It took her a further fifteen minutes to find her way to what was effectively the rear of the house, although this was where carriages drove up and where guests and residents alike entered the ancient building. The front – from where she had just come – faced the park and had a grand staircase leading down to what she supposed had once been an ornamental lake. Its surface was now so weed covered it was indistinguishable from the grass that grew all around it.

The windows on this side were in equally good repair, which was a relief, as replacing the tiny panes inside their lead surround would no doubt be a difficult and skilled job. She walked some way down the drive in order to view the towering red-brick chimneys, built to match the herringbone pattern of the bricks between the black beams to the house itself.

As she scanned the roof she felt the hairs on the back of the neck stand up, became aware that someone was watching her. She spun, but could see nothing. She caught a flicker of movement in the under-growth and then all was still again. Had she imagined it? The sun was beginning to set and the shadows were lengthening, perhaps that was what had caught her eye. She no longer felt comfortable on her own in the empty space of the turning circle. She would go in at once to find the children and inspect the kitchen and the other offices.

The front door was too heavy for her to open and so she was obliged to knock. She hoped her demand for admittance would not disturb Lord Thurston. She had no wish to speak to him again today, or indeed anytime soon.

From his chair in the drawing-room Jack heard the knock and cursed loudly. Surely he was not to be pestered by more visitors? He heard his butler at the door and the soft murmur of voices. He relaxed; it was only Miss Carstairs, nothing to fret about.

He slid down the chair until his feet reached the seat opposite. He grinned as he recalled the girl's reaction when she had inhaled the smell. His stomach gurgled loudly, reminding him that he hadn't eaten since dinner the previous night. Dinner! Good God! Was he to be expected to do the pretty each night and appear in full evening rig and escort Miss Carstairs to the dining-room?

God forbid! No – he settled down again. He would continue to eat in his rooms, as usual, and she and the brats could eat in the dining-room, or in the stables, for all he cared. He filled his glass, his aim erratic, and sadly watched a large quantity of cognac vanish between a crack in the floorboards.

Two months from now Miss Carstairs would depart and leave him alone. He had set her an impossible task; a challenge even a woman twice her age and experience could not hope to complete.

But at least he had given her a chance, not turned her away imme-diately; he would have a clear conscience when she finally packed her bags. It would not be his fault – it would be hers, for failing to improve the estate.

He nodded, and the room spun unpleasantly. He closed his eye and drifted off into a pleasant alcoholic stupor. However, as he began to lose consciousness he saw, for a moment, the image of a lovely girl, her chestnut hair aflame in the sunlight, glaring at him, her large green eyes snapping with anger.

His feet slammed to the floor and he sat bolt upright, his mouth open. Good God! The girl had not flinched at his face, had stared straight at him, seeing through his scar to the man beneath. His mouth curled and for the second time that day he felt a stirring in his groin. The girl, what was the name? Yes . . . Charlotte – that was it. She had treated him as a human being. There had been no pity, no revulsion, in her gaze.

He chuckled as he remembered her anger, relived her tirade in his head. She had no time for malingerers, for self-pitying drunkards. He ran his hand over his unshaven cheeks and recoiled as the stench of unwashed manhood filled his nostrils.

He supposed it would not hurt to have a bath, shave, and change his raiment. He smiled at the thought that, although Charlotte Carstairs hated him, she did not hold him in disgust like another had. It was too long since he had enjoyed the company of a woman, any woman, and he felt his body stirring, waking up after a sleep of almost two years.

He would get cleaned up, have something to eat and then write the letter summoning his lawyers to Thurston Hall. He was going to enjoy watching the delectable Miss Carstairs struggling to be an estate manager. His mouth curled in a predatory smile. He wondered just how far she would be prepared to go to save her family from eviction. Maybe she would except a different sort of challenge when this one failed; one that involved her body not her brain.

Charlotte found her brother and sister sitting at the freshly scrubbed kitchen table munching slabs of warm bread and strawberry preserve.

'Ah! Here you are.' She glanced around the smoke-stained room, her eyes drawn to the massive fireplace upon which various black pots bubbled and hissed. 'Good grief – have they no range here? I cannot believe an establishment of this size still cooks on an open fire.'

Betty laughed, her arms flour dusted, her cheeks red from the heat. 'They have an oven of sorts, and a spit for chickens and such, but I shall manage, never fear, Miss Carstairs.'

'Who has been preparing the food up till now? Is there no cook of any kind?'

'No; the footmen had been taking it in turns. It seems his lordship dismissed all the female staff when he arrived and has not bothered to replace them with extra menservants.'

'It is no wonder the place is a disgrace. But all this is going to change,' Charlotte announced firmly. Four heads turned to stare at her.

'Whatever do you mean, Lottie? Have you spoken to Lord Thurston this afternoon?' Beth asked.

'I certainly have. He has said that if by the end of two months I have made demonstrable improvements to his estate and home then we can stay, make this our permanent residence.' Both children yelled with delight, presuming their sister would have no difficulty completing her task. Annie and Betty, wiser in the ways of the world, exchanged worried glances. Annie raised her eyebrows and nodded towards the scullery. Charlotte pretended not to understand and ignored the request for a private conversation.

With false enthusiasm she explained to them that the lawyers were to be sent for and as soon as they understood that she was now in charge, she would have access to the funds and be able to start work. It wasn't until after Beth and Harry had retired that Charlotte had a moment to reflect on what she had taken on. Improving the estate could not be too hard, could it? Whatever she did would be more than Lord Thurston had done these past two years.

She unpacked her small *escritoire* and found her pen and paper. She would make notes, plan her actions methodically. After all she had been successfully running the Carstairs household since poor Papa had returned from Waterloo. What she needed was a factor, an estate manager, a man who understood how things should be, and could deal with the artisans and labourers directly.

That was it! She would get Meltham to take on some of the men from the nearby village to tame the gardens and the park, and she would interview any of their wives or daughters who might wish to be employed with the herculean task of cleaning Thurston Hall.

She fell asleep, her head awash with unanswered questions. What had happened to Grandfather in his declining years? Why had he neglected his home and land? Indeed, were there any funds available to do the work? One thing was quite sure: she would not go to Lord Thurston for the answers. She would use her initiative; speak to Meltham and the footmen. She would also go and see the vicar and Dr Andrews; they would surely be able to answer many of her queries. There were no end of people she could ask without having to bother the owner of Thurston Hall one jot!

CHAPTER FOUR

C HARLOTTE decided the children could continue their existence
unfettered by schoolwork for a while longer; she was far too busy
at the moment to spend time teaching them. She watched them race off,
eager to be outside in the unseasonably warm autumn sunshine.
September was a lovely time of year, the trees still green, but the bram-
ble leaves already painted crimson and gold. It must be time for
harvest supper. She frowned. It was the lord of the manor's responsibility to provide all his dependants with a celebratory meal when the
crops were safely gathered and the tithe barn filled with their contri-
butions. This was another thing she would have to add to her list.

She had invited the butler to join her in the library at ten o'clock. It
was almost that time and she did not wish to be tardy for her first offi-
cial appointment.

She placed her notes carefully on the freshly polished mahogany
desk, and pulled out the chair. When the expected knock came she was
ready. 'Come in please, Meltham.'

The old man entered warily, not sure why he had been summoned
in this way. 'Good morning, Miss Carstairs, you wished to see me?'

'I do. Please be seated.' Charlotte indicated a chair to one side. He
sat. 'Have you spoken to Lord Thurston this morning?' He nodded.
'Excellent. Then you will know that he has asked me to take Thurston
Hall in hand; to organize its refurbishment. In order to achieve this I
need to employ extra staff. That is the matter I wish to discuss with
you.'

'You wish me to find you the people you need?'

'Yes, I do. What about those women who were laid off, are any of them still in need of employment?'

He smiled. 'Yes, miss, several are still without a position. They will be more than happy to come back.'

'Good; I shall leave it to you to send for them. Do you know if the housekeeper is amongst them?'

'She is, Miss Carstairs. Mrs Thomas is . . .' He hesitated.

'Not a young woman, Meltham?'

'Exactly so, miss. Because of this she has found it impossible to find employment. There are also two parlour maids living locally and some of the kitchen staff, but Mrs Blake, the cook, has a new position elsewhere.'

'That is no problem. Betty' – she paused – 'I suppose she must be referred to as Mrs Gibson now – is more than happy to continue in that place.' This was going to be far easier than she had anticipated. 'What about outside staff? I should like to have the garden cleared and the park restored before winter sets in.'

'I have no connection with such men, Miss Carstairs, but, if you will allow me, I should dearly like a few more footmen. Extra staff inside will mean that they can help with the repairs and the decorations to the interior.'

'That is a good idea.' She stood, terminating the interview. 'I shall leave you to make the necessary arrangements. As soon as Mrs Thomas and the girls are back, cleaning can begin.'

Charlotte was pleased with her first attempt at management. She had no intention of interfering with the farm or villages until the lawyers had been, but she could start on the Hall. No one would consider it odd of her to be running the house.

She stared down at her notes. Betty had given her a long list of essential items needed for the kitchen. Where could she obtain these goods and what would she use for payment? She had no choice; in spite of her determination not to speak to Lord Thurston unless forced, she did not have the wherewithal to fund the improvements. She needed to arrange for money to be transferred to her. Indeed, needed her own banking account if the arrangement was to run smoothly. She could not be for ever going cap in hand to him.

She pushed back her chair, shaking out the skirts of the same green gown she had worn the previous day. She looked around for a mirror in order to check that her hair was tidy, no auburn curls escaping from her chignon. There was a lighter mark above the empty fireplace indicating where a mirror should be but it had been removed. She supposed that Lord Thurston had done this when he arrived. She ran her fingers over her hair and felt the painful ridge of her own recent injury. There was nothing she could do about that. Her mouth curved; he was hardly in a position to object to her unsightly appearance, after all.

She did not ring for a footman to announce her; she knew in which room to find him. She hesitated – could she hear him moving about inside? She knew that he was up as the butler had already spoken to him earlier that day. But if he was drinking in the same fashion he had been last night, he might well be asleep in his chair. Should she leave it until the afternoon when he might be in a better frame of mind? She was so immersed in her thoughts that she failed to hear the footsteps behind her.

'Stop dithering, Miss Carstairs, are you intending to knock on my door or not?'

She shot round, her hands to her chest, but her intended protest at his ill-mannered approach remained unspoken. Shocked, she stared at him. Was this smiling giant, smartly dressed in a navy superfine topcoat, clean buckskin inexpressibles, and, good heavens, polished Hessians, the same Lord Thurston of yesterday?

Eventually she found her voice. 'You startled me, my lord,' was all she could manage. For some reason her pulse was fluttering and her throat constricted.

He bowed. 'I apologize, Miss Carstairs. Did you wish to speak to me?' She nodded, unable to form a coherent reply. Why was he staring at her so strangely? It made her feel decidedly uncomfortable. 'Then let us repair to the library. For although I have improved my own appearance I am afraid I have not yet had the same done to my apartments.'

He took her elbow and she found herself being escorted, firmly, back to the room she had just vacated. She watched him stride over and take *her* place behind the desk, leaving her to sit where she would. Her eyes narrowed. Was his declared intention, to leave her to her own devices, to be so soon abandoned?

'Lord Thurston, I wish to know if the letter to your lawyers has been sent this morning.'

'It has, Miss Carstairs.' He waited, politely, adding nothing more.

She flushed under his scrutiny. 'I have no money,' she blurted out.

'Patently – or you would not be in this predicament,' he answered, obviously enjoying her discomfiture.

'I mean, there is no money to pay for repairs and renewals. I should like some to be made available, if you please, my lord.'

He nodded, all amiability and compliance. 'How much would you like, Miss Carstairs? One guinea? One hundred guineas? More?' He pretended to pat his pockets as if looking for the gold coins.

She stiffened; she did not like to be made fun of. 'I do not require it at this precise moment, Lord Thurston. But it is my belief that trades-men and employees should be paid. I have no time for those with enough to pay who deliberately run up debts.'

He steepled his fingers and nodded. 'Indeed, Miss Carstairs, those are laudable sentiments and I applaud you.' He leant back on his chair and, to her annoyance, swung his feet up on to the newly polished surface. 'However, my dear, I am as impecunious as yourself. Until the lawyers arrive to sort things out, I am afraid that I cannot help you.'

She was aghast. 'No money? Then how am I to begin improvements?'

He shrugged, and although his smile was lopsided, it sent shock waves down her spine. 'I thought we had agreed that your two months does not start until the lawyers have drawn up the necessary documents?'

Her nostrils flared. 'I do not intend to live in squalor whilst I wait on them. This place is a disgrace. Do you not realize that rodents roam around unchecked? That there are holes in the ceilings and—'

'Quite, quite, my dear. Please do not bore me with such domestic trivia. If you wish to instigate improvements then you must do so without the funds to pay. I can assure you no tradesmen will refuse your order. They will be happy to wait for their remuneration.'

She stood up, glaring at him. 'I have told you, my lord, that I do not wish to buy goods that I cannot be sure I can pay for. I shall have to postpone my purchases until the money is available.'

'That is entirely your decision, my dear girl. As I explained, I do not wish to be bothered with the estate.'

He crossed his legs at the ankle and linked his hands behind his head. Charlotte had an overwhelming desire to push him, violently. She began to move forward, her hand raised, her intent written quite clearly on her face.

Realizing he was about to be upended, Jack attempted to remove his feet but, in his hurry, lost his balance and, without her assistance, toppled backwards. The resulting crash and the mêlée of wildly waving arms and legs was accompanied by profanities that only a soldier would know.

Not sure whether to laugh or retreat with her hands clamped firmly to her ears, she hesitated a moment too long. The injured party erupted from behind the desk and lunged forward, grabbing her hand as she attempted to back away.

'Not so fast, Miss Carstairs, we have unfinished business here.'

'Let go of me at once, Lord Thurston; you have no right to detain me.'

'Have I not? I have been reliably informed that I am your legal guardian. So I have every right to treat you in any way I damn well please.'

This was outrageous. He could not pick and choose his duties. Either he was their guardian, or he was not. 'Lord Thurston, am I to understand that you are now accepting responsibility for myself and my brother and sister?'

Instantly he released his grip and stepped back, his expression cold. 'You do not catch me so easily, my dear. You are nothing to do with me.'

'In which case,' she interrupted rudely, 'you shall not molest me a second time.' She nodded her dismissal. 'Pray, do not let me keep you, Lord Thurston. I am sure you have urgent business elsewhere to attend to.'

For an instant he was nonplussed. Then he rallied. 'This is, I believe, my house and this my library. If you do not wish to be in my company, then might I respectfully suggest that you retire to your rooms?'

She almost stamped her foot. 'You are impossible. I think I preferred you in your cups.'

Allowing him no time to reply she flounced out, back straight, her skirts swinging, revealing far more of her ankles than was proper. She barely refrained from banging the door behind her.

Jack rubbed his scar, his head thumping in time with his heart. God – he needed a drink! Sparring with Miss Carstairs was exhausting. He grinned as he recalled how her eyes had sparkled and her bosom heaved with indignation. She had almost tricked him into admitting he had responsibility for her and the brats. Never! He had vowed, when Sophia had rejected him, that he would take no further part in the world, would never marry or produce offspring of his own.

Why should he raise someone else's children? He glared around the book-lined room; why was there no decanter on the octagonal marquetry side table? Meltham was slacking. His brandy had better be waiting for him in his own apartments or there would be hell to pay. He slammed out of the room and strode down the corridor. His sudden arrival scattered Charlotte, two footmen and the butler.

Ignoring them he vanished into his lair. The pungent aroma and semi-darkness eased his agitation. Yes, this was where he belonged. Not dressed up like a popinjay bandying words with a schoolgirl.

Charlotte recovered first. 'As I was saying, Meltham, how far is it to the vicarage? Would it be possible for me to walk there and back before noon?'

'You could, miss, but it would be a wasted journey. The Reverend Foster died a year ago and his lordship has not seen fit to reappoint.'

'Do you mean I cannot attend service on a Sunday? That is scandalous!' She eyed the closed door, but decided one session with Lord Thurston was enough for that morning. 'Well, what about Dr Andrews? Does he reside nearby?'

'He does, miss, about two miles from here. He has a snug mansion with a small estate; I believe it was left him by his uncle.'

Charlotte smiled and waited for him to continue. The old man shook his head. 'But you can not visit him either, miss, as he is not a married gentleman.'

'No matter; I shall request that he calls on me here instead.' She turned to the footmen, lurking in the shadows, watching the drawing-room door in case their master should emerge again. She addressed the younger of the two. 'Jenkins, you shall take a message to Dr Andrews for me. Come to the library in one quarter of an hour to collect it.' The young man bowed. Charlotte hurried off to compose her note. It was only as she was sealing it with a wafer that the significance of the butler's casual comment about the doctor's marital status hit her like a thunderbolt.

She felt the breakfast she had taken earlier threaten to return and swallowed vigorously. Her eyes blurred and she groped in her reticule for her handkerchief. Why had neither Annie nor Betty mentioned it? How could she have been so naïve, so stupid? How long had she been resident at Thurston Hall? Almost a week now – a whole week unchaperoned – living under the roof of a bachelor of uncertain habits and a careless attitude to propriety. She was ruined; her reputation gone, compromised beyond redemption.

She sniffed and blew her nose loudly. Well, it was done now. It was not as though she had had any alternative; it was Thurston Hall or the poor house. She wondered if Lord Thurston realized that he had, albeit through no fault of his own, compromised her? Good grief! Her hands flew to her mouth in shock. What if he felt obliged to offer for her? She shivered, not sure if it was antipathy or anticipation that coursed through her.

She stood up, the folded sheet in her hands, and walked slowly to the grimy window. Idly she rubbed a circle clean with a fingertip and gazed, unfocused, out into the garden. Her mouth curved as she spotted Beth running around amongst the trees. She supposed that the children were playing hide and go seek. Harry was a master at secreting himself.

A tap on the door turned her attention away from the garden. 'Come in, Jenkins. I have the note for Dr Andrews here.' She handed it to the waiting young man. 'If the doctor is at home, then wait for his reply. If he is not, leave the note and return.'

Jenkins took the letter and retreated. Charlotte returned to the desk. What was first on her list? If she kept herself fully occupied, maybe she would have no time to consider the awful implications of her discovery. She was a ruined woman, and only nineteen years of age! She giggled; at least she need no longer bother with proprieties: it was far too late for that. From now on, if she wished to walk alone, then she would do so. She could not damage what had already gone. And she would ride astride as she had as a child; she had no riding habit anyway. It was years since she had had the opportunity to ride, for they had kept no horses in Romford.

She would go and investigate the stables. Harry had said there were four carriage horses, as well as the two stallions that his lordship rode. Perhaps one of those beasts would do. She had been an accomplished rider; Papa had often told her that she had a natural seat on a horse. It was five years since she had ridden, but she was quite certain it was something that you never forgot.

She left the Hall by a side door she had discovered in the corridor, which led to the kitchen and servants' rooms. Outside, the warm sunshine restored her optimism. She stared up into a cloudless blue sky; it was more like summer than autumn. The dry green leaves rustled overhead as she strolled down the shady path that led, she hoped, to the stables, which were situated somewhere to the rear of the building.

She saw an archway ahead and could hear the welcome sound of hoofs on cobbles. Pleased to find she was heading in the correct direction, she increased her pace, eager to discover for her herself what kind of horseflesh Lord Thurston kept.

Charlotte emerged into a large yard. She looked around with delight; the ground was swept, no piles of horse dung to negotiate. There were individual loose boxes and inquisitive equines peered out over the doors. Grandfather had not stinted on his stables; they were obviously of recent construction and housed every convenience.

She spotted a pump in the corner, so there was obviously a stable well. She could hear the sound of shovelling from an open door and, raising her skirt, she went over to investigate. The young groom appeared, shirt sleeves rolled, cord britches tucked neatly into stout boots. 'Good mornin', Miss Carstairs. Have you come to look over his lordship's nags?'

She nodded. 'You must be Jim, for I understand that Jethro is an older man.'

'That's right, miss. He's head groom, but has taken Othello to be shod, down at the smithy in the village.'

'I am sure you can answer my questions just as well as he, Jim.' She glanced into the box. 'This is Lucifer's stable?'

He grinned. 'It is, ma'am. The only time it can be mucked out is when he's absent. All teeth and flying hoofs, is that young man.'

Charlotte turned, walked up to the first of four grey heads, all appearing eager to make her acquaintance. 'These are the carriage horses? The animals that pull the curricle or phaeton? Do any of them go under saddle as well?'

'Yes, Star, the mare you're stroking now, she's fine, but not side saddle, mind, she wouldn't be happy with that.'

The soft lips of the horse nipped playfully up her arm. She reached out and scratched the horse between the ears and the huge animal instantly lowered her head, resting it trustingly against Charlotte's shoulder. 'I wish to ride Star myself, Jim. I am perfectly comfortable astride, for it is how I learnt to ride many years ago.'

'In that case, Miss Carstairs, there's no problem. She's taken to you already, and she don't like many people.'

'Excellent! I shall return in twenty minutes; can you have her ready for me then?'

'That I can, miss. Will you be wanting me to come with you?' It was clear from his tone that he would rather not accompany her.

'No, Jim, I am quite happy to ride alone. I do not intend to go out of the park. It is some years since I last rode, so I do not wish to overdo things on my first outing.'

He beamed. 'If you follow that path over there, it leads round the park, about a mile or so, and it goes through a pretty beech wood. Easy going, and no ditches or hedges to jump.'

'I am relieved to hear that. I am sure that jumping anything would be beyond my abilities today.'

In her room, she ferreted about in her trunk, sure that her old britches, shirt and waistcoat were in there somewhere. She held the britches up. They looked smaller than she remembered, but they were all she had and would have to do. Glad that Annie was occupied elsewhere, for she knew exactly what her maid's opinion would be on the matter of riding astride in boy's apparel, Charlotte carefully draped her discarded gown over a chair back, one of the two that had been found from somewhere. The loose shirt fitted easily accommodating her ample curves – the waistcoat also – but the inexpressibles were a different matter.

It took all her strength to pull them up and when she had finally wriggled her way in, and buttoned up the front, they felt decidedly snug. In fact, if she bent down, she feared they would split down the rear. She tugged at the waistcoat, hoping to drag it down over her bottom but it was too short. Eventually she decided to untuck her shirt-tails and leave them flapping at the rear. It looked untidy, but at least that way she was decently covered.

Next she needed a head covering of some sort. She believed that there had been a hat to go with her outfit. She delved further into the depths of the trunk and emerged triumphant with a flat cap. Hastily she crammed it on, bundling stray curls inside.

She stepped up to the mirror, the only one she had discovered so far. Satisfied she was ready, she left the room and almost ran back through the house, down the ornate carved oak stairs and across the hall.

She did not hear the drawing-room door open or hear Lord Thurston's loud exclamation of surprise as she whisked past, the contours of her pert *dérriere* clearly visible beneath the floating shirt-tails. Neither did she know that, with a gleam in his eye, he was following close behind.

CHAPTER FIVE

CHARLOTTE had come barely half the distance to the stables when she realized that it was not only her britches that were too small; her boots were also. By the time she reached the archway she was hobbling, her toes horribly pinched.

Star was tacked and standing ready in the yard. She tried to ignore the groom's grin but felt her cheeks redden. Perhaps she should have waited until she had had time to let out seams and order new boots. She patted the horse's neck and gathered up the reins, glad that the mare went in a snaffle bit which required only one pair; juggling with two sets of reins on her first venture might have proved too much for her.

She turned her back and bent her leg. Jim, his eyes carefully averted, hoisted her into the saddle. She adjusted the leathers and tightened the girth and then gave her horse the office to move. Less than two minutes after her arrival in the yard, she was away down the path at a brisk trot, eager to distance herself from the sniggering groom.

The path soon meandered under a canopy of leaves and Charlotte lowered her hands and sat back in the saddle. Instantly the mare responded and dropped down to walk.

'Good girl, Star; well done – you are a wonderful horse,' she crooned, patting the smooth muscled neck beneath her gloved hand. The horse shook its head as if agreeing with the praise. In the cool green darkness beneath the trees she relaxed, pleased that her equestrian skills had not deserted her. She could hear the soft cooing of the pigeons and the harsh call of a pheasant or two. She looked around with interest, seeing further signs of neglect and mismanagement. The wood had not been coppiced and a tangle of undergrowth and nettles grew where there should have been clear space.

Star's ears pricked and the mare skittered sideways, almost unseating her. Quickly Charlotte regained her seat and stared around. She could see nothing untoward. Then the horse whinnied loudly and shook its head. Charlotte felt the animal's muscles bunching under her. Something was definitely wrong, but what was it?

She recalled the moment when she had felt that someone malevolent was watching her outside the Hall. Nervously she glanced from side to side but still could see nothing out of the ordinary. She could hear the birds singing – that was a good sign. Then she knew what had disturbed Star. In the distance she could hear the sound of galloping hoofs.

She had to escape. It was not safe alone in the woods. She shortened her reins and dug in her heels. The agitated mare needed no further urging, but took hold of the bit and bolted. Charlotte knew she was being run away with, but could do nothing. The path was too narrow to attempt to circle the horse; all she could do was concentrate on ducking branches and praying that the animal would slow of its own accord before she was unseated.

Fully occupied she completely forgot why she had wanted to gallop in the first place. She crouched over the horse's withers, taking a handful of flying grey and white mane in with the reins for added security. She found she was beginning to enjoy the experience.

Ahead it was lighter; they were coming to a clearing, or maybe an open expanse of grass where she could attempt to turn the mare. No longer in danger of falling, all she needed was to remain calm.

'Steady girl, steady. There is nothing to scare you.'

She tried easing back on the reins, transferring her weight to the rear of the saddle. To her astonishment Star appeared to listen, the black ears flicked back and the wild gallop slowed to an extended canter.

All might have been well if Lord Thurston had not chosen that precise moment to thunder alongside and reach across to take Star's bit. Neither Charlotte, nor her horse, had realized that they were about to be overtaken, their flight had masked the approaching hoofbeats.

The mare, panicked by the sudden appearance of the hand by her head, shied violently, sideways into the trees. Charlotte was swept from the saddle by a jutting branch and deposited headfirst, but unhurt, into a large patch of undergrowth and nettles. She forgot the precarious state of her britches and launched herself backwards. There was an ominous ripping sound and, to her horror, she felt the rear seam give way completely.

Lord Thurston, having vaulted from his saddle, arrived by her side at the precise moment the material parted exposing her bottom to his appreciative eye. Trying not to laugh out loud he reached down and hauled her upright.

'Are you hurt, Miss Carstairs?' His enquiry was polite enough, but she could his sense his suppressed amusement.

'No, I am not,' she snapped, scarlet with mortification. 'If you want to make yourself useful, go and catch my mount.' She could hear him chuckling as he swung himself back on to the second of his fiery stallions.

As soon as she was sure he had left the vicinity, she peered over her shoulder to assess the damage. She had guessed from the draught it was bad, but it was far worse than she had imagined. The seam had ripped from top to bottom and all that was holding the garment up was the waistband. Hastily she tucked her shirt inside; there was plenty of room for it now.

She rather thought the tail was long enough to pull right between her legs and then she could secure it by pushing it into the buttonholes on the front flap. She managed to poke the slippery fabric down to hide her bottom, but soon realized she would have to grope down the front in order to complete her manoeuvre.

Her hand would not fit between her britches and waist. She dare not tug too hard or she would be in an even worse predicament. There was nothing for it, she would have to undo the buttons and pull the recalcitrant shirt through that way. She stared up the narrow path – no sign of Lord Thurston returning – so she was safe for a few moments.

Hastily she unbuttoned herself and reached down between her legs; triumphantly she grasped the material and yanked it hard. At this point in her activities she distinctly heard the sound of jingling bits and the unmistakable sound of horses returning. Frantically she spread the shirt across and was safely restored just as the two horses cantered into view.

Lord Thurston dismounted, his expression bland. 'Are we ready to return, Miss Carstairs? Er . . . have you completed your repairs?'

She felt heat travel from her soles to the tips of her ears. How dare he mention her dilemma! Rigid with embarrassment her answer was forced from between clenched teeth. 'I am quite ready, thank you, my lord.' She stepped up to him and held out an imperious hand for Star's reins. Silently he handed them over, his mirth barely under control.

'Would you like a leg up, Miss Carstairs?'

She was about to present her boot for him to toss her into the saddle when something occurred to her. What if her makeshift repairs came adrift as he did so – her bare behind would be inches from his face. She would not risk that happening.

'I do not intend to ride back. I shall walk.' She had, in her agitation, quite forgotten that her boots did not fit.

'As you wish, my dear; permit me to walk alongside. It is such a lovely day and I shall enjoy the stroll.'

'You shall not—' she burst out. 'I beg your pardon. I mean to say that I would not dream of imposing upon you any longer, my lord. Please feel free to continue your ride.'

He bowed and a lock of dark hair fell across his face obscuring his scar. She caught her breath. He must have been a veritable Adonis before his injury.

'Then I shall bid you good day, Miss Carstairs. It is only a mile or two back to the Hall. You should be safely home in less than an hour.'

He vaulted into his saddle and the huge horse stamped and shook his head, eager to be off. Charlotte remained where she was until all was quiet again. She looped Star's reins over her arm and rubbed the mare's velvety nose.

'Come along, you bad girl, we had better get on.'

Her face still burned unpleasantly from the nettle stings, but apart from that, and a few bruises, she felt she had come through the experience remarkably well.

She hoped she would be able to return to her chamber undetected. As she pictured the spectacle she must have made, face down – naked bottom up – she felt laughter bubbling inside. Did this make her a *fallen* woman as well as a ruined one? She laughed at the absurdity and the noise startled her horse afresh. The animal half reared, lifting Charlotte off her feet.

'Steady, Star, nothing to shy about.' All desire to laugh vanished as her crushed feet thumped back on to the path. How could she walk back in these boots? She knew she could barely hobble a few yards. She had no alternative – she must remove them. Walking in stockings, however uneven the ground, was preferable to having every toe broken.

She spoke aloud to the waiting mare. 'I have to remove my boots, sweetheart; they are so small I am crippled and cannot walk.' The horse nuzzled her shoulder, leaving a trail of slobber behind. 'Good girl! You must remain still whilst I pull them off. Do you think you can do that for me?'

Charlotte leant, experimentally, against the horse's solid flank and the animal did not move. She attempted to lean forward and raise her leg but found she was unable to do so. Her shirt tails were so securely tucked in that it was impossible. She wriggled and fiddled but soon understood that she had but two options: she could try and walk home in her boots, or risk undoing her britches and temporarily exposing herself to the elements whilst she released her shirt.

She had no choice. She would walk even if it broke all her toes in the process. Then a third option occurred to her: she could remount Star and ride home. She glanced around, looking for something suitable to stand on, but could see nothing. Maybe if she lengthened the stirrup leather to its fullest extent she could manage to put her foot in unaided.

She shook her head and unwanted tears spilled down her cheeks. Even if she did find something to stand on, or could get her foot in the iron, she could only manage it by undoing her shirt. Her head dropped and she swallowed a sob of frustration.

She gritted her teeth and set off. The pain after only a few minutes was appalling. She rested her face against Star, unsure how to proceed, or even if she could do so.

Jack continued along the path his mood sombre. Miss Carstairs obviously found him so repellent that even walking beside him was too much. She was a lovely girl – delectable images of her anatomy drifted before his eyes. He chuckled as he recalled her embarrassment. She had handled it well, he could think of no other woman of his acquaintance who would have shown such aplomb. And she was a bruising rider; the fall had not been her fault, but his. He should have apologized not teased her. It was not too late to do so now. She couldn't have gone far on foot.

Decision made, he reined back and expertly turned his mount. As he cantered round the bend he spotted her, further down, leaning against her horse, obviously in some distress. What was wrong? Had he so upset her she was unable to continue? If this was the case his presence would not be welcome.

He stopped. He would not intrude, but he wanted to be sure that she didn't need his assistance before he continued his ride. He watched her straighten, scrub her eyes dry with her gloves and attempt to walk. Instantly he understood. Urging his mount forward he rode alongside. Stretching down he lifted her easily on to his saddle and positioned her in front of him.

'You goose – why did you volunteer to walk home if your boots are crippling you?'

He heard her sniff inelegantly before she answered, 'I had forgotten about the boots.' He tightened his arm around her, drawing her close, loving the soft feel of her back against his chest.

Charlotte stiffened and he immediately slackened his hold. She realized that she still had Star's reins in her hand.

'Give them to me; I can lead your mount.' His voice was brusque, all sign of his previous good humour gone. Had it been her involuntary recoil? Did he not understand that she was inexperienced, unused to being held so intimately by a man? It was not to do with his face. She hardly noticed that anymore.

Forcing herself to relax she settled back into his embrace just to reassure him that she was not repelled by him. He responded by pulling her back so that she could feel his body heat through his shirt, inhale his masculine scent. He smelled good, a great improvement on their first encounter.

'You smell much better now you have bathed, my lord.' Her thoughts had, of their own volition slipped out of her mouth. How could she have mentioned his body or his ablutions? A lady should not appear to even be aware of such things. Horrified, she tried to make amends. 'What I mean – is. . . . Oh! I am sorry. What I said was unpardonable.'

'But, my dear, perfectly true,' he replied drily.

'I should not have—'

'Enough; let us talk of something else. The matter is closed.' His mouth was so close to her ear she could feel his words tickling her neck. 'Perhaps, Miss Carstairs, you could explain to me why you did not wish to ride back to Thurston Hall in the circumstances?'

Good grief! This was an even more unsuitable topic of conversation. She felt her face colour and attempted to move away, to place a decent inch or two between them. She failed as his hold was too strong. Holding herself straight, she eventually answered, 'No, I could not. And a gentleman would not ask.' Had she gone too far – again?

The silence lengthened, the only sound the pad of hoofs in the grass and the birds singing in the trees. Why did he not answer? Becoming worried that she had, once more, mortally offended him, she twisted her head round to see his expression. She regretted her decision.

The wretched man was grinning down at her, his face alight with amusement. He had obviously worked out for himself her reasons for refusing to remount. She glared her disapproval and faced forward, her shoulders stiff with dislike.

He settled her more comfortably against him, and murmured, 'I am a scoundrel for teasing you, sweetheart, but you are so impossibly lovely when you blush, I cannot restrain myself.'

Before she could think of a suitably crushing riposte to his

outrageous comment, he clicked his tongue and Phoenix obediently lengthened his stride and she found herself flung backwards as they cantered the last mile.

Jethro, the head groom, was in the yard to take the horses. Jack lowered Charlotte and released her. Like a frightened fawn she raced off, ignoring the agony from her boots, in her desire to return to the privacy of her chambers.

Thankfully, Annie was occupied elsewhere. That was one hurdle overcome successfully. The second would be to remove her boots herself. She unfastened her ruined britches and removed the shirt tails from between her legs. It was only then she noticed how chafed her inner thighs were. Free from the restriction imposed by the material, she collapsed on to the floor desperate to remove the hated footwear.

She spent a fruitless fifteen minutes before abandoning the task. Her feet must have swollen inside and she knew she would never get them off without assistance. She hobbled over to the bell-strap Jenkins had replaced the day before. She would call her maid – it was too late to worry about receiving a bear-garden jaw for her indecorous exploits. The boots had to come off.

This time she pulled it more gently for she did not want a repeat performance and find herself standing in a fresh pile of plaster. She pulled, knowing she would have a scant ten minutes to cover her semi-nudity. She tugged at the waistband and it tore, making removal easy. In desperation she dropped to her knees and crawled across to the chair on which her green day dress was still draped. She scrambled up, using the chair for support and then sat down gratefully.

She removed the waistcoat and pulled the shirt off over her head. She doubted she could manage to put on her chemise and petticoats before Annie arrived. She would have to wear her gown on its own. The cambric felt rough against her overheated skin but at least she was decently covered. She scooped up her discarded boy's clothes, and used undergarments, then on her knees, she shuffled back to the tester bed and stuffed them under the coverlet.

Next she pulled herself up and sat firmly on the bed, making certain her maid's sharp eyes could not see beneath her. Oh dear! The mud on the soles of the boots. Annie would realize that she had been outside. She swung her legs up and examined the leather – yes – there were tell-tale traces. She groped under the comforter and removed her chemise and, spitting on it, she scrubbed first one and then the other until satisfied they would pass inspection. She pushed the ruined garment back into its hiding place not a moment too soon.

The door in the dark wood panelling opened and her maid bustled in. 'Is something wrong, miss? The bell nigh fell off the wall downstairs.'

Charlotte's eyes checked the ceiling; the bell-strap was still firmly attached. She had not realized how hard she'd pulled. 'There is, Annie. I tried on my old riding boots and find I cannot remove them. Could you please do it for me?'

'Certainly, miss. I'm surprised that you didn't realize they were too small when you put on the first one.'

'It felt snug, but not too bad. It was not until I tried to walk around that I became aware they pinched my toes horribly. And by then it was too late and they were firmly stuck.'

Annie bent down and took Charlotte's right foot firmly in her two hands. She tugged – it didn't budge. She pulled harder and Charlotte shot off the bed landing with a thump on the boards only just managing to hold down her skirts.

'My word, Miss Carstairs. I'm that sorry – I don't know my own strength. Are you hurt?'

Charlotte scrambled up hastily knowing that any assistance might reveal her lack of undergarments and that would be impossible to explain. 'Not at all, it was no more than a bump.'

'I'll try the other way, shall I, miss? I'll turn round and you put your foot through my legs.' Charlotte did as instructed. 'Now, you push on my rear end whilst I pull. I've seen your father's valet remove his boots this way.'

It all seemed very unorthodox but Charlotte was prepared to try anything to remove the wretched things. But however hard they tugged neither boot shifted. Hot and flustered they admitted defeat.

'They'll have to be cut off, miss. There's no other way.'

'Cut off? How? They are so close fitting a blade would cut me as well.'

Annie shook her head. 'Not if it's real sharp. I've seen a doctor do it, years ago, after one of the grooms broke his ankle.'

'That's as maybe, Annie. But the groom's boots would not have been glued on to his legs as these are to mine. I swear they have shrunk since I put them on.'

'Don't fret now, Miss Carstairs. We'll soon have this sorted out. You wait quietly, and I'll send for Dr Andrews to remove them.'

Charlotte flopped back onto the bed with such force that it shook a cloud of dust out of the hangings. She closed her eyes in disgust. It could be some time before help arrived, perhaps she would have a nap to pass the time.

She ached all over, her face stung, her thighs were sore and the pain in her feet, after all the pushing and pulling, was excruciating. In fact she felt thoroughly wretched. She hoped if she kept still, tried to relax, the throbbing would subside.

She was becoming a hoyden. It was scarcely more than a month since her mother had passed away and already she was behaving as though she had no cares in the world. Mama had made her promise not to mourn, to move on with her life, but all of them appeared to have done so with indecent haste. What had come over her since she had arrived at Thurston Hall? She heard voices in the corridor and heavy footsteps. The door opened and Lord Thurston came in his face etched with concern.

'You little idiot! What were you thinking of? You should have asked for assistance.'

Shocked speechless by his sudden appearance Charlotte could only wave her hands, gesturing him away. He ignored her and continued his approach. She found her voice.

'Lord Thurston, this is no concern of yours. My maid has sent for Dr Andrews. He will be here soon. I prefer to wait for him.'

'I do not.' He picked up a chair and dropped it by the bed. Then he slid a silver blade from the top of his Hessian. Seeing her eyebrows shoot up into her hair, he grinned. 'All soldiers carry a blade in their boot. I have not given up the habit.' She edged across the bed, trying to remove herself from his reach. Annie intervened.

'Miss, let his lordship help you. He has done this many times before and I reckon he will be better than a doctor. And he's right here, not two miles away.'

She could not let him; he would discover her state of undress. Had she not suffered enough embarrassment for one day? Sensing her distress, he ducked his head, speaking softly so only she could hear.

'What is it, little one? I promise I shall not hurt you. I have done this many times and have never injured anyone in the process.'

'It is not that,' she managed to whisper, her face a becoming shade of pink. 'I . . . I am . . . not properly dressed.' She glanced down at her skirt and he understood. His smile vanished and he became as impersonal as a physician. He sat back, glancing over his shoulder.

'Annie, come sit on the bed with Miss Carstairs. She is apprehensive and could do with your support.'

'Of course I will, my lord.' The maid came forward.

'Sit there, between me and Miss Carstairs; I believe she will be happier if she cannot observe what is going on.'

Annie did as she was bid. Charlotte closed her eyes and prayed that the ordeal would soon be over. She felt him take her right leg and hold it firmly, then she heard a hiss and the boot was off. She had felt nothing – the blade had not touched her.

'Christ in His Heaven! What a mess!'

Annie almost fell off the bed in horror at his profanity when he saw Charlotte's blood-soaked stockings.

'Hold it. Wait until I have removed the second, then you can deal with it.'

This time Charlotte watched as he deftly slit the boot along the seam and peeled the leather away from her leg. The left foot was equally shocking.

'There, my dear, it is done. I shall leave your maid to tend to your injuries. When you are sufficiently recovered I should like to speak to you in the library.'

'Thank you, my lord. I am sure that I shall be able to get around again tomorrow. I shall send word when I am available.'

He smiled and her heart turned over. Her eyes followed him until the door closed and she was alone with her maid. She sank back on her pillows, her mind full of contradictory thoughts and unexpected emotions.

If Annie wondered how walking around her bedchamber had caused such injuries, she did not say so. Charlotte was just relieved to have her crushed toes free from constriction and she quite forgot that she disliked and despised Lord Thurston and could do nothing but sing his praises whilst Annie bathed and bandaged her mangled feet.

'You will not be able to walk easily for a while, but it looks worse than it is, I'm happy to say.'

Charlotte risked flexing her toes and discovered that the pain was bearable. 'Thank you, Annie. Like Lord Thurston, you have done a splendid job.'

'If you're comfortable, miss, I'll get back downstairs and check how the children are.'

'Yes, please do so. I have been anxious myself about their well-being.'

Left alone in her sparsely furnished room with nothing to read and not even her embroidery to occupy her hands, she stared about her with displeasure. The first thing she must do was send Jenkins up into the attics to find her a *chaise-longue* and a side table, and perhaps a comfortable armchair.

'Good heavens!' She exclaimed aloud, when she remembered that she had, in fact, sent Jenkins out to deliver a note to Dr Andrews hours ago. Why had he not returned? He was a fit young man and could have walked there and back in an hour and a half with no difficulty. Whatever could be keeping him?

CHAPTER SIX

CHARLOTTE was tempted to crawl across to the bell-strap but knew it would be Annie who was obliged to answer her summons and her maid's first concern must be for Beth and Harry. Her curiosity about the tardy footman would just have to wait.

She was too restless to sleep. It could only be a matter of time before someone pointed out to Lord Thurston that he had compromised her. He had not wished her to move in and if she had not been injured by the stone, she was sure he would not have admitted them. This parlous situation was her fault; she could not allow him to sacrifice his freedom because of it.

She banged her hands on the cover. But it was not all her error – if he had done his duty then there would not have been angry villagers and the missile would not have been thrown. She smiled, happy she could lay some of the blame for their predicament at Jack's door. She felt a strange warmth bathe her limbs as she repeated Lord Thurston's given name in her head. Jack – it suited him.

She mentally reviewed his physique and her discomfort grew until her crumpled green gown felt too tight. Why did thinking of . . . Jack . . . she risked his name again and felt a corresponding wave of heat course round her – make her feel so strange?

Admittedly he was monstrously tall, and his shoulders were broad and his chest well muscled. She fanned her hands ineffectually in front of her face, but they did little to reduce the warmth of her cheeks. She could not stay in bed. She needed to be up; she needed something else, but was not sure what it was. All she knew was that her restlessness was linked to him.

She grinned. He might be Jack in her thoughts from now on, but she could just imagine his reaction if she was unwise enough to address him so familiarly to his face. She sat up and carefully put her bandaged feet on the floor. She applied weight, winced and sat back. Her toes were too painful to carry her, but perhaps if she walked on her heels? Holding tight to her bedpost she tried balancing in this way; it was difficult but relatively pain free.

She realized it would be wise to remove the evidence from under the comforter and don some undergarments before her maid returned. She pulled out the discarded riding clothes and her petticoat and chemise then, tucking them under her arm, she shuffled her way over to the closet.

Her heels were sore by the time she'd achieved her objective but at least she had not fallen. She pushed the riding clothes into a dark corner and tossed the undergarments into the laundry basket. It was easier to manoeuvre in here as she had the shelves to hold on to. She edged her way around the tiny room until she could reach the pile of freshly washed and pressed petticoats and chemises.

Shrugging off her ruined gown she stood naked for a moment, enjoying the feel of the cool air on her skin. She stared down critically at her body; was she too plump? Her breasts were full, her ribs tapered to a satisfactorily small waist, her tummy was flat and her hips rounded. She peered awkwardly over her shoulder, almost losing her balance, to check that her bottom was acceptable.

She had always considered herself too tall. She had topped her mother by several inches but next to Jack she had felt almost dainty. A shiver of excitement flicked through her and instinctively she covered her breasts with her hands. Without their support her weight transferred to her injured toes and agony replaced excitement. Her knees buckled and she collapsed to the floor. The touch of the cold boards on her naked skin banished all thought of Lord Thurston. She got to her knees and pulled herself upright. This would not do! What if Beth or Harry had come in and found her cavorting in her closet, totally unclothed?

She snatched a chemise and pulled it down over her head. The ribbons and tiny buttons would have to wait until she could sit down. Next she selected a petticoat and draped it over her arm. She viewed the meagre row of gowns hanging on the rail. She chose a serviceable brown cotton dress, its high neck, long sleeves and lack of decoration, ideal for someone who did not wish to draw attention to her femininity. She ignored the pile of stockings neatly rolled on the shelf. She could not put shoes or hosiery over her bandages.

Twenty minutes later she was dressed. As her hair was hanging in a long braid down her back it did not require any further intervention on her part. She glanced into the speckled mirror to check if she had any stray spots of mud on her cheeks. Her eyes widened in horror. Good grief! She looked positively bracket-faced.

Her cheeks were mottled red-and-white where the nettles had stung and her scar was a livid line slashed across her forehead, the sutures showing black along it. Thoughtfully she ran her fingertips over her face. Perhaps now was a good time to attempt to make her way down to the library. Her appearance was so unimpressive that Jack would no longer find her desirable. He had said that he wished to speak to her and she was eager to know the whereabouts of Jenkins. She decided, however difficult it might be, she would not languish upstairs like an invalid.

Her stomach made a most unladylike noise and she giggled. It was hours since she had broken her fast. Once she was downstairs she would make her way to the kitchen and find something to eat. Then she would send word to Lord Thurston that she was ready for her interview.

She discovered that if she walked flatfooted, the weight on her heels, her toes did not hurt too much. She made slow progress and it was a further twenty minutes before she arrived in the gallery. She paused here to capture her breath and rest her feet. She flopped gratefully against the balustrade forgetting about the intricately carved animals that lurked to damage the unwary. The horn of a unicorn poked sharply into her abdomen.

Startled she reared back, lost her grip, and fell backwards, her arms flailing wildly. Her cry of distress echoed around the vaulted roof and reached the ears of Jack, lounging, brandy glass in hand, in his dilapidated armchair.

Charlotte was shaken by her tumble but not seriously injured, the damage being mainly to her dignity. She sat up and looked for a smooth handhold to pull herself up. She could hear Jack taking the stairs three at a time. She barely had time to cover her legs before he appeared beside her.

'My God! What the hell are you doing here? You should be resting in your room and not wandering unaided about the place.'

She hated being told something she already knew. 'As you have told me several times, what I do is none of your concern, my lord.' It was hard to be cold and disdainful when sitting on one's bottom on the boards.

'You, my dear, are impossible. A sore trial indeed!' He reached down and slid his arms under her, lifting her smoothly.

'Put me down, at once, my lord.' She struggled but he just tightened his hold.

'Keep still, you ninny, do you wish me to drop you down the stairs?'

'I wish you to release me then the question of stairs will be irrelevant.'

He ignored her protests and carried her down. 'I shall take you to the library.'

'No, take me to the kitchen . . . if you please,' she added hastily, as she felt him stiffen.

Again he ignored her and strode down the endless passages to the library. He was forced to put her on the floor in order to open the heavy oak door. How she wished she could pick up her skirts and run away. She did not like being held in his embrace; it made her pulse race.

The door swung open. 'There, it is done.' Without asking her leave he picked her up again and carried her in. He walked across the once blue and green carpet and deposited her on a convenient chair.

'Thank you so much, my lord,' she said caustically.

He reached out for the chair the butler had used earlier and, swinging it round, he straddled it. Then, folding his arms across the back, he stared at her. She bridled; she knew she looked a fright, but it was rude to stare. She lowered her eyes, hiding her face from him.

'Do not look away, sweetheart. I cannot tell you how long it has been since a beautiful woman has looked at me without turning away in revulsion.'

Her head shot up, surprise loosening her tongue. 'What fustian you speak, my lord. You have a scarred face, that is all: your body is magnificent and undamaged. In my opinion it would be far worse if you had lost a limb.'

She saw his expression change and his jaw harden. She wished her words back. He stood up gently placing the chair to one side, his expression unreadable. Charlotte could not move. Was he going to strike her for her insolence? She felt her stomach contract with fear and she closed her eyes, too frightened to watch his approach.

But he did not raise his hand, he dropped to his knees beside her. He was so close she could feel his breath on her face. Then his fingers touched her cheek and she shuddered, but it was not fear that shook her. Something she did not understand was happening. Her limbs felt weak and her eyelids too heavy to lift. A delicious warmth ran through her, pooling in a most unexpected place. Her hands left her lap and without conscious thought they found their way to rest tentatively on his chest.

'Open your eyes, sweetheart. Look at me, please. I need to see your lovely green eyes. Need to know you do not find me repulsive.'

She forced them open. His face was inches from her own. She sighed and the fingers of one hand reached out to gently trace the scar from the corner of his mouth up to his forehead. She felt him tremble under her touch and wondered at it.

With his thumbs he traced the outline of her lips, her cheeks, and she felt her insides melt. Her lips parted and she buried her head in his thick dark hair, glad he had not had it cut short as was the current fashion.

He bent his neck and his mouth brushed across her, sending spirals of pleasure twisting down her spine. Then his tongue followed the same path and she tugged his hair, pulling him closer, unconsciously demanding that he kissed her properly.

His lips crushed hers and she was transported to a place she had never dreamed of. Now she understood why poets wrote of physical love, why men and women risked their very lives for it. After several blissful minutes he unlocked her fingers, removing them from his hair and sprang to his feet. His voice, when he spoke, sounded husky, different.

'My God, Charlotte – Miss Carstairs! What was I thinking? I have run mad.' He turned his back on her giving her time to compose herself, to rearrange her ruffled clothing. When she was still behind him, he folded himself on to a chair on the far side of the room.

'My dear, I must apologize once again for my outrageous behaviour. You are a green girl, not a society sophisticate, and I took shameless advantage of you.'

'No, my lord, you did not. The . . . the embrace was reciprocated, I can assure you.' Charlotte knew she sounded too earnest, like a pleading schoolgirl caught out in a misdemeanour, but she did not wish him to feel in anyway that he had offended her.

His rich laugh filled the space between them, removing the tension and awkwardness. 'I rather think it is time you call me by my given name: it is Jack, by the way. I am heartily sick of hearing "my lord" and "Lord Thurston" tumble from your lips at every opportunity.'

'The use of a given name is only permissible between close relatives and siblings. It would be very forward of me to call you thus.' She giggled. 'However I am prepared to call you Cousin Jack, or perhaps Uncle Jack might be more appropriate?'

'Uncle! You had better not, you baggage! I am eight and twenty, not in my dotage.'

She grinned. 'Then Cousin Jack it shall be. And you may call me Cousin Charlotte, if you wish.'

'I shall call you Charlotte. You may do as you please.'

She gave in – it was pointless to argue with him – he was obviously a man used to having his own way. 'What rank were you, Cousin Jack?'

'Major, I was a major in the Hussars.'

'My papa was a major also.' She nodded. 'But in the infantry. We travelled with him until my mama. . . .' She hesitated, then ploughed on, it was far too late to worry about propriety. 'Until my mama was expecting Harry, and then we were forced to return to England.'

She frowned as she recalled the cramped dark house in Romford, their lack of horses, the lack of sunlight. 'I much preferred it in Spain and Portugal, in spite of the deprivations we encountered.'

'You are a constant surprise, Charlotte, but the fact that you followed the drum explains a lot. You are obviously not a young lady who allows convention to hold her back.'

Her eyes flashed. 'Are you impugning my honour, Lord Thurston?'

'Do not poker up, sweetheart, I was referring to your bravery and excellent seat on a horse.'

At the unfortunate mention of her seat she flushed crimson and to her chagrin he threw back his head and roared with laughter. Reluctantly she found herself joining in.

Meltham had to knock twice in order to make himself heard. 'Come in, damn you,' Jack shouted, resenting the interruption.

'I apologize for disturbing you, my lord, but I have urgent need to speak to you in private.'

Jack was on his feet as he spoke. 'What is it, man? What has happened? Speak freely – Miss Carstairs needs to know as well.'

'It's Jenkins, my lord. I was becoming anxious about his lateness and sent a groom to seek him out.' The old man stopped, too overcome to continue.

'Tell me, what has happened to Jenkins?' Jack enquired softly, his arm resting on the butler's shaking shoulders.

'He's dead! Murdered most foully, my lord. Some wicked person has struck him down.'

Charlotte attempted to get to her feet, her face ashen. 'The children! Jack, I must check on the children. They have been out on their own all morning.' She attempted to step forward but the pain was too great, and with a soft cry, she sank back into her chair.

'Meltham, are the children inside?'

The butler nodded as he blew his nose vigorously. 'They are, my lord; they have been indoors this past hour helping Annie with her duties.'

Jack returned to her side and dropped down, taking her cold hands in his. 'I must leave you here, my dear. Do not try and walk. I shall send the children to talk to you. And also have a tray brought up from the kitchen.'

She watched him stride out, talking quietly to the butler. It was hardly credible how much they had both changed over the space of a few days. She had grown up, discovered what it meant to be a woman and he had metamorphosed from a bad-tempered drunkard to a formidable soldier, a man well able to take charge.

She shook her head in disbelief. How could Jenkins be dead? He had been here, conversing with her in this very room, but a few hours ago. Her eyes filled; he had had all his life ahead of him. Why would anyone wish to snuff that out? What evil was stalking this place? First, the attack on herself, a stone thrown that could have killed her; next, the unseen watcher at the front of the hall and now poor Jenkins had been cruelly killed.

She heard childish voices in the hall and Beth and Harry burst in, their faces tear-streaked. She held out her arms and they flung themselves at her.

'Oh Lottie, it is terrible! Poor Mr Jenkins has been killed,' Beth sobbed, 'and he was so nice to us. How could anyone do such a terrible thing?'

Charlotte stroked the girl's hair. 'I do not know, Beth, but Cousin Jack will find out. He will bring the perpetrators to justice, never fear.'

Harry sat back, scrubbing his eyes with his fists. 'Who is Cousin Jack, Lottie? Is he coming to stay here, too?'

'No, darling, Cousin Jack is Lord Thurston. We have decided to dispense with formality. In future you must address him in the same way.' This astounding news dried Beth's tears.

'Does this mean we are staying here for ever, Lottie?' Harry asked eagerly. 'Then I should like a puppy and Beth would like a kitten.'

Pleased they were so easily distracted, for Charlotte did not wish her siblings to dwell on the murder of the footman. 'I see no reason why not, but we also need two full-grown cats and a terrier to catch the rats.'

'And he told us that new staff are coming later today. Parlour maids, kitchen maids, extra footmen and also a housekeeper, is that true?'

'It is, Beth. Cousin Jack has agreed to allow me to organize the refurbishment and repair of the house. In a few weeks we should be living in a clean and luxurious establishment.'

'Not a pigsty!' Harry added innocently.

'Harry! That is quite enough. Things are not as bad as that.'

'But Betty and Annie said it is, so it must be, for they wouldn't lie to me, would they?'

'Beth, I said that is enough on that subject. Now settle yourselves down and tell me what you have been doing all morning and I shall tell you how I come to have damaged feet.'

Up to this point neither child had noticed this interesting fact. Harry scrambled down and peered closely at her bandages. 'You have no stockings or shoes on,' he observed seriously.

'No, Harry, I do not; my feet are too sore.'

The next hour was happily taken up by shared explanations and a light repast. Charlotte's eyes turned repeatedly to the ormolu mantel clock. Why did Jack not return?

The children left, chattering happily and Annie arrived soon afterwards. She gave Charlotte some disturbing news. It was not good – indeed matters were far worse than she could possibly have anticipated.

CHAPTER SEVEN

'N<small>O</small> money? None at all, Annie?' Charlotte was almost too shocked to speak.

'Well, as to that, I don't rightly know, miss. It was Mr Meltham who overheard his lordship's comment.'

'And lost no time telling everyone else, it would appear.'

Her maid shifted uncomfortably. 'He was that upset, Miss Carstairs, what with poor Jenkins and everything that he couldn't help himself.'

'What exactly did you overhear?'

Annie helped Charlotte back into her chair before answering. 'Let me think. He came back into the kitchen white as a ghost, muttering to himself. Betty fetched him a drink of water—'

'I do not need to know the details, just the substance, please, Annie.' Charlotte was beginning to lose patience.

'He said, "The ships went down", that's it – it was to do with ships. "The ships went down and Thurston's fortune went with them".'

'So Grandfather did not gamble away his money or invest it unwisely; it was unforeseen circumstances that caused this neglect, not poor management. I am glad about that.' Charlotte blinked as her vision blurred and she rubbed her temples. 'I fear I am getting a megrim, Annie. I have been trying to ignore the pain building over my right eye, but it is getting worse.'

'I'm not surprised, miss; there have been too many shocks and upsets today.' They both knew what was coming next. Charlotte did not get sick headaches often but when she did she was prostrate, some-

69

times for days. 'Come; let me take you back to your chamber. I'll get Betty to make you a tisane and bring it up immediately.'

'But I need to know what the lawyers have said – to know just how bad things are.'

'Whatever it is, miss, it will be the same when you're well again. The sooner you're resting quietly, in the dark, the better.'

Jack poured himself a large brandy, downed it in one swallow then refilled his glass before settling back into his chair. He stared morosely at the flickering flames, sunk once again into despair. He had thought his life turned round and that he had finally come to terms with his injuries. He could move on with his life. Seeing a lovely girl with her eyes sparkling, her lips swollen from his kisses he had felt like a whole man again.

Then some bastards had ambushed the footman and now he was dead. He thought he had dealt with that efficiently, more like the old Major Griffin. He had sent one groom to bring back the militia who were stationed in Ipswich and sent the remaining footman and the second groom to recover the corpse.

In the midst of this drama the carriage containing Messrs Blower and Thomas, the lawyers, had arrived in answer to his summons. He gulped down his drink; the alcohol beginning to serve its purpose, dull the pain as it had been during these past two years.

One of the black crows informed him that there was no money – that the old lord had invested heavily in shipping and that his fleet had gone down in a tropical storm taking his fortune with it. Jack swirled the dregs of his cognac around the crystal glass. He needed another brandy. He would get drunk as a wheelbarrow, return to his alcoholic fog. He didn't feel better in his cups, but at least like that he didn't have to think. He had consumed his fourth glass before he began to forget his despair.

His world had fallen apart for the second time. Without funds there could be no improvements, no restoration of Thurston Hall. Even if he wanted to, how could he offer for Charlotte when he was as destitute as she? He reached out and after several attempts, managed to grasp the decanter. It was almost empty. Devil take it! He could not get through the night without refreshment. He tipped the remains into his glass not spilling a drop. He nodded, smiling at his skill.

He had been ignoring the repeated knocking at his door, not wishing to speak to anyone. Even in his befuddled state, he realized that if he answered he could send whoever was there for more brandy.

'Enter,' he shouted, not bothering to turn his head.

'My lord,' Meltham said nervously, 'the lawyers are still waiting in the library for your return.'

'Tell them to go to hell. I do not wish to speak to them.'

'Shall I ask them to return tomorrow, my lord?'

Jack ignored the question. 'Refill this; in fact, bring me two bottles and then leave me in peace.'

He heard the butler depart leaving the door open, which allowed him to hear the worried whispering outside.

'Lord Thurston's indisposed, sir. Perhaps it would be best if you return tomorrow, or the next day?' The lawyer's reply was too indistinct for Jack to hear but he heard Meltham's reply. 'It is certainly good news, Mr Thomas. I shall make sure his lordship sees the documents as soon as he is well.'

Jack pushed himself upright, replacing his glass clumsily on the side table. Good news? How could there be any when the old crows had said all his fortune was beneath the waves? Should he enquire further before they left? No – tomorrow was soon enough. All he wanted at that moment was to drink himself into oblivion.

'Annie, place the bowl on the bed where I can reach it, then leave me alone please.'

'Yes, miss. I shall put the little brass bell next to your bed. I shan't be far away.'

Feeling too sick to answer, Charlotte rolled over on her side, praying she would fall asleep and wake up feeling well again. The shutters were closed and what was left of the bed hangings had been drawn round. But the room was still too bright. She tried pulling the comforter over her head, but with her face covered she felt even worse and uncomfortably warm.

She twisted on to her other side, turning her back to the windows, and without the light flickering across immediately felt a little better. There was so much to think about. What would happen to the new staff, would they be sent away? Her head throbbed and the pain over her eye intensified, feeling as though a hot needle was being plunged into it. She gave up any attempt to reason and resigned herself to enduring a miserable twenty-four hours.

Charlotte slept through the afternoon and into the night. She woke in the small hours to discover to her delight that her headache was waning, her brain ready to function. Glad she had not had to use the china bowl, she sat up. She felt a trifle weak but otherwise quite restored.

She wriggled her toes experimentally and found they, too, appeared to have recovered. Slipping out of bed, she groped for the tinderbox on her bedside table. Deftly she struck the flint then lit the candle. Her wrapper was draped over the end of her bed and she pulled it on. It was chilly in her room; there was a definite autumnal nip in the air.

Standing up, she walked carefully about the chamber testing her toes. They bore her weight quite happily. She picked up the candlestick and, holding it aloft, went in search of supper. It seemed a long time since she had enjoyed the meat pasty and bread and cheese in the library with the children.

The house was silent, everyone asleep. Then she heard the patter of small feet above her head and knew that the rats were awake and busy about their own business. She crept along the empty passageways, not wishing to disturb the children by her nocturnal ramble. The flame of her candle threw eerie shadows up and down the walls. A woman of weaker nerves might believe that she was seeing ghosts, but she was not given to missish vapours of that kind.

The hall with its high ceiling seemed alarmingly large. She paused in the small pool of light from her candle, trying to get her bearings. The passageway that led to the kitchens was on the far side to the left of the entrance. The stairs faced the front door so she needed to follow the wall to her right until she found it.

She squeezed her eyes closed and opened them again hoping her night vision might be improved. One of the after effects of her headaches was impaired vision and tonight was no exception.

She could not stand on the stairs all night; if she wished to go to the kitchen to find herself something to eat she would have to be brave, step out into the darkness and trust that her memory was correct. She fingered her way around the newel post then back until her feeble light showed she was standing in front of the dark wood panelling of the wall.

She raised her candle again; she could see a door ahead – that would have to be Jack's. She would make certain she was even quieter than the mice as she passed. She already knew him well enough to know that if she appeared in his domain dressed in her nightgown, he would take that as an invitation to continue what they had started earlier. She knew that in the eyes of the world she was a woman of loose morals, but as long as she knew it to be without substance, she was content.

She negotiated the endless panelling, avoiding all three doors, until she reached the far side and could see she was facing a corridor, but was it the correct one? Did it lead to the kitchen, or somewhere else entirely? In this rabbit warren of a house it was hard to be sure.

She walked a little way down, sniffing the air like a hound. Yes – she could faintly detect the smell of food – this had to be the right direction. Feeling more confident, she increased her pace, knowing that the butler's pantry, housekeeper's rooms and the servants' quarters all led from this passageway and that the old-fashioned kitchen was at the far end.

Charlotte glanced over her shoulder nervously. She suddenly had the feeling that someone was behind her, but when she spun and held her candle high, she could neither see nor hear anything suspicious. The silence and the darkness were beginning to unnerve her. The light from her candle did not shine far, it would be easy for someone to wait, quite close, but remain out of her sight. By the time she reached her destination she was almost running.

She pushed harder, the kitchen door was stuck. It was difficult to lift the latch with one hand but she was reluctant to put her candlestick down. She looked over her shoulder, checking to see she was alone, and then risked placing it on the floor beside her. She gripped the heavy latch with both hands and managed to lift it clear of the hasp. Triumphantly she threw her weight against the door.

It flew open and, losing her balance, she tumbled forward to find herself enveloped in the arms of the one person she had been at pains to avoid.

'Charlotte, my dear, what unexpected pleasure.' Jack's words were slurred and his breath pure alcohol.

'You are foxed, sir. Let go of me at once, before we both fall.'

He released his hold and stepped back, swaying alarmingly. She was glad to see that he had managed to light two oil lamps without setting fire to himself or the kitchen.

'I have come down to find food; are you on a similar errand, Cousin?' She rather thought a good meal would be exactly what he needed. She could recall her father once telling a young lieutenant that he had to eat in order to sober up. She frowned, or was it to eat before he drank in order to remain sober?

Jack dragged out a chair and subsided. 'Actually, sweetheart, I forget why I came here. But I expect you are right; I came in search of food.'

She smiled, relieved he was no longer looming over her, breathing brandy fumes down her neck. 'In that case, I shall make us both a meal. No, do not look so surprised, you will discover I am a proficient cook, even in such an antiquated kitchen.'

She busied herself finding the makings for an omelette. The bread was still fresh. She would ask him to cut it; it would keep him occupied, stop him staring at her in that disconcerting manner. She put the bread, the board and a sharp knife beside him.

'Do you think you could cut us some bread without slicing off your fingers?' She smiled, as obediently, he began his task. It was taking all his concentration to hold the blade straight. Satisfied she had achieved her aim, she returned to her cooking.

A short while later the impromptu meal was ready. She had found the butter dish in the pantry and he had hacked off two thick slabs of bread. She divided the creamy yellow omelette between two plates, added the slices of thickly buttered bread and placed one on either side of the table. The appetizing smell of eggs wafted across the room.

Jack looked at it with distaste. 'I find I am no longer hungry.' As she watched she saw his complexion pale to an almost greenish tinge. Then he kicked back his chair and, hand to mouth, headed for the scullery. She tried not to listen to the unpleasant noises. Her own nausea threatened to return and she pushed her plate away.

She heard him washing his face and then he returned, his colour restored, and quite unrepentant. To her horror he sat down, picked up his fork and started to shovel down his meal with obvious enjoyment.

He paused just long enough to say, 'If you are not intending to eat yours, may I have it?'

She nodded, too disgusted to speak. He was behaving with the same disregard for another's feelings as her little brother Harry. Had he no delicacy at all? The kettle hanging on a trivet over the fire began to hiss. She supposed she could make him a cup of tea. It might help to dilute the brandy he had consumed.

She rose, forgetting she was not dressed, and her wrapper gaped open, revealing far more than she considered proper to the interested spectator munching his way through *her* supper! He made no comment. Angrily she pulled the edges together and retied the belt. The man was a Philistine – more interested in filling his belly than anything else.

She unlocked the tea caddy and put three spoonfuls into the pot. She was reaching over to lift the heavy black kettle when he spoke sharply.

'No, Charlotte, wait. I will do it.'

So he had been watching her after all. 'I can manage. I am not a milk sop.'

'Leave it!'

She froze at his command, her hand poised over the handle. She heard his chair scrape on the tiles and then he was beside her. He took her hovering hand and drew it back.

'Charlotte, you ninny, you have no protection. Your hand would have been burnt and the kettle dropped.' She stared at her hand lost in his and found she could not withdraw it. Her breathing was erratic and she trembled. 'Are you afraid of me, sweetheart? Is that why you shake like a blancmange?'

Instantly she snatched her hand from his. Her voice was commendably composed. 'Of course not. Why ever should I be frightened of a giant ex-soldier with a penchant for brandy and distressing habit of manhandling me?'

'*Touché!* I am indeed all you say. I can assure you that at this precise moment it is not brandy I have a desire for.'

There was no mistaking his meaning. She felt her cheeks turn crimson and hastily returned to her tea making. 'Well, are you going to tip the water on the leaves or not, Cousin? I would like a dish of tea to go with my bread and butter.'

He swung the kettle over and tipped the boiling water, one-handed, into the china pot. Then without a word he replaced it by the fire.

'I have my tea weak, is that acceptable?'

'Perfectly.'

Then Charlotte found the strainer and tipped the tea into the waiting cups. Jack was moving about behind her. Whatever was he doing? She expelled her breath with a relieved sigh as she heard him leave the room. Carefully she carried the tea over to the table and put it down. It was then she noticed the two plates which had contained the eggs were gone, as had the bread and butter. Botheration! She had been looking forward to eating that.

She did not look round when he came back from the direction of the pantry. She held her breath as he stopped behind her. Then he leant forward and his face brushed hers as he dropped a plate in front of her.

'Here you are, sweetheart, not as good as your delicious omelette, but I hope it will be enough to satisfy you.'

On a clean white plate was the errant bread and butter, crusts removed, accompanied by a large wedge of cheese and a spoonful of chutney. Her mouth curved in delight. 'Thank you. That looks wonderful.' She picked up a fork and prodded hopefully at the relish. She raised an eyebrow.

'I know; it must be over two years old, but I can vouch for the fact that it tastes none the worse for that.'

Charlotte set to with enthusiasm. She interspersed mouthfuls of bread, chutney and cheese with swallows of tea. She was aware that he had sat down opposite and was watching her wolf down her food.

'I do like a female with a healthy appetite,' he announced to the ceiling.

She choked on her tea. 'It is impolite to comment on such things. Have you no manners?'

He chuckled. 'None at all, sweetheart. I am merely an uncouth soldier so I shall have to rely on your superior knowledge of such matters to rectify my failings.'

She grinned. 'You are incorrigible, but I am glad to say that I am replete. I could not eat another morsel.'

'Excellent.' He was about to place his boots on the table but seeing her frown he pushed his chair back and folded his arms instead. He half smiled at her. 'Perhaps you can explain why you found it necessary to sneak downstairs in the middle of the night to find sustenance?'

She nodded. 'I went to bed with a megrim yesterday afternoon. Usually I'm too sick to eat for at least a day and so my maid did not bring me a supper tray.'

'And I was too drunk to eat, but now we are both well fed and I am sober.' Charlotte shuddered as she recalled the reason he was no longer in his cups. He openly smiled at her look of disgust. 'Quite so! Did your maid tell you what the lawyers said?'

'She said there is no money, that Grandfather invested heavily in shipping and everything went down in a storm.'

'That is correct. We are at an impasse. I cannot give you the money to restore the Hall, or employ new staff.' He paused assessing her reaction. 'It seemed pointless asking them to draw up documents if there were no funds for you to work with.'

She stilled. What was he telling her, that their bargain was cancelled? That the challenge was no longer valid? 'You intend to turn us out because of this? We will manage somehow. We do not eat very much, you will hardly know we are here.'

He stared pointedly at her empty plate. 'If the bantlings eat as much as you I shall be bankrupt within a se'ennight.' His face was solemn but she knew he was funning.

'And you drink enough brandy to fill a bath so I consider we are equal on that score.'

He laughed. 'But, my dear, I can stop drinking brandy, but you cannot stop eating.'

'Do not be ridiculous, Jack. This is a serious matter. Have you no funds of your own at all?'

He was instantly serious. 'I have a major's half pension and I believe there is something from my grandfather, but altogether it does not amount to very much.'

'And I have a tiny annuity. I am afraid that both pensions stopped on my mother's death.'

'Then, my dear girl, shall we starve here together, or part company?'

'Together, if you please. There is a walled vegetable garden, it is overgrown but it can easily be brought round. We can purchase some chickens and a milk cow and perhaps a hog or two. I believe that we could provide most of our own food and it would hardly cost anything.'

'Good God! You are serious – do you really think we could succeed?'

She nodded, beginning to believe that their life at Thurston Hall could be viable.

'And I can shoot even with one working eye and there is game aplenty in the woods.' He stood up, his expression animated, his enthusiasm making him appear younger, less austere. 'Miss Carstairs, you are a bloody marvel! There is no money, the place is falling down around our ears, but together I think we might pull things round.' He held out his arms and she walked into them.

At first he just held her; she felt safe, protected by his strength. His body heat seeped through her thin wrapper and nightgown taking away the chill. Then a different kind of heat started to flow around her limbs. His chin was resting lightly on the crown of her head, his hands moving gently up and down her spine. With a sigh of pleasure she relaxed further into his embrace.

His arms tightened and his mouth nibbled at her hair; his hot breath sent shock waves down her back. She moved, but he raised a hand and tilted her head allowing him free access to her mouth. She drowned in his kisses, oblivious to all but the passion they were sharing. Then she felt him stiffen and in one fluid movement he threw her down to the floor, landing on top of her, crushing the breath from her body.

Furious at his crude attack she was about to protest when there was a flash of light, a bang, the sound of breaking glass and the room was full of smoke.

'Lie still, we are being shot at,' he hissed in her ear.

CHAPTER EIGHT

CHARLOTTE was too frightened to answer. She closed her eyes and prayed fervently for deliverance. Jack dropped a tender kiss on the back of her neck then she felt his bulk shift and he was gone. Why had their attackers not spoken? Identified themselves – come in search of them? After all they were unarmed and helpless beneath the table, or at least she was.

Where he had gone she had no idea and dared not move her head to see. She knew he was an experienced soldier well used to being ambushed; he would know what to do, she had to lie still, keep praying and listen.

She thought she heard a slight movement outside the kitchen window but could not be sure. There was a cool draught on her face and she guessed someone had opened the back door. Was it the assassin coming in, or Jack going out? Her heart was beating so loudly she could hear it. Her legs were jutting out; they felt exposed, vulnerable, easily seen in the flickering lamplight. Inch by inch she drew them in until she was curled tight, hugging her knees. Somehow the smaller she made herself the safer she felt.

She rolled into the space that ran down the centre of the table and came up on all fours using the chair legs as protection. She carefully turned her head. She could see no sign of either an attacker or of Jack. The smoke had cleared but the smell of cordite remained. From her hiding place she saw that there were shards of broken pottery on the floor under the huge dresser opposite.

Did this mean the bullets had struck there? They must have been fired from the outside, through the window. She considered the implications. The kitchen, unlike the rest of the house, did not have tiny leaded panes; it had clear glass and wooden frames. The ideal place, in fact the only place, a gun could be fired with any hope of hitting a person inside. She folded her hands on the chair seat, resting her head on them in contemplation. There was something odd about the whole thing, but she could not quite think what it was.

She sat up abruptly, forgetting she was under the table, and the sound of her head cracking against the wood echoed round the room. She sank back with a startled cry, rubbing her bruised crown. She remained frozen, expecting to see a pair of boots, or a pistol, jammed under the table, but all was quiet.

She waited for a few moments then decided it was safe to emerge. As a precaution she crawled out keeping the table between herself and the window. She didn't attempt to stand, merely rested her back against the dresser, brushing away the broken china first. Then, stretching out her legs to ease her stiffness she waited for the pain in her head to subside.

She returned to the idea that had caused her to have the accident. The attackers must have been watching the house and had seen the lights go on in the kitchen. She shivered violently, recalling the feeling she had had that someone was in the passage with her on her way to the kitchen. Was it credible that an intruder had been inside already?

Surely this was not possible? The doors were locked; the windows stout; the only way anyone could have entered was through a secret passage and this would mean the person was familiar with the building. The most horrific explanation was that it was a member of their staff who was attempting to kill them.

She shook her head, regretting it as a searing pain shot between her eyes. She could not believe that Smith, the remaining footman, a pleasant middle-aged man, could be involved. And the butler was above suspicion. The two grooms were accommodated above the stables so they could not have been involved either. She was being fanciful.

She stopped, shocked to the core. Could Jenkins have been killed because he had unmasked Smith as a potential murderer? She felt perspiration trickle down her spine. It was all too complicated, too outlandish for her to make sense of it. Why should anyone, especially a footman, wish to kill them?

Then she remembered the unprovoked attack on herself; the three incidents had to be connected. She shivered again and her teeth began to chatter. It was cold sitting on the flagstones in her nightwear so far away from the fire, and the broken windows were letting in a steady stream of cold air.

She wished Jack would come back. Beneath his dissolute façade he was a formidable man, with a lifetime of command behind him. She clenched her teeth to stop them rattling her already aching head. It was freezing – attackers or not she had to get up and warm herself.

Cautiously, she pulled herself upright, peeping over the table edge to ensure the room was empty. If Jack was prowling about outside she was certain that whoever had shot at them would have vanished into the darkness.

She picked her way carefully through the debris of broken crockery and glass. She did not need to add lacerated feet to crushed toes, bruised head and partially healed cut. The kettle was warm and full enough to push back over the glowing coals. She would make a second pot of tea; extravagant, but in the circumstances allowable.

She sensibly kept as close to the fire as safety allowed by standing inside the cavernous grate where, in olden days, a boy would have stood to turn the spit. From her vantage point she surveyed the wreckage of the kitchen. The floor was easily fixed; a good sweep and a scrub would put that right. The window could be repaired, if there was glass to be found, otherwise the broken panes would have to be replaced with wood.

She stared at the dresser. Betty and the children had spent hours polishing the copper pans and bowls that hung there and the majority of these were undamaged. She realized that in the glow from the oil-lamps she could see a reflection of the window. She smiled, that was how Jack had known they were in danger. He must have caught a glimpse of something in the surface of the pan and his instincts had done the rest.

She felt herself blush. How could she have thought that he was hurling her to the ground in order to ravish her? She giggled. She had been reading too many romances. Mama had warned her that they were not suitable for a gently bred young woman. She blinked back her tears as she thought of her mother. She missed her so much and it was hard to keep to her vow not to grieve.

Her mother had been desperately unhappy after Papa's death and had made no effort to fight the fever she had contracted. She had welcomed her demise, hurried towards her end, happily abandoning her children. A flair of anger shot through Charlotte. She would never pine away for a dead lover. She would put the needs of the living first. No man was worth dying for, even Jack.

Jack? What had he to do with anything? Yes, she had allowed him to take liberties with her person, behaved in a most unseemly manner, but that was all. It was just the natural reaction of a woman to an attractive man, was it not? Her feelings were not engaged, how could they be? She had only known him a few days and for most of those he had been drunk and frequently unpleasant. In future she would be more circumspect and keep a proper distance, behave in the way she knew she ought. And she would inform him of her decision when he got back.

She was sitting at the table sipping her tea when he returned. He called to her as he closed and bolted the back door.

'It is quite safe now, Charlotte. Whoever it was has vanished – there is no one outside.'

She gestured to the teapot and he nodded, glad to have something hot to drink. 'You should wear your jacket, you look like a buccaneer in your shirt sleeves.' She had quite forgotten her determination to remain aloof.

'No doubt you would like me to wear a stock and a diamond fob as well?'

She giggled, he sounded so affronted at the thought. 'How you dress is none of my concern, Cousin. I was jesting; you know that I would not presume to criticize your attire or behaviour.'

He laughed out loud. 'You can say what you please, my dear, I am immune to criticism. I live purely to please myself.'

She snorted inelegantly, spraying tea across the table. 'That is absurd! But, never fear, I shall remind you of your words next time you fly into a rage because I have inadvertently upset you.'

She became serious as he sat down, the tea cup too small for his hand, the saucer left deliberately on the dresser. 'Jack, are you certain that there is no one hiding inside? I thought there was someone following me when I came here earlier.'

'In the Hall?' He frowned. No, I am sure you were mistaken. However, I shall search the place thoroughly as soon as I am armed.'

'Thank you. I shall sleep more soundly knowing we are, at least, safe indoors.' She drank her tea in silence. 'Who do think was out there? Why would anyone want to kill either of us?' Her earlier considerations now seemed too far-fetched to mention.

'I have no idea, but I aim to find out. I suspect that it is disaffected locals inflamed by the seditious literature that is being circulated in many parts of Suffolk.'

'They certainly looked sullen and unfriendly and one threw a stone at me, did he not?'

'He did indeed. And Jenkins . . . he must have been a second victim. But I can assure you he will be the last.' He reached over the table to capture her hand but she removed it.

Surprised he raised his eyebrows. 'Have I offended you? Are you upset with me, Charlotte?'

'No, Cousin, far from it. I like you exceedingly.' That had been quite the wrong thing to say for she watched his jaw clench and he began to push back his chair. 'No, you misunderstand me. I am trying to explain. I like you; you are a brave and resourceful man, exactly the person to solve this mystery, but I do not wish to repeat what has happened between us.' She stared at him, her expression severe, her huge green eyes sincere. 'I wish to remain a cousin to you, nothing else; do I make myself clear?'

He nodded. 'You are right, as usual. And, as usual, I apologize for suggesting it could be otherwise.' He shrugged, as if indifferent. 'You are a beautiful woman, eminently desirable, and it has been far too long since I—' He stopped and had the grace to blush. He had been about to say something exceedingly indelicate. 'Stay where you are until I come back for you.' His voice was gruff and he couldn't meet her eyes.

It was a long lonely wait in the kitchen and it gave Charlotte too much time to think, to consider her options, to decide what would be best for Beth and Harry. The promise to her mother to bring them to Thurston had been fulfilled. There had been nothing said about staying permanently once they had arrived. She had done as she had vowed, now she had to make her own decisions.

She remembered the letter she had sent to her grandfather, the one that had been returned unread, that had coloured her feelings about Lord Thurston. His rejection had almost persuaded her not to come, despite having given her word. Grandfather, she belatedly realized, had already been dead. So who had read the letter addressed to him and sent it back? It could not have been Jack, he had not been in residence then.

Another unpalatable thought occurred to her: Mama had been left nothing in the will. Lord Thurston had never relented, even in death he had rejected his only child. She swallowed the lump in her throat and got up to see if she could squeeze a third cup of tea from the cooling pot.

Finally she made her decision. There was no question of her seeking employment and leaving the children, and Annie and Betty, to face the danger alone. Whatever she did it would have to include all of them, but at that precise moment she could see no fresh path to follow. She had no option; she was stuck at Thurston, for the moment anyway.

She heard footsteps in the passageway. There was one thing she did know: would-be assassins were not the only danger she faced – Lord Thurston posed an even greater threat. For some unaccountable reason her sense of propriety went out of the room when he walked into it.

'I am sorry I have been so long, Charlotte. I wished to be quite sure the house was secure. I had not realized just how big it was until I was obliged to poke and pry into every room.'

She averted her eyes from the pistol he held. 'Goodness, I hope you have not disturbed the children. The last thing I want is for them to know what happened here tonight.'

'Charlotte, be sensible. How can you not tell them? They are bound to notice the damage to this room.'

'Oh! I had not thought. But, Jack, they were so upset about Jenkins, and remember, Harry is only four.'

He started to walk over, to offer comfort, but on observing her recoil, remained in the doorway. 'They will have to remain indoors anyway, until the militia come tomorrow and flush the buggers out.'

'Jack!'

Her shocked exclamation made him laugh. 'I am a rough soldier – profanities slip out. But I apologize, again. In future I shall endeavour to curb my tendency to pepper my conversation with inappropriate words.'

'Thank you, it would be appreciated.' She tightened the belt of her wrapper. 'If it is safe, I shall return to my rooms. I am decidedly cold after sitting around in here.'

She reclaimed the candlestick and kindled it from a taper pushed into the fire. 'Listen, did you hear that? I do believe it was a cockerel crowing somewhere in the village. It will be full light soon.' The blackness outside had slowly turned to grey during her long vigil.

'It is five o'clock; you have been up for far too long. Come along, I shall escort you to your room.'

She shook her head making her plait dance down her back. 'I am quite capable of finding my way back. I shall bid you good night, Cousin, or should it be good morning?'

Jack allowed her to ascend, but remained alert on the stairs until he heard her bedchamber door close behind her. He did not return to his rooms but headed purposefully to the library. He had thinking to do and plans to make. He was used to going without sleep; he had done so many times before when fighting in the Peninsula. He had a campaign to organize, a battle to win. He grinned; two battles in fact, and he rather thought that disgruntled villagers were going to be easier to overcome than Charlotte's reservations.

Her ideas for rescuing them were sound, but could not be put into practice until the other matter was settled. They were far too exposed at the moment; there were not enough men to keep watch. He desperately needed ready funds.

He rested his head on his folded arms; he would have a quick nap, ten – fifteen minutes – no more. Leaning on a desk was as good a place as any. He was wakened by the sound of footsteps in the passageway, women's voices, and the clank of pails. He pushed himself upright. Good God! It was past six o'clock. He had slept for over an hour; he was out of condition, his body not responding to his will. Too much brandy, too little food and not enough exercise. But all that was going to change; from now on he was a new man; he had a purpose in life again.

Irritated by the clatter in what was usually a silent house he yawned, stretched and strode over to open the door. Two young women, sacks tied round as aprons, were on their knees scrubbing the boards. They all froze; he too surprised to react, the girls too frightened.

The older one started to scramble up. 'My lord, we did not realize you were in the library, or we wouldn't have started cleaning here.'

'It is of no matter. I am glad you woke me; I have work to do. Is Meltham up?'

'He is, my lord, in his pantry sorting out the duties of the new footmen.'

He nodded politely and, stepping round their buckets, went to find his butler, delighted at the news that there were to be extra men working and living inside. He knocked sharply on the pantry door. The butler appeared, looking more animated than he had for years. He beamed on seeing who was disturbing him. Not a reaction Jack was expecting.

'Lord Thurston, I'm delighted to see you up so early. I have some documents from Messrs Blower and Thomas. I believe they will please you.' He held out a rolled parchment, neatly tied with blue ribbons.

Jack took it. 'Could you organize a jug of strong coffee and have it served to me in the library? And get those girls to clean my rooms. I am sick of living like a hog.'

Meltham's face appeared about to crack. 'Perhaps, my lord, I could suggest one of the new men to act as your valet? Robert has had experience in this field.'

Jack was about to refuse; he had always looked after his own gear, never bothered with a manservant. But he was a lord and things were different. 'That is a sound idea. Get him in there with the girls; he can sort out my clothes, find me something clean to wear. And I shall require a bath as well.'

'I shall arrange it right away. Young Robert will suit you perfectly. Shall I arrange for something more suitable for him to wear? A footman's uniform is not appropriate for a valet.'

Jack waved his hand in assent. 'Whatever you like; send that coffee straightaway.'

On his return to the library he spread out the parchment on the desk moving the candelabra nearer. His heart beat heavily; his skin prickled with anticipation. He had remembered hearing the butler's words to the lawyer last night, he had spoken of good news.

He scanned the spidery black writing, absorbing its contents instantly. He banged his fist on the desk in triumph. There was money, not a lot, not the hundreds of thousands that there used to be, but, by God, sufficient for his purposes.

It appeared that the old lord had left a few thousands in the funds and this had been untouched by the commercial disaster with the ships. Over the next hour he did some rapid calculations, gulping down coffee to keep himself awake. If he spent wisely, was miserly with his resources, he thought he could restore half the property, but would close down the rest.

By employing local labour to clear the grounds, mend the fences, do all the outside jobs, he rather thought the discontent would go. With repaired cottages and food in their bellies not many men would still be prepared to risk dangling on the end of a rope.

He got up, satisfied he was ready to explain to Charlotte how things stood. He glanced at the bracket clock, it was thirty minutes past seven.

He doubted if she would appear before noon. This gave him ample time to bathe, change his garments, and, God help him, even to put on a jacket and neckcloth!

Chuckling he tossed the paper to one side and, as he did so, a second sheet, secreted behind the first, dropped on to the desk. He almost ignored it, believing it was merely a letter confirming the financial document, but something prompted him to pick it up.

The first paragraph of the letter merely informed him that Messrs Blower and Thomas were returning the following day in order for him to sign the paper that would release the remaining money. This was excellent news; he had not dreamt that he would be able to begin improvements so soon. He continued reading and his stomach lurched and he felt his face drain of colour. Horrified he collapsed back on to the chair. For a moment he stared blankly into space hardly able to assimilate the words. With shaking hands he held the letter up, reading the bold black script.

We feel it is our duty to bring to your attention the fact that Miss Carstairs has been residing under your protection, unchaperoned, for the past two weeks and this is already giving rise to unpleasant gossip. Therefore, we respectfully suggest that we should find Miss Carstairs, and her family, an alternative establishment in Ipswich, before her reputation is irreversibly besmirched. We are yours, respectfully. . . .

Jack threw the letter down and dropped his head into his hands. How could he have been so stupid, so immersed in his own misery, own gratification, that he had all but ruined an innocent young woman? As Charlotte's only male relative, however remote the connection, it was his duty to protect her, not cause her ruination. The lawyers, for all their impertinence, had the right of the matter. It was his responsibility to rectify matters and he would do so immediately. He was not sure how Charlotte would react to his solution.

CHAPTER NINE

A<small>T</small> ten o'clock, Charlotte, dressed in her brown cambric dress, children at her heels, was on her way to the freshly cleaned breakfast parlour.

She could hear activity downstairs and hurried to the balustrade to discover what was going on. In the hall were two unknown footman, on their knees, scrubbing the boards. 'Good heavens! I did not realize men servants cleaned.' Charlotte smiled down at her brother and sister. 'Thurston Hall will soon be clean and tidy and then it will feel much more like a home to us.' But she feared that the house was just too big and too old to be made truly comfortable.

Both footmen jumped up, damp sack-aprons flapping. 'Good morning, Miss Carstairs, Miss Beth and Master Harry,' they chorused, obviously well rehearsed.

She nodded. 'Good morning; you are doing an excellent job here, well done.' They bowed and Charlotte swept through feeling rather like royalty, not an ordinary soldier's daughter.

There had been a buffet laid out on the sideboard; which included several china plates containing sliced ham, sweet rolls, bread, plum cake, jars of preserves, butter and a jug of milk. Such extravagance surprised her in the present financial circumstances. The door opened in the panelling and another new member of staff emerged.

'Good morning, Miss Carstairs. I'm Mary. I'm to ask as to what you would like to drink. There's tea or coffee or chocolate? And would you like some coddled eggs, or such like?'

'Thank you, but I think we have more than enough here already. I would like chocolate; what about you two?'

They were seated around the white damask-covered table when Lord Thurston strolled in. Harry was the first to spot him. His eyes rounded and his mouth fell open allowing a half-eaten mouthful to tumble out. Automatically Charlotte corrected his table manners. 'Harry, that is disgusting. Kindly eat with your mouth closed in future.'

The little boy swallowed hastily before speaking. 'But, Lottie, Cousin Jack's here and he's all dressed up.'

Charlotte's head whipped round. 'My word, Cousin, you look smart as paint; I feel quite drab in my work gown, beside you.' He bowed, pleased his appearance met with approval.

'You're wearing a stock, Cousin Jack, and your boots are polished. Is there to be a party here today?' In Harry's limited experience such sartorial elegance always heralded a celebration of some sort.

'No, young man, not today. But the militia are here. Would you like to come and see the soldiers, when you have finished breaking your fast?'

Without waiting for permission from his sister Harry threw down his cutlery and jumped off his chair.

'Will you join us? There are things we need to discuss, Charlotte.'

'I need to meet with Mrs Thomas, the housekeeper, but I shall come directly from there to join you outside.'

'Excellent. I shall be watching for you.' He ruffled Harry's hair. 'Come along, bantlings, we must not keep Captain Forsythe waiting.'

The door closed behind them, leaving Charlotte confused. The urbane gentleman dressed in navy-blue superfine, waistcoat and neatly tied stock, with his buff breeches spotless, his Hessians so shiny you could see your face in them, was almost a stranger. Crossly she glanced down at her own shabby dress and was tempted to run upstairs and change. She did have another morning gown, a fetching sprigged muslin in daffodil yellow, but it was not suitable for the domestic chores she envisaged being involved in that morning.

She smiled; Jack had also got someone to cut his hair. She rather liked the shortened style, and having the thick dark hair brushed forward obscured much of his scar. Why had he taken the children? Up to this point he had avoided them. What had caused this *volte face*? Intrigued, she abandoned her half-eaten breakfast, dabbed her lips with a napkin and hurried to her appointment with Mrs Thomas.

Her meeting was brief and she left certain that the housekeeper would be able to run the place far better than she. Delighted that was one responsibility she could safely delegate, she rushed through the house to keep her rendezvous outside. The double front doors were standing open and she could see the soldiers grouped in the turning circle. She ducked her head, trying to assess how many there were. It was hard to tell, but she rather thought that there were at least two dozen horses milling about.

Where were the children? Then she saw Jack, Harry in his arms, conversing earnestly with a man, who by his appearance was obviously Captain Forsythe. Beth was close by, mesmerized by the array of military splendour. She was too young to remember their time on the Continent when such sights were an everyday occurrence.

Charlotte realized that he must have sensed her coming, as his head turned and he smiled a welcome. Her chest constricted and her knees felt strangely weak. She almost turned and went in, to the safety of domestic issues, but something compelled her to walk across to join him.

Both men bowed politely. 'Miss Carstairs, may I present Captain Forsythe to you?'

The soldier bowed. 'Delighted to meet you, Miss Carstairs, but I wish the situation could have been otherwise.'

She nodded. 'And I am pleased to meet you, Captain Forsythe.'

Formalities over, Jack told her what was to happen next. 'The troops are going to search the grounds, but if they find nothing suspicious, they will widen their search to the surrounding villages.'

'How long will this take?'

Jack looked to the captain for an answer.

'We will be thorough, Miss Carstairs. Three incidents in two weeks indicate a serious breach of the peace. We will bivouac in the barns and continue searching until we apprehend the culprits or are certain they have fled the vicinity.'

'That is good news, Captain. It is not a pleasant feeling being constantly under threat.' She turned to Jack. 'You wished to speak to me? Shall I wait in the library until you have finished here?'

He nodded. 'I shall not be long. If you would wait a moment, I shall come with you.' He put Harry back on the ground. 'Harry, you must go in with your sister. Charlotte and I have things to discuss.'

Charlotte had watched this exchange with annoyance. The children were her responsibility; it was to her they should look for permission. They were all the family she had and she was not going to allow Lord Thurston to usurp her authority. Knowing she was overreacting, but unable to stop herself, she did not wait as requested, but left, head high, and stalked back into the hall, displeasure obvious in every step she took.

Puzzled, Jack watched her go. What burr had lodged under her saddle this time? She was as unpredictable as a windmill in a storm. Impatiently he turned back to the waiting captain.

'Report to me at noon, Captain Forsythe, I wish to be kept fully informed of your progress. Is that clear?'

'Yes, my lord.' The captain clicked his heels and bowed.

Jack spotted a horse cantering down the drive and cursed under his breath. It was the damn doctor; what did he want? Charlotte was recovered and Jenkins was beyond medical aid. Scowling, he stepped forward to greet this uninvited guest.

'Good morning, Dr Andrews, are we expecting you?'

The young man swung down from the saddle tossing his reins to a newly arrived stable boy. 'Good day, Lord Thurston. Miss Carstairs sent a message to call when I was in the vicinity. I believe she wants some local information from me.'

Jack didn't like this man; he was too young, too personable. Far closer to Charlotte's age than he was; just the sort of man to turn her head. Why would a young girl of nineteen summers want to marry him, an impecunious, imperfect specimen, when she could have someone like the doctor?

'Miss Carstairs is not receiving today. The shock of the murder yesterday, you understand. Perhaps you could call back in a few days' time?'

Doctor Andrews appeared confused. Jack glanced over his shoulder and was annoyed to see Charlotte waving merrily from behind the library window. He could hardly send him packing after this. He fixed a smile to his face. It did not reassure the young doctor.

'It would appear that she has changed her mind. I have estate business to attend to, so I shall bid you good day.'

Charlotte shook her head in disbelief as she watched Jack storm away like a petulant child. Sometimes he was more immature than Harry! She supposed their talk would have to wait until he recovered his temper. She moved over to the chairs grouped informally in front of the empty fireplace. She supposed she ought to have a chaperon; it would not do to be thought to be involved in two illicit relationships. She was still giggling at the absurdity when Dr Andrews was announced by one of the footmen.

'Come in, sir, it is good of you to ride over. I expect you have heard about poor Jenkins?'

He nodded, his face serious. 'I have, Miss Carstairs; a bad business indeed. I see the militia are here, no doubt they will catch the perpetrators if they are still in the area.'

'I do hope so. But this is not why I asked to see you. Please be seated, sir.' She waited until he was settled before continuing. 'I would normally have approached the vicar, but as you are aware, we do not have one in Thurston at the moment.' She paused, marshalling her thoughts.

The doctor appeared rather uncomfortable, glancing frequently at the open door. To reassure him she smiled, quite unaware of the impact this had. She was a lovely girl and smiling, she was a diamond of the first water, an incomparable, even dressed in her oldest gown. She watched the young man flush and fiddle with his stock as though it was too tight.

'Are you quite well, Dr Andrews?' She stood up and tugged at the bell-strap, relieved it did not pull away from the ceiling in a cloud of dust. 'I shall send for some refreshments. It is very remiss of me not have done so at once.'

He found his voice. 'I am not ill, thank you for enquiring so kindly, Miss Carstairs. It is a little warm in here, that is all.'

'Please feel free to open a window, sir.' Charlotte supposed he was overheated by his ride; it certainly wasn't especially warm in the library.

A parlour maid appeared in the doorway and Charlotte arranged for coffee to be fetched. 'Now, sir, where was I? Oh yes, information about this area. Could you tell me how long Thurston village has been so neglected?'

The doctor was happy to talk of anything as long as it wasn't his state of health. 'I do not imagine you would have been aware, Miss Carstairs, that old Lord Thurston became unwell in his declining years. Confused mentally and unable to run the estate.'

'I understand, but did he not have a factor, a bailiff, or estate manager to organize things for him?'

'No, at least there was none when I arrived a little over three years ago.' He smiled. 'My small estate, which runs parallel to Thurston Hall, provides me with sufficient income to live comfortably. I practise medicine as a hobby, not a necessity.'

She nodded, glad that mystery had been explained. She had wondered why a physician should wish to carry out his trade in such a poor locality. 'Then I am delighted you decided to do so, sir.' She touched her scar. 'My situation might have been far worse without your intervention.'

'It is kind of you to say so, Miss Carstairs. I had intended to call on you in a day or two, to remove the sutures, as they are more than ready to come out, and I believe you will feel far more comfortable when they are.'

She smiled. 'I admit they do pull; it will be a relief to be able to put my hair up once more.' Her intention, when she had sent for the doctor, had been to ask for advice about hiring labour. But as Jack was obviously up to snuff again, and intended to take over responsibility himself, her questions were redundant.

'I wished to ask you where the nearest church is. I do not wish to miss another service, if it is possible to walk there.'

'I go to the next village. It is a drive of about thirty minutes, and I should be delighted to escort you and the children tomorrow morning, if you should wish to accompany me?'

She hesitated; she would dearly love to go, and with the children as chaperons surely there could be no breach of propriety? 'I should love to accompany you, sir; how thoughtful of you to offer.'

He stood, bowing low, his eyes glowing with pleasure. 'In that case, Miss Carstairs, I shall take my leave. My carriage is commodious so there will be ample space for your maid as well.'

'Thank you, there does not appear to be a suitable vehicle here. It is something I shall have to look into.' She fingered her scar. 'I do not suppose you have your bag with you, Dr Andrews? I should dearly like these out before I appear in public tomorrow.'

Immediately he became professional. 'I have what I need in my saddle-bag; but I must boil my instruments, I have found that this avoids the risk of infection.'

Charlotte rang the bell for a second time and a maid appeared.

'Kindly show Dr Andrews out, but wait for him to return and then escort him to the kitchen.'

She sat down again to wait for the doctor to return with his equipment. Then she heard footsteps in the passageway and braced herself for a lively confrontation with Jack.

'Charlotte, have you been alone in here with that man, all this time?'

'I have, Cousin, however the door was wide open, and *he* behaved like a perfect gentleman.'

In answer he slammed the door. He turned to face her; she shivered, waiting for the next tirade.

'You will not see that man alone again; do I make myself clear?'

She glared at him. 'I shall see whomsoever I please, in whatever manner I please. My behaviour is none of your concern.'

He stepped closer. 'God's teeth! Do not argue with me. I am master in this house and I expect to be obeyed.'

'If it is acceptable for you to be in here alone with me, then why is it not for my physician to do the same?' She hoped the tremor in her voice was not apparent.

He closed the gap between them in one stride. 'It is acceptable, as you so quaintly put it, my dear, because you are to be my wife.'

Charlotte gasped and sank deeper into the sofa, closing her eyes in shock.

'God damn it to hell! That is not how I meant to tell you.' She felt the sofa dip. 'I am sorry, sweetheart, that was clumsy of me.' Still she kept her face averted, but his fingers closed around her chin and forced her head up. 'Look at me, please. Good, that is much better. Now, listen to me. You have been totally compromised. Staying here, alone, unchaperoned has all but ruined your reputation. I cannot allow that. For all your accusations, Charlotte, I am no rogue. I know what is expected of a gentleman.' He paused, studying her reaction. 'Well, what do you say?'

She drew a shaky breath. 'I do not wish to marry you, nor anyone else, for that matter.'

He smiled and gathered her trembling hands in his. 'I know you do not, and neither do I, but we have no choice, my dear. You have the children to consider; although Beth is only ten, she will be tarnished by this if we do not rectify matters immediately.'

'Is there no other way, nothing else we can do?'

Jack shook his head firmly. 'No; I have sent word for Reverend Peterson, from the next village, to call. I shall have him read the banns at Thurston church tomorrow. That will allow you three weeks to prepare your trousseau.'

'Trousseau? How can I make new clothes with no money to purchase the materials?' She attempted to remove her hands but he, for some reason, was running his thumbs up and down the backs, making her pulse skip erratically.

'I have good news, Charlotte. There are funds, not a lot, but sufficient for our needs. The lawyers are returning on Monday with the necessary papers.'

She tried again to extricate her hands. Reluctantly he let her go. 'You have no carriage, Jack. I shall not be able to go to Ipswich to purchase what I need. I cannot be married without replenishing our wardrobes.' She sat back believing she had, at least, managed to postpone the ceremony. Three weeks – it did not bear thinking of!

'There is a gig somewhere – I saw it in the barn – all it needs is cleaning. A pair of my greys will happily pull it.' He stood up abruptly. 'Then it is settled? You agree that we must be married, that we have no choice?'

She nodded. 'If there is no alternative, if by marrying you I can protect Beth's reputation as well as my own, then I agree.' She tried to stand but her legs felt weak and would not hold her. Before she could protest he took her elbows and lifted her to her feet.

'It will not be so bad, little one; we are becoming friends, are we not? We want the same things – to restore Thurston – give Beth and Harry a decent home?'

She was finding it difficult to think with him so close. She was unable to step back, the sofa blocked her path. 'Yes, we are getting to know each other, but I never thought to be obliged to marry in this fashion. I have always considered that marriage should be a union of souls, of minds, not a business arrangement.'

He stepped back, staring at her as though she had just escaped from Bedlam. 'You, my girl, have been reading too many romances. Marriage is a business, like any other. If you invest sufficient time and effort it will succeed; souls and minds and all that nonsense do not come into it.'

'And love? Does that not come into it either?'

His expression changed and he moved, fast. Before she could voice an objection her breasts were crushed to his chest. One hand held her captive the other tilted her face to receive his kiss. She tried to turn her head away, not respond, but his lips were insistent. The tip of his tongue running up and down until her own mouth relaxed and she was once more carried away, made to feel she belonged in his embrace, her mouth was made for his kisses.

Doctor Andrews coughed loudly a second time. Jack heard him and, without relinquishing his hold, half turned, sheltering Charlotte from view. Anger and dislike crackled in the air. Jack spoke first.

'You are *de trop*, Andrews. My fiancée and I do not wish to be disturbed.'

The doctor stood his ground, his pale-blue eyes icy. 'Miss Carstairs asked me to call, Lord Thurston. It is a medical matter. I shall wait in the hall, until she is free.' The door banged behind him.

Charlotte felt Jack's fury and knew if she did not intervene he would do something they all regretted. 'Doctor Andrews is correct; he has come to remove my sutures. I asked him to.' She believed it unwise to mention the doctor's suggestion that he take her to church the next day.

He dropped his arm and laughed – it was not a pleasant sound. 'I shall remove those for you. I have done it more often than that quack. I have a set a medical instruments in my pack somewhere.'

This was too much; first she was forced to marry him and now he wished to be her physician as well. 'No, thank you. It will not be necessary: Dr Andrews is here and his instruments are clean and ready. Goodness knows what infection you would pass on to me if you attempted it.'

'I do not like it, Charlotte. That man—'

'That man,' she interrupted, 'is an excellent physician, and that is all he is. Please ask him to join me here as you leave.' She waited for the explosion at her summary dismissal.

He nodded, his expression guarded. 'I shall ask Mrs Thomas to sit in with you.'

'Very well; it is unnecessary, but, this once, I shall agree to your demands.' She knew she'd said too much and wished her words back.

He strode over, and she shivered, this time from fear. 'I think you are under a misapprehension, Charlotte. I will brook no disobedience from you or anyone in this establishment. Is that understood?'

She did not answer, her teeth were clenched to stop them chattering. His voice dropped an octave, became almost menacing. 'I am waiting for your answer, Charlotte. Did I make myself clear?'

She nodded, forcing her words from between frozen lips. 'Yes, my lord, you did.'

'Excellent – do not forget it.'

Charlotte groped in her reticule for her handkerchief and, with shaking fingers held it to her eyes. She collapsed on to the sofa and buried her head in her hands. She had just agreed to marry a terrifying stranger, no vestige of humour or gentleness apparent. What had happened to him to change him so drastically overnight?

The tears fell faster as she considered the implications. Was she to be linked for the rest of her life to a man who thought marriage was a business, did not believe in love, only lust?

When the housekeeper came in five minutes later she was still crying, the small white cotton square sodden with tears.

Mrs Thomas was shocked. 'Come along, Miss Carstairs, you will make herself ill. Are you feeling unwell? Does your head hurt?'

Charlotte swallowed drawing several shuddering breaths before answering. 'I believe I am suffering a reaction from all the upsets of the past twenty-four hours, Mrs Thomas. The murder of poor Jenkins, the attack last night, and thinking of my head wound reminded me of the stone that was thrown at me.'

'Lord Thurston told me that he had been shot at, and I saw the state of the kitchen. I was deeply shocked, miss. It is hardly surprising you're overcome. The doctor's waiting, but shall I send him away?'

Charlotte shook her head. 'No, please ask him to come in. I am quite well now.'

CHAPTER TEN

JACK'S anger carried him to the stables where he demanded that Phoenix be saddled. He needed to gallop out his blue devils or he might be driven to his room and down a decanter of brandy. No groom dared meet his eye; they hurried about their duties heads down, hoping to remain invisible. Jethro led the huge chestnut horse out of the loose box, barely avoiding being stamped on.

Jack took the reins, placed one hand on the horse's massive withers and vaulted into the saddle. He only just managed to ram his boots into the stirrup irons before the stallion took off, scattering grooms and gravel in equal proportions. It took a mile or so to calm both horse and rider.

He sat back in his saddle applying pressure to the reins. Obediently, the horse dropped into a canter, then down to a trot and, finally, to an easy, long strided walk. He could hear the sound of the militia in the distance quartering the park in their search. He guessed he was safe from interruption for a while. He dismounted and, looping his reins over his arm, walked across to a log lying conveniently under a tree. Ignoring the moss and fallen leaves he sat, stretching out his legs, and rested his head on the trunk.

He could hear himself snarling at Charlotte, issuing orders, demanding her obedience like an enraged parent. What had he been thinking of? He knew what had triggered his appalling behaviour: it was her mention of love. His head had immediately been filled with images of Sophia, of her rejection, of his heartbreak and humiliation.

He had no heart to give her, no love left; it had withered and died when the sabre had sliced into his face. He could offer her companionship, friendship, even passion, but love . . . that was never going to be part of their relationship. When he had been rejected by the woman whose face was forever burnt on his soul he had vowed never to allow another to enter his heart.

Charlotte's unexpected arrival had turned his plans to chaos. He had been forced to abandon his hedonistic lifestyle and return to reality, take charge of not just his life, but three others as well. He had no choice: he must marry the painfully young, inexperienced girl. He had not sunk so low that he could allow an innocent to be ruined by his actions, or lack of them. For some reason he did not even consider the lawyers' suggestion that Charlotte move out and set up her own establishment with a female companion.

Phoenix nudged him and he laughed. 'Are you bored, old fellow? Come along, let us go back. I have some serious fence mending to do and it does not involve hammer and nails.'

Doctor Andrews left after completing his task.

'Do you wish me to assist you to your room, Miss Carstairs?' Mrs Thomas enquired.

'No, I'm quite recovered, thank you. I wish to see the children. They are spending far too much time in idleness at the moment.'

'They are prettily behaved, miss, if you don't mind me saying so. No trouble to anyone and ever so polite.'

Charlotte's lips curved. 'That is good news. I am hoping that now you are here to run the house and supervise the cleaning, I can resume my role as their governess.'

'I have it all in hand. I can't believe how the situation has deteriorated since Lord Thurston . . . since I left.'

'Is there sufficient staff to rectify matters?'

The housekeeper nodded. 'I believe so, Miss Carstairs. I have four parlour maids at my disposal and Cook has a scullery maid and two kitchen maids, and Mr Meltham has a full complement of footmen. Between them and my two cats we will soon rid this place of vermin and restore it to a pleasant place for you to live in.'

'I shall be going upstairs to the nursery and schoolrooms after I have spoken to the children. I shall require a footman and a maid to assist me.'

An hour later the three of them were on hands and knees, sharing pails of sudsy water, scrubbing out the schoolroom. Mary, a maid, was clearing the years of neglect and cobwebs, and a footman was filling in the rat and mice holes with gravel and brick, then smoothing over the whole with a mixture of mud and lime. Charlotte hoped the makeshift repairs would hold until Mrs Thomas's cats could do their work.

'Harry, try not to slop water on your sister, she is quite damp enough already,' Charlotte admonished.

'But my cloth's all wet, Lottie, and I can't help it,' Harry whined.

'Of course it's wet, stupid boy; you can't clean floors with a dry cloth,' Beth answered crossly.

'That is enough you two – please do not argue, I am so pleased with the hard work you have done, do not spoil it now by churlishness.' Charlotte realized that they were all fatigued. It was past time to stop for refreshments. 'That is enough for today. We should get washed and go downstairs for luncheon.'

Beth was so relieved to be able to get up from her knees that she jumped to her feet without checking and tripped over a pail of filthy water. To her horror Charlotte watched it vanish between the boards before she could attempt to mop up the spill.

Harry was astonished. 'Where's my water gone, Lottie?' He pressed his nose to the floor as if expecting it to be visible.

'Oh dear! What a disaster – so much water has to come out somewhere.' Charlotte scrambled up, untying her apron as she did so. She tried to remember which rooms were directly underneath the schoolroom. There was no point in asking the servants; they knew even less about the geography of the house than she did.

She shrugged. 'It is too late to worry, children. If it comes out in our bedrooms, then so be it.' She left the cleaning up to the staff and hurried down the winding stairs to their bedchambers.

Annie was waiting for the children. 'His Lordship is inspecting the rooms along this passageway with Mr Meltham. I think he's seeing which should be redecorated and which are too far gone to bother with.'

Charlotte felt her insides lurch unpleasantly. Surely they could not be so unlucky? The missing water could not possibly reappear in the very room in which Jack was? She bundled the children into their room. 'Hurry up and wash, children. I shall do the same. I have sent Mary to ask for some refreshments to be set out in the breakfast parlour. And water or no water I am as hungry as a hunter.'

'I am hungry as a horse,' Beth added.

'Me, too – I'm as hungry as ... as a haystack,' Harry finished triumphantly.

Charlotte, still smiling at Harry's remark, headed back to her own chamber. She noticed that at the far end, directly under the schoolroom, the door was open. Jack and the butler were obviously inside; she could hear the murmur of male voices. Should she go and warn them about the possible deluge?

She hesitated. Jack had been so abrupt with her, so angry, so dictatorial. They were going to be married in three weeks and somehow, in that time, she had to convince him that she needed a husband in the fullest sense and not another father. It would seem that he thought of her as a child one moment and a woman grown the next. It was up to her to convince him that she was the latter, but how she was to do this she had no idea. She giggled. Would it be considered childish to leave him in ignorance, or mature to ignore the whole episode? She stopped outside the door; she would risk a peek to see what was happening.

The only reason she could think for his presence upstairs was that he intended to move his quarters to this level, to abandon his lair on the ground floor. Cautiously she stuck her head around the door, her eyes drawn irresistibly to him, standing in the middle of the room gesticulating, whilst Meltham wrote notes on a pad. He was talking too softly, and the room was too big for her to catch what was being said.

Then her glance strayed upwards. She frowned. He was standing directly under a large bulge in the plaster, a suspicious damp bulge, one that was certainly full of the missing dirty water.

'Jack,' she called tentatively. He didn't hear. 'Jack,' she shouted.

This time he spun round his expression anxious. 'God's teeth, Charlotte! What is wrong?'

'Nothing, er . . . well, I came to warn you. Look out!' She alerted him too late as, with hardly a sound, the ceiling exploded, covering him with a mixture of dirty water, plaster and rat droppings.

Charlotte watched in fascinated horror as he stood, his fine clothes ruined, water dripping down his face. Like a dog he shook his head sending drops across the room. It was far too late to retreat; she knew exactly how fast he could move.

'I am so sorry; I came to warn you. Beth knocked Harry's bucket over upstairs . . .' Her voice trailed off as he came towards her. He stopped within arm's reach.

'Do you know these are the only respectable garments I own?' His tone was conversational. She assumed the question to be rhetorical and shook her head, offering no answer. He held out a sopping arm. 'This coat is wet – whose responsibility is that, I wonder?'

She was unsure whether she was required to speak. She risked a cautious comment. 'Mine?'

'Exactly, my dear. Here I am doing my very best to impress you and you pour scorn, or in this case, filthy water and a large part of the ceiling, on me. Am I to understand from this that my efforts are to no avail?' He sounded so earnest, so sincere, that she almost believed him. She was about to explain again, apologize profusely, when she noticed a strange rigidity about his shoulders.

'You wretch! You are bamming me!'

He exploded with laughter and, lunging forward, gathered her in a bear hug thus transferring a goodly portion of his dampness to her own person.

'Let me go, you are making me wet!'

Ignoring her protests, he picked her up and swung her round, much to the consternation of the elderly butler. Such goings-on were unseemly, even between a recently betrothed couple. Finally he set her down, having achieved his objective, that of making Charlotte as wet and dirty as he.

'There. Now I consider we are even.' Jack released her and walked back to stare up into the gaping hole that had once been the ceiling. 'Meltham, I think we shall have to find another room, this is no longer suitable.'

'Yes, my lord. But the hole will have to be repaired, or the rats will pour down into the house. Even good ratters like Mrs Thomas's cats will not be able to prevent us being overrun.'

'Good grief! Surely there are not so many rats up there?'

'There are, my lord; a veritable colony has taken root in the attics. It is going to take more than two cats to dislodge them, I fear.'

Jack scowled; this was not the news he wanted to hear. 'Could we smoke them out?'

The butler considered and shook his head. 'We would be more likely to burn down the house, my lord. It is tinder dry, and riddled with woodworm up there.'

Charlotte had heard quite sufficient about rats and woodworm. One or two was bad enough, but an army? It did not bear thinking about. 'I am going to change my clothes, my lord. I suggest you do the same.'

'If I do, it is unwashed clothes or my old uniform; which would you prefer?'

She pretended to give the question due consideration. 'As I do not intend to spend any further time in your company today, I suggest the unwashed garments will suffice. There are more than enough soldiers here at present.'

'Forgive me, my lord, but your new man can clean and press your clothes in no time,' Meltham told him.

Jack nodded. 'Thank you, I had forgotten that I am now equipped with a manservant of my own. Charlotte do . . .'

But she had gone, taking the opportunity to return to her room, not wishing to be the recipient of any further juvenile behaviour. The children were relieved to hear he had taken his dousing so amiably. Annie was more concerned with the state of Charlotte's gown.

'Miss Carstairs, let me help you change.'

Charlotte stripped off her brown dress and held up her arms for her maid to drop a fresh gown over her head. Annie made a suggestion.

'Miss Carstairs, would you consider taking on one of the new girls as your abigail? As you are to be Lady Thurston in a few weeks, you should have your own lady's-maid.'

'I liked Mary, the girl who helped me this morning; perhaps she would do? Could you ask Mrs Thomas if she could be spared?'

'Good gracious, miss, you don't have to ask. You're the mistress here; Mrs Thomas will do as you tell her.'

'It is hard to believe that I shall be Lady Thurston soon.' She smiled. 'It's a great shame his lordship does not have the wherewithal to maintain my improved status.'

'Lord Thurston is a resourceful man; I have no doubt he'll provide for you all comfortably.'

'I do hope so, Annie. It would be delightful to have sufficient funds to purchase gowns and bonnets whenever the whim took me.'

She seated herself in front of the scratched, half moon table upon which the speckled mirror rested. 'That reminds me, Dr Andrews is calling tomorrow to take us to church in Nettleworth. I should like you to accompany us. The service is at nine o'clock. You need to have the children downstairs and ready by eight o'clock. Please make sure they have had their breakfast in the kitchen before we depart.'

'Yes, miss, that will be grand. It is far too long since I've attended a service and sung the Lord's praises.'

Reassured that her maid had not thought the arrangement to be out of the ordinary, and had not immediately suggested they apply to Jack for permission, Charlotte decided she would not bother him with the information. Time enough to tell him, if he appeared tomorrow morning, demanding to know where they were going.

'Excellent, thank you. It is to be hoped that Mary has such a deft touch with my hair as you.' She admired herself from every angle. The modestly scooped neckline showed no more of her bosom than she was happy with; the darker green silk sash exactly matched her eyes and complimented the dress perfectly.

She wriggled her toes, they were almost fully recovered and her dainty green slippers hardly pinched at all.

'Are you ready yet, Lottie? We're almost dead from hunger,' Beth called plaintively from the window seat.

'I am, darling. What do you think?' Charlotte twirled, sending her diaphanous skirts floating out in a soft green cloud.

'You look like a princess, Lottie. Is that your best dress?'

'Are we having a party?' Harry asked hopefully.

'No, Harry. I have nothing else to wear, apart from a morning gown which has seen better days and my very best gown.' She smiled. 'Cousin Jack has promised we can go to Ipswich on Monday or Tuesday and purchase fresh garments.' She had not told the children about her betrothal. The staff knew because Jack's shouted proposal had been heard quite clearly in the corridor even with the door of the library shut. How could she have forgotten? It was mainly for their sake she had agreed to his preposterous suggestion. There was no point in prevaricating.

'We all need new clothes because I am to marry Cousin Jack in three weeks' time.'

This announcement was greeted by total silence; for once Beth had nothing to say. Charlotte tried to explain. 'We decided we are an ideal match. Thurston needs a mistress and we all need a home.'

Beth chewed her lip thoughtfully. 'But you hardly know him, Lottie, and if you ask me, you don't even like him overmuch. You're always shouting at each other, you know.'

Charlotte did not need her sister to point out the obvious. 'Marriages are arranged for many reasons, Beth, and more often from expediency than anything else. I admit that Cousin Jack and I have had some lively exchanges, but that shows our life together will not be dull.' She knelt down, bringing herself to Harry's level. 'What about you, Harry? Are you happy about this?'

'I like Cousin Jack, Lottie. And he said I can have my own puppy.'

'That was good of him.' She stood up, shaking out her skirts, relieved this section of the first floor had been freshly scrubbed. 'So, you are both content?' They nodded and Charlotte felt it was safe to resume their journey downstairs.

Their tardy arrival had been observed and they had hardly arranged themselves comfortably around the table when the door opened and two parlour maids entered carrying trays. She was not certain if she was disappointed that Jack didn't join them for luncheon. Secretly she was eager to see his expression when he saw her in her finery. Dressed as she was, further cleaning was impossible so it was decided that they would take a stroll around the park.

They left through a side door that led directly to the gardens. If they had used the front door they would not have missed Jack who wished to accompany them and to put himself out to be charming.

When Annie informed him his quarry had already left for her constitutional, his face darkened. How could he persuade her that he was not an irascible, arrogant bastard if she flitted off on her own at every opportunity? He was wondering if he should go after her when Meltham appeared at the library door.

'Lord Thurston, the reverend gentleman from Renford is here to see you.'

'Thank you; show him to the library, I have urgent matters to discuss with him.' His bid to woo his lovely young fiancée would just have to wait.

CHAPTER ELEVEN

Sunday morning was overcast; although the heavy rain had stopped, it was a cold, damp morning. Charlotte met the children and their nursemaid in the hall at five minutes to eight.

Beth had been keeping watch, her face pressed against the window pane. 'Doctor Andrews is coming, Lottie. He has a closed carriage, so we shan't get wet if it rains again.'

A footman appeared from the shadows to open the door. Charlotte glanced nervously over her shoulder, expecting an irate Jack to appear at any moment from his lair demanding to know where they were going. Thankfully the door remained closed and they were able to descend the front steps without incident.

She noticed that the doctor was resplendent in a bottle green topcoat, snowy cravat and black waistcoat. Charlotte thought it improper to drop her gaze to his nether regions but assumed he was wearing trousers and boots. Her outfit was the pale gold cambric, with matching chip straw bonnet, she had worn on her ill-fated arrival. Annie had worked her usual magic and restored the gown; no one would know it had ever been covered in blood.

'Good morning, Miss Carstairs, children. I hope that I have not kept you waiting?' The young man bowed.

Charlotte curtsied. 'No, Dr Andrews, you are in perfect time.'

He handed her into the carriage and stood aside politely as Annie shepherded her charges inside. When they were comfortable he jumped in and the footman folded up the steps.

'Is it far to Nettleworth, sir?' Beth enquired.

'Not as far as Ipswich, but considerably further than Thurston village,' he answered, smiling, well satisfied with his wit.

'I expect it will take more than the usual thirty minutes today, will it not, sir? The lanes are so muddy this morning.' Charlotte said, quietly supplying the information Beth wanted before her sister forgot her manners and commented on the doctor's evasive and irritating answer.

The coach rocked violently as it traversed a deeper puddle and Harry squealed with delight. The jogging and bouncing made chitchat all but impossible. They were all too busy staying in their seats. After twenty minutes the carriage ride became bearable as it reached the outskirts of the village.

'Look, children, this is the pretty place we passed where a little boy waved to you,' Charlotte told them. Harry peered hopefully from the window.

'There's no one here today; where is everyone, Lottie?'

Doctor Andrews replied, 'The church is outside Nettleworth, in the grounds of Nettleworth House, the home of Sir Reginald and Lady Sinclair.'

Harry looked puzzled; this did not answer his question at all. He turned back to Charlotte, ignoring the doctor. 'Lottie, where's everyone gone?'

'They have to walk to church, Harry, so will have set off before us. I expect we shall see some of them in the lane as we get near the church.'

'I should like to walk. I don't like this carriage anymore,' Harry announced and, before Annie or Charlotte could react, he turned the door handle and fell out. Pandemonium followed his abrupt disappearance. Beth screamed and Annie attempted to get up, blocking both Charlotte and the doctor's passage. The coachman on hearing the noise reined back fiercely and the two horses plunged to a halt, throwing the remaining occupants back on to the squabs.

Charlotte was the first out. Without waiting for the steps, or the doctor's assistance, she jumped from the carriage and ran back down the lane. Frantically she searched the verge, the narrow road – there was no sign of a crumpled body or crying child. Harry was not there.

Panting, she halted, bonnet hanging down her back, the hem of her dress mired. 'Harry, Harry, where are you?' she called but received no answer. Beth arrived beside her.

'Where's he gone, Lottie? Why isn't he here?'

'I have no idea, Beth,' she forced her mouth to smile. 'But at least we can be sure he is unhurt. If he had been injured by his fall he would still be lying in the lane, would he not?'

Doctor Andrews appeared, his face alight with amusement. From his taller viewpoint he had been able to see the missing child. 'Miss Carstairs, I can see him, he is unhurt. He is being ministered to by a cottager. He must have flown over the hedge and landed in her garden.'

As he spoke, a wicket gate, all but hidden in the overgrown hedge, opened and an elderly lady appeared, with Harry holding her hand. 'Here he is, madam. No harm done; apart from the mud on his clothes, he's as good as new,' the old lady said with a gummy smile.

Charlotte was unsure whether to scold her little brother or embrace him. 'Harry, what were you thinking of? You could have been killed.'

Believing he was safe from retribution, Harry stepped forward, saying earnestly, 'I'm sorry, Lottie, I never meant to fall out, it just happened.'

'If you are silly enough to open the carriage door when it is in motion, what else do you expect?'

The little boy grinned. 'It was capital fun, Lottie; I flew over the hedge and landed in the flowerbed.'

'You are lucky your sister is so forgiving, young man,' Dr Andrews said sternly, feeling it was his place as a gentleman to admonish the child. 'If you were my responsibility you would be soundly beaten for your stupidity.'

Tears filled Harry's eyes and he hid his muddy face in Charlotte's skirts, adding fingerprints to the already ruined dress. She glared at the doctor. 'Then it is a good thing, sir, that my brother's behaviour is none of your concern.'

Doctor Andrews realized his error and blushed. 'I beg your pardon, Miss Carstairs.' He cleared his throat and brushed invisible dust from his jacket. 'Do you wish to continue to the church, or would you prefer to return home?'

'I should like to go back to Thurston, if you please; but do not think of accompanying us, Dr Andrews. There is no need for you to miss the service as well. Your coachman will be back in ample time to collect you.'

He nodded, his expression formal. 'If you are sure, then I shall do exactly that. The carriage can turn on the green and I shall walk the remaining mile. Good day, Miss Carstairs.'

She watched him stride away. She sighed; he was a pleasant gentleman and she had not wished to offend him, but the children were her concern, no one else's; he had no right to interfere, to threaten to chastize her little brother.

Jack was not pleased, in fact he was furious. He had risen early, with a clear head, ready and eager to breakfast with Charlotte and the children. What did he discover? That they had gone out, gone to church with the doctor, in a closed carriage.

Meltham had pointed out that the nursemaid had also accompanied Miss Carstairs, and the children, but that had not tempered his annoyance. He should have been informed, asked, before they accepted the escort of another man. Charlotte was his responsibility, his fiancée. If she wanted to attend Sunday service it was he who would take her, no one else. The fact that he had not set foot inside a church for years was immaterial.

Yesterday, Peterson had agreed to bury Jenkins on Monday morning and to post the banns of his forthcoming nuptials at the same time. Jack paced the study, his expression thunderous. What he needed was his own church back in use on a Sunday; he needed to appoint another incumbent. God knows how he was to do that! He stopped, and chuckled at his absurdity. His speech was liberally peppered with blasphemy; he had little time for churchgoing of any sort, but maybe the Almighty was taking a hand, leading him back into the fold after a period in the wilderness.

His anger slowly dissipated as he considered this astounding premise. Charlotte and her brother and sister had arrived at exactly the point in his life when he needed a jolt, needed to be dragged out of the destructive cycle his life had become.

She was nothing short of a bloody miracle; he had never expected to feel a young woman melt in his embrace again, thought his physical needs would, in future, have to be paid for. But Charlotte responded to him, enjoyed his lovemaking, indeed it was he who had stepped back before things got out of control.

He nodded; yes, the lawyers were coming tomorrow; they would know how to find him a new vicar. But in the meantime he would expedite the cleaning and repair of the gig, then he could drive them to church next Sunday. For the first time since his injuries he was prepared to go out in public, brave the stares of strangers; if Charlotte was beside him he could do anything.

If he started to employ the disgruntled villagers on repairs to their own properties, he was fairly sure whoever was trying to harm them would disappear back into the underworld. It would not be somebody local, but a radical hoping to stir up further trouble as was happening elsewhere in East Anglia.

Happier than he had been since Waterloo, he went out to the barn to supervise the cleaning of the gig. He was there when he heard the carriage approaching. It was scarcely ten o'clock; it could not be the church party returning, but who else would call, especially on a Sunday? He grabbed his jacket and shook his arms back in, then strode through the stable yard, to the front entrance. The carriage was unknown to him but its occupants were not.

It was Harry who spotted him approaching the stables. 'Lottie, it's Cousin Jack. He doesn't look very pleased to see us.'

'I expect he is concerned that we have returned unexpectedly early, my love. Annie, take the children in, quickly now.'

The maid needed no further urging; she grasped the hand of each child and hurried away. Charlotte smiled up at the coachman. 'Thank you, Mr Taylor; I should get back for Dr Andrews, he will not wish to be kept waiting.'

The man touched his hat with his whip handle, clicked to the matched bays, and the carriage trundled off, leaving Charlotte alone on the gravel.

'Good morning. We were on our way to church at Nettleworth and Harry had a slight mishap and we were obliged to come home again.' She hoped he would be satisfied with this explanation, assume it was a matter of damp britches that caused their early return and not enquire further.

'What sort of mishap?' He was not to be fobbed off so easily.

She was tempted to lie, but knew Harry would discuss his misadventure with all and sundry. 'He inadvertently fell from the carriage and—'

'He what? Is he hurt? For God's sake, Charlotte, what were you thinking of to let such a thing happen?'

She bristled with annoyance. 'Harry was unhurt by his tumble, thank you for asking, my lord. If you knew the slightest thing about small boys, you would understand exactly how such things can happen to the most conscientious carer.' She picked up her skirt, straightened her bonnet and, turning her back, marched off, nose in the air.

He was dumbfounded – nobody spoke to him the way Charlotte did – they would not dare. He surged forward catching her in two strides.

'A moment please, Charlotte, this conversation is not over.'

She kept her head straight, hiding her face inside the brim of her bonnet. She didn't want him to see how nervous she was. 'I have had no breakfast, sir, and if you wish to speak to me, then you must do so after I have eaten. I shall join you in the library later.'

Meltham, ever vigilant, had the door open as they arrived and she sailed in, pausing just long enough to issue her instructions. 'Have coffee and scones sent to the parlour, please.'

'Very well, Miss Carstairs.' The butler was obliged to hop out of the way, narrowly avoiding being mowed down by his lordship.

'Charlotte.' His voice was quiet, but his tone demanded her attention. 'I wish to speak to you. Now. We shall repair to the library where we can be private.'

Charlotte stopped dead and he almost cannoned into her. 'I do not wish to go to the library. I wish to eat.' She knew she sounded more like a child than a woman grown.

Exasperated, he put a restraining arm on hers. 'If I have your food sent to the library, will you come with me?'

She capitulated; she was in no position to argue. She knew he was quite capable of picking her up and transporting her bodily if she continued to obstruct his wishes.

'Meltham, send the tray to the library. And set a cup for me; I believe I am in need of a strong coffee to settle my nerves.'

Charlotte's head turned in surprise. Since when had he suffered from nerves? He was leaning, relaxed, against the wooden panelling, a faint smile flickering across his lips. Her mouth curved in response. 'Jack, you are a nincompoop.' She tossed her head and her bonnet slipped sideways. He reached over and gently untied the ribbons at her neck, his fingertips brushing her cheek as he did so.

'And you, my love, are a baggage! I shall be grey before my time if you continue to behave in this way.'

She assumed that he did not require an answer; she was incapable of making one anyway, her throat was constricted and her heart leaping like a caged bird in her chest.

'Come, sweetheart, we cannot remain dithering in the hall, let us go to the library.' With her bonnet swinging casually in one hand and the other resting firmly in the small her back, he ushered her down the passage.

On this occasion one of the new footmen had followed and darted ahead to open the door with a flourish. The young man was sure protocol demanded that the door be left open, but Jack had other ideas.

'Shut the door – we wish to be private.' He waited until the door clicked to before dropping his hand.

'Where would you like to sit, my dear?'

Charlotte looked at him suspiciously; he was being far too polite, too conciliatory. She stepped over to a small, upright chair, its rattan seat sadly in need of repair, but it was ideal for her purpose. She picked it up and carried it to the centre of the room. There she placed it and sat down, satisfied he could not sit within arm's reach. Her chair was the only portable seat in the room, the rest were overstuffed, unwieldy armchairs.

She waited for him to make the next move. He appeared undecided, for a horrible moment she thought he might cast himself at her feet like a lovelorn swain, but instead he dropped into a chair, stretching out his long legs, crossing them at the ankle, as though he had no cares in the world. His head was lowered so she could not see his expression. Why didn't he berate her? She found his reticence unnerving and she did not know how to react.

'Sir, if you intend to ring a peal over me, then please do so. I wish it to be over before my tray appears.'

He raised his head and she swallowed; it was not anger or amusement she saw reflected there, it was a more dangerous emotion. He made no move towards her and she relaxed a little. She believed she would prefer his anger to his passion.

'Charlotte, you did not ask my permission to go out. Was it because you were going to church in a closed carriage with Andrews and knew I would forbid it?'

'I need not ask your leave to speak to God, it is my right to do so. You have no suitable carriage, so of course I accepted the doctor's kind offer to take us.' She paused, then unwisely added, 'And it is none of your concern what I do, we are not married yet.'

'I see – is that what you believe, my dear, or what you hope is the truth?' His voice was cool, his tone pleasant, but she wasn't deceived, he was furious.

She knew it to be more sensible to remain mute, to sit and simper, apologize, promise never to do it again, but he made her so angry it was impossible not to speak. 'I merely repeat what you told me not long ago: you said you wished to have nothing to do with any of us, we were not your responsibility.'

He nodded, as though agreeing. He drew in his legs and slowly stood up, towering above her. Her stomach lurched and she felt cold perspiration trickling between her shoulders.

'But that, my dear, was before you agreed to marry me, before you willingly put yourself and your brother and sister under my control. I take my position seriously. I do not wish to be made a fool of in my own house.'

She jumped to her feet. 'I went to church, not to the theatre, or to a private supper party, and I had two children and their nursemaid as company. How can that diminish your status?' She was almost shouting by the time she finished.

He closed the distance but she didn't back away. She stood her ground. She knew when she was in the right. He appeared to be having difficulty breathing, and beads of perspiration were gathering on his forehead. Was he unwell, about to have an apoplexy?

Without conscious thought she stretched out and ran her gloved hand across his cheek, her eyes concerned. 'Are you ill, Jack? You are breathing rather loudly and your skin is decidedly overheated.'

He forced out his answer through clenched teeth. 'I am in two minds, Charlotte, whether to put you across my knee, or make passionate love to you.' His breath was tickling her ear. 'Which would you prefer, do you think?'

Her hand stilled; she could feel the roughness under her fingers through the thin kid leather of her gloves. She heard his laboured breathing, but her brain refused to assimilate his outrageous remark. Then she gasped, and her hand left his face to return with a slap that knocked his head sideways. Aghast at her behaviour, her hand burning as though it had been plunged in a fire, she stumbled backwards forgetting about the small chair behind her.

Even his lightning reactions were not fast enough and, her feet tangling in the chair legs, she lost her balance, crashing heavily to the floor. He was on his knees beside her, his anger at her defiance and his shock at her blow temporarily put aside in his concern for her well-being.

'Do not try and move, my dear. Stay still and recover your breath. Let me check if you have broken any limbs.'

Charlotte felt her chest begin to function normally. She kept her eyes closed, trying to blot out the memory of her hand striking his cheek. What had possessed her? She was not a violent person, did not believe in physical punishment, had never raised her hand to either of her siblings, however vexed they made her. Why did Jack bring out the worst in her?

She vaguely heard his voice murmuring soothing words but did not register their meaning. She was lucky he had not retaliated, slapped her back. She deserved it. Then she became aware that his hands were taking unwanted liberties with her lower limbs – he was running his fingers up her right leg. How dare he do so when she was indisposed? The man was a depraved monster to take advantage in this way. Her eyes flickered open.

'Let go of me, sir; have you no decency? No gentleman would attack a defenceless woman in this way.' She gasped her accusation to the back of his head, and did not see his expression, but she heard his reply.

Indeed the whole of Thurston Hall heard it, and the unfortunate parlour maid bringing in the coffee and scones was so shocked she dropped the tray. In the resulting chaos, the maid weeping amidst her broken cups, Jack swearing as he scraped strawberry preserve from his head, and the butler and footman flapping about trying to help, but only getting in the way, Charlotte picked herself up and slipped unobtrusively out of the room.

She raced upstairs, ignoring her bruises and lumps, and didn't stop until she was safely in her own chamber. Her heart was pounding, her hands shaking. Frantically she searched the door for a key as she knew she would need to bar the door to prevent him getting in. He would not respect the privacy of her boudoir. There was no key, no bolt to push across, she would have to drag the chair and jam it under the latch and hope that was sufficient to keep him out. Then she heard a sound behind her and her legs almost gave way in terror.

'Miss Carstairs, is something wrong?' Mary, her new abigail, enquired, her face anxious.

Charlotte began to breathe more easily, Mary was here, surely her presence would keep her safe? Shakily she smiled. 'Mary, I had forgotten you were here. I have come up to change my gown, as you can see it is sadly mired.'

If her maid thought it odd that her mistress had felt the need to change so urgent she had run up to her room, she wisely held her tongue. Charlotte was standing in her chemise, her arms raised above her head, waiting for Mary to drop over a fresh gown when the chamber door burst open – no knock, it just flew back. Lord Thurston froze Mary with his stare.

'Get out. I wish to speak to Miss Carstairs.'

Mary released her hold on the gown and fled, leaving Charlotte smothered by yards of limp muslin unable to find a hole through which to put either head or arms.

'Oh, let me assist you, my love,' he said silkily, but instead of pulling the material down he lifted it clear, leaving her shivering in her undergarments.

CHAPTER TWELVE

C HARLOTTE felt the warmth of humiliation spread from the tips of her toes to the crown of her head. She burnt with shame, quite forgetting that he had already seen her bottom totally unclothed. She kept her eyes shut, like a child, pretending she wasn't there, that he wasn't prowling round her, so close she could feel his body heat.

He ran his fingers down her arm and she flinched; then, more boldly, he encircled her neck, his thumbs caressing her chin and tracing the outline of her lips. She shuddered – hating him for his effrontery but her treacherous body beginning to enjoy the sensations he was sending coursing round her limbs.

'Please, Jack,' she pleaded, her voice little more than a whisper.

'Please, Jack, do not, or please Jack, do more?' His words slipped like silk across her cheek and she swayed.

'You must not, not until we are wed, it is not right.'

He laughed softly and began to drop feather-light kisses along her jaw, finally engulfing her mouth with his. He lifted her from the floor, crushing her to his chest and, even innocent as she was, she could not mistake the telltale hardness pressing into her belly.

His lips covered hers, forcing them apart, and then his tongue was inside her mouth exploring every intimate crevice. Charlotte couldn't breathe, couldn't swallow, felt as if she was being invaded, taken over, ravaged. It was not enjoyable, in fact it was abhorrent, and she changed from compliance to fighting for her purity.

She began to struggle, but her legs were trapped between his thighs and her hands pinioned to his chest. She was helpless. She could not stop him; he was too strong for her. Then Jack, wishing to complete his lovemaking horizontally, slackened his hold, intending to swing her round and carry her to the bed.

Charlotte seized her opportunity, bringing her knee up hard into his unprotected groin. The result was better than she could have dreamt. He released her, doubled up in agony, his hands to his injured parts. Nimbly she stepped around the writhing form and, grabbing her gown from the floor, ran across the boards and out through the servant's door.

It was pitch dark and she had no candle. She paused, listening. She could hear him cursing but he didn't appear to be coming in her direction. There were grunts and shuffles, then the bedchamber door opened and heavy footsteps faltered down the passage towards the gallery. He had gone; she had escaped unscathed. Cautiously she pushed open the door. The room was empty. Clutching her dress she crept back in and quickly pulled the garment over her head. It was the work of minutes to adjust the neckline, shake out the skirt and tie the sash.

Then she realized she only had on one slipper, the other must fallen off when he lifted her. She spotted it under the bed and knelt to retrieve it. Her face felt sore where his beard had rubbed and she could taste blood in her mouth from his kisses. She sank back on to the stool in front of the mirror. She hardly dared to raise her eyes to stare at her reflection. Horrified, she saw a wanton stranger gazing back, a hoyden with huge green eyes, swollen lips and russet hair tumbling in disarray around her shoulders. She didn't have the appearance of a woman who had been fighting to save her virtue, but looked like a courtesan who had just bid farewell to her lover.

She put two fingers to her mouth and felt a tremor run through her. She was no better than a light skirt. Had she encouraged him to behave in that way, given him permission to make love to her? Tears trickled down her cheeks and she dropped her head into her hands and rocked from side to side in her grief. She had not lost her virginity, but she might just as well have done. She had certainly lost her self-respect, and probably his, by her behaviour.

She did not hear her maid returning. 'Miss, oh, Miss Carstairs, I'm that sorry I ran away. I should have stayed, fetched someone to help you.'

Charlotte sniffed and sat up, accepting gratefully the linen square Mary handed her. 'It is not your fault, Mary. And I am unhurt; Lord Thurston and I were settling a difference of opinion in a rather unconventional way.' She offered a watery smile. 'However, I believe Lord Thurston came off worse in this particular encounter.'

She tossed the screwed up handkerchief on to the tabletop. 'My hair has come down, please will you dress it for me?'

As the girl removed the remaining pins and began to brush it out, Charlotte's jangled sensibilities settled. She had come out of her confrontation physically unscathed. It was he who had received a slap, a tray of scones and coffee on his head, and her knee in his most delicate place. Maybe he would think twice about molesting her again. Satisfaction at her thwarting of his authority buoyed her up, pushed reality aside.

It was as Mary pushed in the last pin, and she saw herself restored to her usual tidy, unflushed appearance, that she realized the full implication of what had transpired. Jack was not the man she wished to spend the rest of her life with. She could have tolerated his filthy temper, arrogant manners, if he truly loved her as she loved him. Her head flew back in shock, knocking the silver-backed hairbrush flying from Mary's hand.

In the time it took the girl to scramble about under the bed to retrieve the brush, Charlotte managed to recover. How could she have fallen in love with a man who shouted at her, bullied her and almost forced her to share her body with him? But that was only a small part of the whole; he was also kind and gentle, caring and sensitive, intelligent and charming and, when he wasn't angry, his kisses made her head spin and the blood fizz through her veins.

But she could not marry him, not even to save the children. Mary returned. 'Thank you, Mary. My hair looks splendid. I am going to write a note, then I shall require you to deliver it for me. I shall ring when I am ready.'

Charlotte opened he escritoire, selected a quill and sharpened it, then uncorked the ink bottle. This was going to be even more difficult to write than the letter she had sent to her grandfather two years ago. It was strange writing to a different Lord Thurston.

Dear Lord Thurston
It is with deep regret that I find I can no longer agree to become your wife. I wish to be released forthwith from our engagement. I shall remove myself and my brother and sister from Thurston Hall as soon as I can make suitable, alternative arrangements.
Yours sincerely
Charlotte Carstairs, Miss.

She read it through a second time. It would have to do. She sprinkled sand to dry the ink and folded it. She had no sealing wax, so tied it neatly with a red ribbon. She rang the brass bell and her maid appeared.

'Please take this down to Mr Meltham. Ask him to hand it to Lord Thurston, but do not, under any circumstances, deliver it yourself, is that clear?'

'Yes, Miss Carstairs.'

Charlotte handed her the square of paper, her heart heavy. She had done the right thing; she had been given no choice in the matter, for a loveless marriage was worse than no marriage at all. Whatever he said about 'business arrangements' she wanted none of it. Unless he told her he loved her, she would not marry him. She snorted inelegantly, knowing that was as likely as snow in July.

Her small ormolu mantel clock chimed the hour. Good gracious! Was it only eleven o'clock? How could so much have happened in just an hour? She decided to go down to the kitchen. Betty would find her something to eat and, surrounded by servants, she was fairly sure she would be safe.

She knew that if Jack managed to find her alone he was quite capable of charming her into changing her mind. She paused on the gallery, checking the hall was empty. Had the butler delivered the letter yet? Was he about to erupt from his chambers in search of her?

It was strangely quiet downstairs. Perhaps Jack had been relieved to have the matter taken from his hands. After all he had only offered for her because he was concerned about her reputation. She met no one, not even a footman, on her way to the kitchen. She lifted the heavy latch and pushed open the door.

The heat hit her like a wave, the permanently burning fire glowing in the enormous grate. The kettle was hissing gently, an aromatic stew bubbling over the flames, but the room was empty. Where was everyone? She heard voices outside in the yard and smiled. It was the children and Annie returning from somewhere. Her smile faded as she wondered if they had heard about the incident. Had Mary run downstairs to gossip about what she had witnessed? She sincerely hoped not, trying to explain to a four-year-old would have been nigh on impossible.

Harry entered first, dressed in clean clothes. 'Lottie, we wondered where you were. Cousin Jack has ridden off with Captain Forsythe and he wouldn't take me with him.'

Beth laughed. 'Of course he wouldn't, you ninny. They were going to speak to the villagers at Thurston and he could hardly take a little boy with him.'

'I'm not little . . .' Harry whined.

'That will do, Harry,' Charlotte told him sharply. He stopped, his mouth round. He was unused to hearing his beloved sister speak like that.

'Yes, Lottie, I'm sorry. Do you have the headache coming?'

'No, sweetheart, I'm just a little out of sorts. I was really looking forward to attending service this morning and I am disappointed we missed it.'

'Miss Carstairs, we beg your pardon, but we went out to wave off the militia,' Betty said. 'They are escorting his lordship to the village and then they are returning to Ipswich. A handsome body of men, if ever I saw one.'

'They have obviously found nothing untoward. Let us hope their presence here has driven, whoever it was, away.'

'Amen to that, Miss Carstairs,' Annie replied.

'Mrs Thomas says that more girls and women will be here tomorrow to begin a real clean up, and the men from the village will be starting on the outside at the same time.'

'That is good news, Betty. Now, I have come down to find something to eat. I am afraid your delicious scones were dropped.'

Charlotte ate her belated breakfast and then left the children with their nursemaid. She had to know if Jack had received the letter before he left. She was also concerned about the imminent arrival of daily workers, for these always had to be paid at the end of each day and, as far as she knew, there was no money in the house to do this.

She hoped the lawyers would bring some ready cash with them. If it had been someone from the village behind the attacks, it would not help the situation if they did not receive their wages at the end of their labour. Meltham was exiting Lord Thurston's room as she arrived in the hall.

'Has Lord Thurston read my note, do you know?'

'Yes, miss, he read it before he went out.'

She knew it was not correct etiquette to question a member of staff in this way, but she had to know. 'Er . . . how was he – how did he react?'

The butler smiled, pleased he could pass on good news. 'He was happy to receive it, miss. He laughed and tucked it into his waistcoat pocket, close to his heart.'

Charlotte felt herself blushing. Good grief, Meltham believed it was a *billet-doux* he had delivered. 'Thank you. I am going to go for a walk. If Lord Thurston asks for me, please tell him I am not available.'

She decided to retire early. Jack had not yet returned and she wished to be in her bedchamber before he did so.

Charlotte was in the library when the door opened and his lordship strolled in, as though yesterday's incident had never happened. He tossed her note on to the desk.

'You are a pea-goose, Charlotte. I have no intention of releasing you;

we are to be married, as planned, three weeks from today.'

'I cannot marry you, you are—'

'A depraved monster, a brute! Yes, yes, my dear, that is stale news. But, my love, you have no choice. You have nowhere else to go, and can hardly tramp the streets with Harry and Beth in tow, so accept it; I have.' He perched on the desk, smiling in a way that made Charlotte forget her firm intentions. 'It is far easier when you have swallowed the pill, the anticipation is much worse. Did your mama never tell you that?'

What was he talking about? 'Pills? Jack, I have no notion what you mean. What have pills to do with anything?'

'Swallow them, then you cannot taste the noxious centre, I have always thought it an excellent analogy.'

She was even more confused. Should she be outraged that he compared marrying her to taking unpleasant medicine? Or had she completely missed his point?

'Are you suggesting I am unpalatable, that you have to force yourself to marry me?'

'Yes, my love; you see, I have no wish to marry anyone, your objections are to myself alone, therefore it is much harder for me. And,' he finished, openly laughing at her, 'if I can be happy then so can you.'

Charlotte frowned. 'I have absolutely no idea what you're talking about. And please do not laugh at me, I do not enjoy being a figure of fun.'

He flicked her on the cheek affectionately. 'Then, my dear, do not behave like a ninny hammer.' He straightened. 'So, that is settled. By the way, the gig will be ready tomorrow so you can go to Ipswich to buy your bride clothes.'

She threw her hands up in exasperation. 'Very well, I surrender. You are right, I have nowhere else to go, but I promise, Jack, if a viable alternative presents itself I shall leave, and you cannot stop me. I am marrying you out of necessity, not because I take any pleasure in the thought.'

He bowed. 'That is all I ask, all I expect. We can be friends, partners and lovers, which will be more than enough for me.' He turned to go.

'Jack, what happened in the village yesterday? Did you uncover anything interesting?'

'No; I am certain no one living there was responsible for the attacks. If the threat came from that direction then it was an outsider, a seditious malcontent from elsewhere.'

'I am relieved to hear it. I am sure once the cottages are repaired, and they have food on the table, no one in Thurston will be unhappy with their lot.'

'I must go, Charlotte; I have men to organize. Not all the villagers are involved with the repair of the cottages, some are here to start clearing the park.'

She smiled, this was the man she found so irresistible. 'Are we out of danger? Can we relax our guard?'

'I think that is possibly premature, my love. However, whilst there are so many men about the place, it should be safe to walk anywhere within the grounds.'

Charlotte was uncertain how she felt, for without the slightest difficulty he had outmanoeuvred her. He was so alluring when he was being playful. She sighed, gathering up the book she had come down to collect. Lessons were resuming, thus the need for books. She had noticed a large illustrated book on the flora and fauna of East Anglia which would interest the children, and they could look out for the plants and animals they read about, on their daily walks.

A parlour maid disturbed them just before noon. 'Excuse me, miss, but Mr Meltham says, as the legal gentlemen are here and are wishing to speak to you.'

Puzzled by this message, Charlotte asked, 'Is Lord Thurston not available?'

'No, miss, he's nowhere to be found; he's out in the park somewhere.'

'Very well, I shall be down directly.' She got up. 'You can finish your handwriting, Beth, and you, your drawing, Harry. When that is done, Annie can bring you down for luncheon. I shall join you in the parlour when I have finished my meeting.'

On her way down Charlotte wondered why the lawyers should

wish to speak to her. Jack's ridiculous challenge had been abandoned and, as far as she knew, never mentioned to Mr Blower or his associate.

The two gentlemen were waiting in the library. They bowed deeply at her entrance. The older man, obviously Mr Blower, addressed her. 'Thank you for coming down so promptly, Miss Carstairs, and I apologize for disturbing you.'

'How can I be of assistance, sir?'

'We have the funds Lord Thurston requested and the papers to release the remainder when he requires it.' He cleared his throat. 'But it is on another matter that we wish to speak to you. We wish to know your decision regarding the house in Ipswich.'

'I am sorry, sir, I have no knowledge of a house in Ipswich. I am afraid you will have to wait until Lord Thurston returns for your answer.'

'This is somewhat delicate, Miss Carstairs. Do I have your permission to speak of this?'

She was tempted to refuse, but curiosity overcame her distaste. 'Very well, what is it that you wish to tell me?'

'We have acquired a fine house, in the best part of town, and it is available for you and the children, and your staff of course, to move into straightaway. Your residence unchaperoned at Thurston Hall is causing speculation and gossip.'

'A house? Somewhere I can live on my own with the children? Not only am I under age, but I have no funds with which to run such an establishment, as I am sure you are aware.'

Mr Blower smiled. 'There was an annuity left for your mother, in Lord Thurston's will, and that will be more than enough for your needs. And a suitable companion will be easy to find; there are dozens of impecunious gentlewomen looking for exactly this sort of position.'

Charlotte stood up, terminating the interview. 'Please leave details of the house, and the annuity, and I shall decide whether I am going to move after I have discussed the matter with Lord Thurston.' There was something about these men, their oily smiles and shifty eyes that she didn't trust. 'Lord Thurston and I are betrothed; we plan to marry in three weeks, so such an upheaval hardly seems worthwhile now.'

She saw the lawyers exchange glances and began to feel uncomfortable closeted alone with them. 'If you will excuse me, sirs, I have matters to attend to elsewhere.' She nodded and hurried from the library.

In the corridor she paused, trying to sort out her conflicting emotions. Jack should have told her about the house, given her the option of moving. Why had he not done so? If he was as reluctant to marry her as he had professed, then being offered an honourable alternative should have seemed like a godsend.

Did she not have a right to decide for herself? The more she considered it, the angrier she became. She forgot her disquiet about the lawyers, the possible reasons why he might have decided to marry her and not send her away, and allowed her righteous indignation, at his highhanded behaviour, to sweep her along. When his lordship returned from his gallivanting around the countryside she would confront him with his perfidy and tell him that their marriage was cancelled. She had her alternative accommodation, and the funds to support herself; she had been given exactly what she wanted.

For some reason being offered this opportunity did not fill her with the excitement she had anticipated. In fact, if she was honest, her heart had sunk to her boots at the thought of her imminent departure from Thurston Hall.

CHAPTER THIRTEEN

C HARLOTTE had no time for a private word with Jack until evening. When he returned from his duties on the estate and had spoken to the lawyers before they departed, it was time for him to don his black jacket and attend poor Jenkins's funeral. All the male servants attended, and a few folk from the village, but it was a quiet affair. The young man had no family locally and no one had ever asked him where he hailed from, and now it was too late to do so.

Thurston Church had been hastily cleaned for the occasion so the pallbearers, Jethro, two grooms and a footman, had no difficulty carrying the plain wooden casket down the aisle. The vicar completed the service at the graveside in the churchyard and, when it was over, Lord Thurston gave Meltham a handful of coins and told him to take the mourners to the village inn for a drink. Then he followed the reverend gentleman back inside the tiny Norman church to hear the banns of his marriage read out for the first time.

'Thank you, Reverend Peterson; I apologize for the state of the building, but it has not been used for over a year. I promise it will be pristine on my wedding day in three weeks' time.'

'I am looking forward to performing that ceremony, my lord. It is far too long since a Thurston married in this little church.'

A brisk wind rustled the beech trees showering Jack with crimson leaves. He smiled; was this another nudge from the Almighty? To his astonishment, at that precise moment, the black clouds parted and the sun shone down, bathing him in bright light. He stared, awestruck, and felt the hairs on his arms stand up. He bowed to the beam of light, not sure if he was witnessing a miracle or a series of incredible coincidences. Whatever it was, it was remarkable, and convinced him that it was time he mended his ways. He must give up for ever his military habits of swearing and shouting when he was annoyed, and stop issuing orders to Charlotte as though she was a private under his command.

He grinned – it would be hard, he had spent all his adult life in the service of the Crown. There had been no necessity for drawing-room manners in the army. Of course, he had attended numerous balls and soirées, card parties and routs, but always in his regimentals, hiding behind his persona as a major. Who the real Jack was he had no idea, but he was sure he was not the irascible, foul-mouthed man his self-pity had allowed him to become.

The Reverend Peterson handed him the key to the church. 'You will require this, my lord, if you wish your staff to get in to clean and arrange the flowers before the big day.'

'But Sunday's service, and next week, the second reading?'

'I shall call for the key, my lord, never fear. I have been considering your suggestion that I should take care of both parishes until you can appoint a new incumbent.'

'And your decision?'

'I should be delighted to help. I can hold a morning service at thirty minutes past eleven o'clock each Sunday. Unfortunately time does not allow me to return to do evensong. However, I shall be available to perform baptisms, funerals, and of course, marriages as requested.'

'That is excellent news, and a great relief. Miss Carstairs will be delighted that she can walk to church.' Seeing the kindly old gentleman's enquiring look he quickly added, 'and I shall accompany her, of course.'

He strode off to the Hall, a short walk along an overgrown, bramble-infested path. The vicar returned to Renford in his pony and trap, both pleased with the outcome of their meeting.

Jack's brief conversation with his lawyers had also been satisfactory. He was looking forward to handing Charlotte a bag of coins to spend in Ipswich the next day. It was getting late. It would be dinnertime soon and tonight, for the first time, he had asked for it to be served formally. He knew the only room available was the breakfast parlour, not very grand for a celebration meal, but it was better than nothing.

The message he had left instructed her to be dressed appropriately ready to dine with him at six o'clock. This gave him barely an hour to organize a bath and change of clothes. He smiled; he had no evening dress, so it would have to be his dress regimentals. He hadn't worn his uniform since he had attended the ball the night before Waterloo. He remembered that some officers had stayed so long they had been obliged to fight in their best. He was glad he had not been one of them.

Beth clapped her hands. 'Lottie, I've never seen you look so beautiful. Is that the gown you made from the ball dress Mama had for her come out?'

Charlotte nodded. 'It is, Beth. Because the skirt was worn over hoops there was ample material. All I had to purchase was the gold sarsenet to make the over skirt.'

'Did the pretty bugle beads you have sewn in swirls around the hem and along the neckline, come from that dress as well?'

'No, they were in a box, in that old trunk with the carved lilies on the side. I believe they might have belonged to Grandmother.' Charlotte smoothed out her silk evening gloves. She examined the stain on the edge of one glove closely. It was so small she was certain Jack would not notice.

Harry had been watching the men from the village clean their scythes before they departed for the day. Satisfied they had finished he scrambled down from his position in the window seat and came over to admire his sister.

'How do you eat with gloves on, Lottie? Won't the food go all over them?'

Charlotte smiled and held up her hands for him to examine. 'See, Harry, they have no fingers, the material ends at the knuckles.'

'And why do you have a bit hanging out of your skirt at the back, Lottie, none of your other gowns have one?'

'It is a *demi-train*, Harry, all evening gowns have one, don't they, Lottie?' Beth informed him smugly.

'What's that? Why's it a train?' He had never seen a formal gown before and knelt down to examine the skirt.

'Are your hands clean, Master Harry?' Mary enquired anxiously.

' 'Course they are, I washed them this morning.'

Beth reacted. 'Harry, don't touch Lottie's gown, you will spoil it.' Her shouted warning was accompanied by a violent push, sending him sprawling. Annie bustled in and removed both children, scolding them for misbehaving.

Charlotte felt much better. The fracas had released her tension wonderfully. She was sorry she had not had the opportunity to speak to Jack about the house in Ipswich, tell him she was determined to move there, but in the excitement of wearing this gown for the first time, she had forgotten to be cross.

Meltham, in his habitual black, and two footmen, smart in freshly pressed green and gold livery, waited to greet her. She smiled, such formality, and to dine in the breakfast parlour!

The butler bowed. 'Lord Thurston is in the drawing-room, Miss Carstairs, if you would care to follow me.'

It seemed that it required the two footmen and Meltham to escort her across the width of the entrance hall. Trying not to laugh, she followed them as instructed. Outside what had been Jack's domain, the butler halted. The footmen ceremoniously opened the double doors.

'Miss Carstairs, my lord,' Meltham announced grandly.

Scarcely suppressing her giggles, Charlotte entered. What a change! The room was restored to something resembling a drawing-room. The disgusting armchairs had vanished to be replaced by two *chaise-longues*, a love seat and several spindly-legged gilt chairs, more suited to a ballroom.

Then all desire to laugh evaporated. She spotted Jack, standing by the mantelshelf, watching her, his face alight with appreciation. She hardly recognized him; he looked magnificent in scarlet jacket, skin-tight calfskin britches and top boots with flamboyant tassels. His hair was swept forward, almost covering his scar.

He bowed deeply and she curtsied low. On offering her hand to him he gripped it, carrying it to his mouth. His lips burnt across her folded fingers and her heart somersaulted. Her closely fitting bodice felt constricting. He gazed into her eyes and she could not resist. Her feet carried her the three steps needed to reach his arms. His hold was gentle and his lips, when they found hers, were tender. She felt bereft when he lifted his head.

'I had not intended to do this, sweetheart. I was going to be the perfect gentleman tonight, treat you with the utmost respect.' He smiled his lopsided smile and shrugged. 'But you are so utterly *ravissant*, I could not help myself. Forgive me please?'

At that moment Charlotte knew she would forgive him anything. Maybe marrying without his love would not be so bad. 'Of course I forgive you. It was I who came to you, not the other way round.' She smiled, her eyes glittering. 'And tonight, dressed as you are, I find you quite irresistible.'

He gestured around the room. 'What do you think? A vast improvement, is it not?'

'It is indeed. Where are your quarters now?'

'I have moved upstairs, there are one or two chambers habitable. I thought to have made it the room where the ceiling collapsed, but I have found another.' He led her over to the *chaise-longue* and waited for her to be seated. 'May I offer you a glass of champagne? Meltham has unearthed a dozen bottles.'

'I have never tasted champagne,' Charlotte answered shyly. She was finding him rather overwhelming this evening.

'I did not ask you, my love, if you have tasted champagne; I wish to know if you wish to share a glass with me now?'

Charlotte recovered her equilibrium; being cross with him was so much easier. 'Do not bandy words with me, Lord Thurston. Of course I would like a glass.' As she watched the butler deftly remove the cork and pour the golden frothing liquid into tall crystal glasses, she recalled why she had wished to speak with Jack earlier in the day.

'Mr Blower tells me that there is a house in Ipswich waiting for me and the children and a legacy from my grandfather to pay for its upkeep.'

135

He sat up. 'The house I knew of, but the legacy is news to me. I wonder why this was not mentioned earlier.'

'And why did you not inform me of its existence, give me the option to remove myself there?'

He chuckled. 'I am sure you know the answer to that, my love. As I had already made up my mind to marry you there was no necessity to mention the house. But I am puzzled by the sudden appearance of a legacy.'

She recalled the unease she had felt in the company of the lawyers. 'I did not like those men, they have a shifty manner that I cannot trust.'

Meltham interrupted the conversation to serve the wine on a silver salver. She took a few exploratory sips and placed the glass aside. 'I find I do not like this; it has too many bubbles and a rather dry taste.'

Jack followed her example and put the glass down. 'I have always thought this overrated. You can have a glass of claret with the meal; perhaps that will be more to your liking?'

'I have had both red and white wine on many occasions, it was often the only safe drink to be had.'

'I had forgot you had accompanied your father on his campaigns. But to return to the lawyers, do you know if they knew of your whereabouts prior to your arrival here?'

'Oh yes, Lord Thurston would have had it. I wrote to him when Papa died, to ask for his help. Of course, I did not know that he was already dead and that is why I received no reply.' She frowned. 'But it is odd, is it not, that the letter was returned opened but unanswered?'

'Decidedly odd. It had to be Blower who returned it. Why did he not inform you of your legacy then?'

'I wish he had; it would have made such a difference to our lives. I would not have needed to come here; I could have remained in the house in Romford.'

His expression became serious. 'Then I am glad they were derelict in their duties; your arrival here has changed my life, and all for the better.'

She flushed with pleasure. This was almost a declaration of devotion, maybe he felt more for her than he was prepared to own. 'Another thing, have you wondered where all the silver plate and decent furniture and paintings have gone? Mama did not speak often about her life here, but I do know that it was a grand place, and she experienced every possible luxury.'

Jack called across to the butler, standing unobtrusively by the sideboard. 'Meltham, how long have you been here?'

'Thirty years, my lord. I started as an under footman.'

'Then you can answer a question for us. What has happened to the silver, furniture, in fact anything of value?'

'The lawyers took it when Lord Thurston died, my lord. Mr Blower said it was at risk in a house with no master.'

'And the furniture and paintings, did they go into storage as well?'

'Yes, miss. The only thing that remained was the cutlery. I am surprised they have not returned the rest as you have been in residence, my lord, for more than a year now.'

'Thank you, Meltham, you have been a great help.' Jack waited for the man to retire to his corner at the far side the room before continuing. 'There is something havey-cavey about this, Charlotte. I shall accompany you to Ipswich tomorrow and speak to the lawyers.'

'Could you not ask to see the will? See the accounts, and the extent of the debts incurred by the loss of the fleet?'

'Excellent suggestion, my dear. I have been remiss in all this. Had I not been so lost in self-pity this past year, I would have investigated the matter and discovered the truth for myself.'

A footman came in and spoke to the butler, who promptly moved forward. 'My lord, Miss Carstairs, dinner is served.'

Charlotte detected a certain tension in Jack, a suppressed excitement. He held out his arm and she placed it on his, his forearm solid beneath her fingers. She smiled up. 'What is it? What are you hiding from me?'

'Wait and see, my love. I have a surprise for you, a pleasant one, I hope.'

Meltham led them from the drawing-room and, instead of turning right to the breakfast parlour, took them across the corridor and stopped in front of a room she had not been in. The two footmen hurried forward to open the double doors. The butler bowed and stepped aside giving Charlotte a clear view of the chamber.

'Oh my! You have opened the dining-room for us.'

Jack led her in and she glanced around in wonder. The long table was covered from end to end in snowy white damask and a large vase of beautifully arranged late autumn flowers and golden leaves occupied the centre. Candles stretched its entire length bathing the room in a romantic glow. At the far end two settings were laid, the crystal sparkling and the ornate silver cutlery reflecting the flickering light.

'It looks beautiful, thank you so much.'

'It is a mirage, my dear. The candles have been placed down the centre of the table deliberately. The rest of the room is in a parlous state, I can assure you.'

For Charlotte the meal passed in a haze. Betty had surpassed herself and managed to produce two courses and several removes. Jack put himself out to be charming and kept her entertained with a series of amusing anecdotes about his life on the Peninsula. She had no need for claret, she was drunk with happiness.

It was late when they parted in the gallery. Charlotte had been anticipating his goodnight kiss all evening but Jack disappointed her. 'I was thinking of having the gig brought round at nine o'clock tomorrow. Is that too early for you?'

She shook her head. 'No, I am an early riser, as are the children. I shall be ready in time. Is there room for all of us and Annie?'

'I am riding, that means there will be ample room inside.'

He took her hands and squeezed them gently. 'I must bid you goodnight here, sweetheart. I cannot trust myself not to follow you into your chamber if I come any further.'

Charlotte flushed. 'You are a reformed character, my lord; if you continue in this way I shall not recognize you.'

Her oblique reference to his previous invasions into her chamber did not pass unnoticed. 'It is twenty nights until I have the right to enter your chamber and stay there. I can wait. I count myself a patient man.'

Charlotte's chuckle escaped without her permission. 'If you are a patient man, my lord, then I am the Queen of Sheba.' Still laughing, she pulled back her hands and ran down the passage to her room where Mary was waiting to prepare her for bed. She glowed all over at the thought of him joining her in her chamber on their wedding night and exactly what that would entail.

The drive to Ipswich the next morning was uneventful. Jack's huge stallion provided plenty of entertainment for the children as it did its best to tip him off on several occasions. On the second of these alarms, she realized that he was armed. He had a pistol holstered on either side of his saddle. She was uncertain if she was reassured by his foresight or perturbed by the idea that he believed there was still a danger of being attacked.

The carriage slowed to join the queue of other vehicles heading into town. Jack rode alongside, his horse having finally settled. 'The lawyers have an office in Fore Street. I have asked Jethro to arrange refreshments for us all in the Crown at midday.' He grinned. 'Is it possible you might have completed your purchases by then?'

Charlotte laughed. 'I sincerely hope so. Neither Beth nor Harry enjoy shopping overmuch. I might have a rebellion on my hands if I do not stop for luncheon.'

The shopping expedition was agreed by all concerned to be a success. Just before midday Charlotte and her party returned to the Crown Inn laden with parcels and boxes. These were stacked tidily in the corner of the private parlour Jethro had bespoken for them.

'Annie, I declare I am delighted with my purchases. I had not expected Ipswich to have such an excellent range of emporiums.'

The maid rubbed her back. 'The four gowns you got will hardly need any alteration to be a perfect fit, miss. It was a stroke of luck that a lady cancelled her order. I just hope we have time enough to complete the sewing of your undergarments and nightwear before you are wed.'

'We have almost three weeks, which is plenty of time. And I intend to ask Mrs Thomas to loan me a couple of the new girls to help.'

Harry jumped up and banged on the window making them both jump. Charlotte opened her mouth to scold him but saw Jack waving through the glass obviously unbothered by Harry's rudeness.

'Look Lottie, Cousin Jack has boxes as well. I can hardly see Mr Jethro under all the parcels.'

'And Cousin Jack is carrying two boxes himself,' Beth announced, her tone expressing her astonishment that such a top-lofty person as a lord should deign to carry his own purchases.

Charlotte got up and pulled the bell-strap. If he was here it was time to have their refreshments served. Annie moved over to join the children at the small table leaving the larger one for her employers. Two maids staggered in with trays stacked high with food. Charlotte surveyed the mountain in dismay. When the girls had set out the repast and departed she spoke of her concern.

'We shall never consume all this; there is enough to feed an entire army.'

'Jethro obviously did not know what we like so ordered a small amount of everything they serve.' Jack grinned across at the children. 'Come along, you two, let me serve you first. I can see you are bursting with curiosity to see that what there is on our table.'

He gestured towards the parcels. 'I see you have not wasted your morning, my dear.'

'Indeed, I have not.' She rummaged in her reticule and produced the soft leather pouch he had given her that morning. 'I am sorry, but I have spent almost half the money. I had hoped to return far more to you.'

His eyebrows shot up. 'Good God! I did not expect to see any change. You must be the only female in creation capable of restraint when shopping for gowns.'

She pushed the bag across the table, but he dropped his hand over hers, restraining her. 'No, sweetheart, it is yours, keep it. I am certain you will need pin money of your own. I do not wish you to be obliged to come cap-in-hand to me whenever you have personal needs.'

'Are you sure? I thought we were short of funds, we had to economize?'

'We do, but things are not at such a pass that I cannot give you an allowance.'

They ate in companionable silence until Charlotte replaced her cutlery on her plate. 'I am replete. I could not eat another morsel. I am not used to consuming so much in the middle of the day, but it was all delicious. How did you know this place served such excellent food?'

'I have to admit that I did not. I asked the redoubtable Meltham – he is a fount of all knowledge – and this is his recommendation and an excellent choice it was too.' He stood up and strolled across to the children. 'Well, bantlings, are you finished?'

'I'm bursting out of my britches,' Harry announced happily.

Beth, shocked at his improper comment, interrupted him before he could embarrass her further.

'It was a lovely luncheon, Cousin Jack, thank you.'

'Excellent. Annie, I have something outside with Jethro that might interest these two. And I think a well supervised run around the yard will help to settle their meal before we begin our return journey.'

The door closed behind the children and the two maidservants completed clearing the table leaving Jack and Charlotte alone.

'Charlotte, we need to talk. I have spent an informative hour with the lawyers and wish to share my information with you.'

'What have you discovered? I do hope it is not bad news, you look so serious.'

He removed a packet of documents from the inside pocket of his topcoat and handed them to her. 'Read these, my dear. I should be interested to hear your views, see if they coincide with mine.'

Charlotte carefully untied the ribbon and opened the first paper, smoothing it flat with trembling fingers. There was something amiss, Jack's expression told her so and she hoped it was not too shocking. There had been too many unpleasant revelations and events in the three short weeks she had known him, and she did not wish to experience anymore.

CHAPTER FOURTEEN

CHARLOTTE flicked through each document quickly. She noticed the ones detailing the sale of the silver and paintings and others relating to essential expenses that had to be met, debts that had to be paid. They all seemed to be in order; what was Jack hoping she would discover?

'Take your time; I did not see anything amiss on my first perusal,' he informed her helpfully.

She spread them out, side by side, across the polished tabletop; perhaps she would see something when they were viewed in this way. She sorted them into a logical order and began to study them again. The black spidery handwriting was easy to decipher, her grandfather's signature clear on each. She studied the dates. The documents went back over several years, apparently cataloguing a reckless disregard for economy and the tendency to invest in uncertain enterprises.

She smiled – she knew what it was. Triumphantly she looked up. 'These were all written by the same person and, judging by the clarity of the ink, all at the same time.'

'Well done! I am certain you are correct. These are forgeries.' He leant over and took her hand. 'You realize what this means, my dear? Blower and his partner are rogues; they have been systematically stealing from the estate for years.'

'My grandfather was unwell in his declining years and unable to make decisions because of his mental confusion; Dr Andrews told me so. This would have made it easier for them; he would not have queried anything they did.'

Jack picked up one of the most recent papers and studied the signature, then he compared it to another earlier document. 'Then these signatures have been forged as well. I can detect no difference between the ones done when he was well and when he was ill.'

Charlotte found this unpleasant revelation hard to accept. Lawyers were people you trusted with your money – they should be above suspicion. 'Perhaps there is some mistake? Did you confront Mr Blower when you were there?'

He shook his head. 'No, I studied them at my leisure in a coffee house nearby. It was only then I noticed the discrepancies.'

She felt the band around her chest begin to slacken. 'Then, I think I have the answer. Mr Blower has supplied us with copies of the relevant material, not the originals. That is why they all look the same.'

He was not convinced. 'But why would they all be written at the same time? No, there is something underhand going on here, I am sure of it.'

'Think. They knew you would wish to see documentation, proof of the legitimacy of their transactions. I expect that they have had their clerk scribbling away making these for you, ever since you first contacted them.' She pushed back her chair. 'There is one way to discover the truth: let us go back there and ask to see the originals.'

'And if they insist these are they, what then? I am not taking you into a situation that could prove unpleasant. I shall return alone; you must wait here with the children.'

'Jack, have you stopped to consider the other side of the matter? What if you charge into the office accusing them of chicanery and they are innocent? You could be arrested for slander. Imagine the embarrassment? And the problem of finding another firm prepared to work with you after that.'

He rubbed his cheek, his brow creased. 'Very well,' he said after a few moments, 'I capitulate. We shall go together.' He sounded so fierce, she laughed.

'We shall stay here until you have recovered your temper. Consider, if they are villains, we do not wish to alert them to our suspicions, or they could abscond with your money before you have them appre-hended.'

'Charlotte, you are wise beyond your years and, as always, quite correct. Do you wish to tell Annie where we are going?'

His mention of the nursemaid reminded her of his intriguing comment to the children. 'What did you buy them? I hope it was noth-ing extravagant; I do not wish to see them spoilt.'

'I purchased a terrier puppy for Harry and a pair of tortoiseshell kittens for Beth. Neither gift was costly, I can assure you.'

She was overcome by his thoughtfulness and forgot they were not in the privacy of Thurston Hall. She flung her arms around him. 'Oh, thank you, that is the kindest thing. We have never been able to keep pets because Mama could not be near one without wheezing dread-fully.'

With commendable restraint he released her. 'It was my pleasure, sweetheart.' He took her hand and looped it through his arm. 'We shall go outside and inspect the new members of the household before we go and see Blower and Thomas.'

Charlotte declared the puppy adorable and the kittens sweet. The children were perfectly content to stay in the yard while getting acquainted with their pets.

The cobbled street they had to cross was filthy, its surface liberally strewn with dung. Charlotte viewed it with dismay. Jack, seeing her hesitation, swept her up into his arms and ignoring the scandalized looks from several passers-by, strode over, depositing her neatly on the other side.

'That was outrageous.' She fanned her scarlet cheeks with her hands. 'You promised me you would behave with propriety in future; that vow did not last long.'

He was unrepentant. 'I am a soldier; I do not procrastinate. You did not wish to walk in the sh— the manure, so I carried you.' He was highly amused by her annoyance. 'If you like I shall carry you back and you can then traverse the road on your own feet.'

She almost stamped her foot in vexation. 'You are impossible. I do not wish to stand here making a spectacle of myself any longer.' She glared, daring him to return a flippant answer. He too had become aware they were attracting an unwarranted amount of attention. 'The lawyers' office is situated around the corner, no more than a few minutes from here. Shall we go?'

Reluctantly she placed her hand on his proffered arm and they completed their walk in silence. She was too cross to trust herself to say anything civil and he too engrossed in studying the delightful curve of her cheek, her extraordinarily long lashes and eminently kissable mouth.

'I dislike that bonnet, Charlotte. I do not wish you to wear it again.' He had not intended to speak his thoughts aloud but it was too late to retract them.

She stopped, snatching her hand from his arm. 'It took me two days to line this bonnet with the pleated silk that matches my gown. It is my very best one. You are the rudest man I have ever met.'

He had the effrontery to chuckle. 'I think it is a delightful confection; my objection is to the fact that the large brim obscures your lovely face when I am walking beside you.'

Somewhat mollified she replaced her hand. 'It is the first stare, you know; I copied the design from a fashion plate in *La Belle Assemblée*. And it was made to be worn with this ensemble.'

He patted her gloved hand. 'Now, the gown I thoroughly approve of, but I preferred it with the spencer left unbuttoned.' He prevented her from removing her hand a second time by placing his own on top. This was the first time either had mentioned the incident in the inn yard when they had first seen each other.

'I remember that you stared at me in an ungentlemanly manner. I was quite unnerved.'

'Not as much as I was when I heard you say you were all coming to Thurston Hall. I galloped home determined to deny you access, to send you packing when you arrived.' He caressed her fingers tenderly. 'I thank God every day that I did not do so.'

She reached out and brushed his cheek with her free hand. Her impropriety caused a passing matron to miss her footing and step into the road. In the confusion, as her maid helped her back on to the path, they were able to slip past and avoid further embarrassment. Breathless they arrived at the steps that led up to the offices they sought. Charlotte's bonnet was askew and Jack's beaver had slipped over his forehead at a rakish angle.

'We are a disgrace, my lord. I do not believe we should be allowed out in public.' She straightened her bonnet and retied the ribbons. 'I do not understand it at all. I was always a model daughter, never gave my parents a moments worry.' The mention of her mother sobered her. How could she behaving like a hoyden so soon after her beloved mama's demise? She felt her eyes filling and looked down, hoping to hide her distress. She was not quick enough.

'Here, little one, take this.' A large cotton square was placed in her hand and she mopped her eyes. He stood protectively in front, his bulk effectively screening her.

'Thank you, I am quite recovered. I am not usually such a watering-pot. I promised my mother I would not cry for her, but it is so hard to keep my vow.'

'It is an impossible one to keep. You loved your mother; you cannot just pretend she did not exist. I am sure repressing these feelings is what is causing you to act so out of character.'

She managed a watery smile. 'Do you think so? Then I shall stop worrying about it and try and get on with my life as I promised.'

He turned to head up the steps. 'This is damned odd! The shutters are closed and the door is locked.' He knocked loudly but there was no answer.

'I expect they are away on business; their absence might not be anything sinister.'

'I shall come back tomorrow. If they are not here then, I shall inform the militia and have them arrested.'

'I am certain it will not come to that. Everything will be explained to your satisfaction tomorrow. However, I think we should go back to the Crown; the wind has turned chilly and the carriage has no protection if it rains.'

The traffic was less dense on their return and they were soon out of town and bowling along the lane. The clouds had thickened and although it was barely two o'clock already dusk was setting in. Charlotte was grateful for the rugs Jethro had provided.

'There, Harry, snuggle under this, pull it up to your chin. You will be warm enough then.'

Annie glanced nervously at the lowering clouds. 'I don't like the looks of the weather, miss. We could be in for a drenching before we get back to Thurston.'

Jack was riding behind them, the lane at this part was narrow, the high hedges making it impossible for him to be alongside.

Harry, from his cocoon of blankets, posed a question Charlotte couldn't answer. 'Lottie, what happens if we meet another coach, we would get stuck. Would we have to go backwards?'

'I have no idea, Harry, I was wondering about that myself. The hedges are far too high for Jethro to see ahead and I believe that is how they normally avoid such problems.'

'If you'll excuse me for speaking out of turn, Miss Carstairs, this lane is not used much so I doubt we'll meet anyone this afternoon,' Jethro called back.

'Thank you. I should imagine backing down this winding lane would be extremely hazardous.' She shivered; she would be glad when they had completed this part of their journey. It had not seemed nearly so dark and threatening on their passage through a few hours ago. Things looked different in the sunshine, she decided, it is the same lane, no more dangerous than before.

She relaxed back onto the squabs pulling the rug closer around her knees. It was so cold; the weather had turned from summer to winter overnight. Jack must be freezing on Lucifer; he had not thought to bring a riding coat with him. She turned round to speak to him.

'Are you very cold? I have a spare rug here you could drape around your shoulders.' The wind carried her words away and he urged his horse closer to the rear of the vehicle and leaned forward over the animal's ears.

'Say that again, I did not catch what you said.' His parade-ground voice carried so well he all but deafened the occupants of the gig. They were all laughing when there was a loud report and a bullet whistled over Jack's head, missing him by inches.

'Get down on the floor. Do it now!' he roared.

She grabbed Harry who was sitting beside her and gripped Beth's arm and together they toppled off the seats and into the well in the centre of the carriage. Crouching on the floor in a tumble of blankets, her arms around Harry, she waited for the next explosion.

From her position she could not see what Jack was doing, and the roaring of the wind meant she could not hear him either. What was the coachman doing? Even the horses were still, no snorting, no jangling of harness. Just the sound of the wind in the branches rustling and creaking. She could feel Harry shaking and drew him closer.

Jack heard the report and reacted instinctively. He rolled sideways from his horse pulling out his pistols as he did so. They were primed and ready, all they needed was cocking. He crept forward, scanning the hedge for telltale movement. From the trajectory of the bullet he knew that one assailant was hidden on the left-hand side, but he had to be sure there was no one else on the right.

This was not a casual hold-up, this was a professional job, a deliberate ambush, and it could only mean one thing: whoever was out there was not after their property but their lives. He tensed, was that a flicker of leaves? Yes! He aimed and fired, his one eye as good as another man's two.

He heard his victim scream and there was a crash as a body fell through the bushes. Ice cool, he stuck the unfired pistol into his boot whilst he reloaded by touch alone. He was watching the hedge and the far right of the gig. He was certain there was another villain, biding his time. He needed to draw his fire, make him show himself.

Should he risk it? Expose himself in the hope that they would reveal their position? If he was shot, Charlotte and the children would be left unprotected, at the mercy of whoever was out there. His heartbeat slowed; his brain cleared. He was a veteran of the Peninsula and no bastard was better than him in a skirmish.

Decision made, he straightened and, keeping his guns out of sight, he walked round the stationary vehicle. His head and shoulders were visible, a clear target, and he had his blindside to the danger area. But his ears were sharp – he could hear as well as most people could see. He called to Jethro, keeping his voice even, trying to sound like a man who believed the danger was over.

'Jethro, I hit him. I am going to check the bugger is dead.'

The coachman was at the horses' heads, his hands over their muzzles, keeping them quiet. He knew his lordship was relying on his hearing. 'On your left, my lord, two of them,' he hissed.

Jack swung round and fired both guns into the hedge. He heard the ladies' screams of terror but ignored them. He ducked back and retraced his steps, managing to reload one pistol before he reached the rear of the vehicle.

He dropped to his knees and slid underneath, intending to make his next attack from below, from between the wheels. He crawled on his belly until he reached his position. He could hear Beth crying and the sound made him even more determined to kill the men who dared to frighten his family.

He moved forward cautiously and could see the hedge, had his first two bullets done the job, or were there still unseen killers hiding there? At first he could see nothing, no bodies, no live men, but then he detected a darker patch amongst the leaves. With a triumphant grin he raised his pistol, squeezed the trigger and saw the leaves explode outwards as a masked figure fell forward to crash, dead, inches from his face.

Jack was a soldier, so lay still before reacting. It would not do to break cover until he was certain the murdering bastards were dead or had fled the scene. He heard the sound he was waiting for, men moving backwards through the hedge. Whoever it was, their progress was slow. He smiled, he had winged at least one of them, so they should not be hard to track.

'Jethro,' he yelled, as he shuffled swiftly out from his hiding place. 'Get back up; it is safe to resume your journey.'

He felt energized, renewed by his battle, all his doubts about his abilities, his manhood, had vanished. He had killed two men and winged another, not bad for a man with one good eye.

*

Charlotte had no time to consider her own terror, her concern was for the children. Harry had soiled himself in his fear, and was shivering as though afflicted with the ague. Annie could take care of Beth; she would concentrate on her little brother. Gently she wrapped him in the blankets and lifted him back on to the seat pulling him on to her lap as soon as she was settled.

'There, darling, it is all over now. Cousin Jack has saved us, is he not a hero?'

Harry was incapable of speech. His hands clutched her jacket and he continued his silent crying. Charlotte felt something warm wriggling under her feet. The puppy – she had forgotten all about him. The kittens had been returned to their box but Harry had insisted that he cuddle his new pet on his lap. She groped about in the middle of the blankets and found the tiny animal.

'Come along, you are needed.'

She placed it on Harry's chest and was glad to see him release one hand from his vice-like grip on her spencer in order to hold the dog. The puppy licked his young master's fingers and then snuggled down inside his jacket.

By this time Annie had Beth back on the opposite seat and was comforting her. Normally the child hated to be fussed but she burrowed into her nursemaid's side, burying her face in the well-padded shoulder. The carriage rocked as Jethro returned to his seat and Jack opened the door and climbed in beside Charlotte.

'Sweetheart, the danger is over for the moment. I am sorry you had to undergo this experience.' He gathered her and Harry into his embrace and held them to his heart. 'I promise no harm shall come to any of you. This is the last time anyone takes shots at my family.'

Charlotte relaxed in his arms for a moment, his strength, his warmth, slowly restoring her. Then she glanced over his shoulder and saw the body prostrate in the dust. Before she could speak the skies opened and the threatened rain came down in torrents.

He shot out of the gig and closed the door. 'Renford is closer than

Thurston, Jethro. Who lives there who could take us in?'

'Doctor Andrews, my lord; he's about half a mile from here.'

'Then get going, the ladies and children are too shocked to withstand a soaking as well.'

He vaulted on to Lucifer and forced the horse to squeeze past the vehicle. 'Charlotte, I am going ahead to alert them, but I shall return to escort you.'

She saw him vanish into the rain but was too wet and cold to worry about being left temporarily unprotected. Jethro whipped up the horses and the coach rattled off at a spanking pace. No one minded the jolts and bumps, they were all too concerned with trying to keep the rain out.

Jack was back to escort them the last few hundred yards. The manor house was ready to receive the unexpected visitors. Doctor Andrews's housekeeper had hot bricks heating and towels and dry clothes ready in a guest chamber. A bevy of chambermaids and footmen were, at that very moment, hurrying up the backstairs with jugs of water to fill two baths; one for Charlotte and the other for the children.

Doctor Andrews would have taken Harry but Jack was there first. Ignoring his smelly state he swung him up, being careful to include the puppy in his hold. 'Off we go, young man. What you need is a hot bath and some dry clothes.' Harry was strangely silent, his face pinched and white, and in no state to respond.

The doctor assisted Charlotte from the carriage. 'There is a hot bath waiting for you, Miss Carstairs, and for the children. As your physician I can tell you that the sooner you all get out of your wet clothes the better. Being soaked to the skin after such a horrible experience will not help at all.'

Charlotte checked Beth was following before allowing him to escort her into the house. There the housekeeper took over.

'If you'll permit me, Miss Carstairs, I'll conduct you to a guest chamber. I've put the children in the adjoining room.'

Charlotte nodded her thanks, finding it was taking all her remaining energy just to mount the stairs. She ignored the room she had been allocated and followed Jack.

He placed Harry and his pet on the day bed. 'I must leave you, sweetheart. I have to find the men who attacked us before they can make good their escape.'

She roused herself sufficiently to answer. 'Please take care. I wish you God speed and a safe return.'

He pulled her close and his mouth covered hers in a fierce kiss, sending welcome waves of heat coursing through her icy limbs. 'I shall be, my darling. I have a family to come home to and I intend to be around to enjoy the experience for many years to come.'

He released her and strode off, gratefully accepting the loan of the doctor's many caped drab-coat. He was also glad to add two grooms, stout cudgels strapped to their saddles, to his search party. Jethro had borrowed a saddle and was mounted on one of the grey carriage horses. The four men thundered off down the drive, ignoring the driving rain, determined to find the attackers before full dark.

CHAPTER FIFTEEN

HARRY fell asleep cradled in Charlotte's arms and she was able to carry him over to the bed whilst Annie took Beth to the other guest room to bathe and rest.

'He is finally asleep, Annie. Thank God! I shall go and have my bath and see what Mrs Baker has managed to find me to wear. Please sit with him until I get back.'

A chambermaid had topped up Charlotte's bath and it was still pleasantly warm. She sank back, allowing the lemon-scented water to soothe away her stress. It had taken so long to settle Harry that her beautiful gown had all but dried on her. She feared it would never recover from the experience. She tried to block out the image of guns firing and bodies littering the lane, but whenever she closed her eyes, they were all she could see. A sound behind her made her jump but it was only the chambermaid.

'Mrs Baker has found you something to wear whilst we clean and press your own clothes, Miss Carstairs. They are ready on the chair.'

'Thank you. Is Miss Beth sleeping comfortably?'

'Yes, miss. Mrs Baker said I should sit with her until her nursemaid comes back. I can hear her from the dressing-room if she stirs.'

Charlotte was glad of the girl's assistance. Her limbs were leaden, her head heavy, and it took all her willpower to get out of the comfort of the tub. She raised her arms and legs as instructed, not noticing, nor caring, what she was being dressed in.

'There, miss; not exactly what you're used to, but at least you're warm and dry now.'

Charlotte glanced down at her gown – it was a plain grey bombazine, with a low waist, long sleeves and high neck. It was a trifle loose but served its purpose. Rose, the chambermaid, brushed and braided her hair, and wound it around her head in a neat coronet.

'That is excellent, Rose. I am going back to sit with Master Harry. Annie will be here directly to relieve you.'

'Mrs Baker said to tell you she would send up a tray, seeing as you missed out on dinner.'

The thought of food nauseated Charlotte, but she knew it would be impolite to say so.

She discovered Dr Andrews in the bedchamber examining Harry. She hurried forward, her heart racing. 'What is it? Is he worse?'

'His temperature is going up. I fear he could have contracted an inflammation of the lungs.'

'So soon? He was fit and well this morning. How can he be so ill now?'

The doctor's face was grave. 'Shock does dreadful things to a person's health, Miss Carstairs. The horrific events he witnessed today, coupled with his prolonged exposure to inclement weather, have lowered his resistance.'

'But he will recover? He is a healthy boy; he is never unwell. Indeed he has not even had a head cold in his entire life.'

'Unfortunately he is only four, a delicate age. I shall do my best to save him, Miss Carstairs, but must warn you I cannot promise a happy outcome.'

Charlotte ran to her brother's side. She placed a hand on his forehead, it was warm, but not unduly so. Puzzled, she turned to find the doctor standing close behind her. Too close.

'Doctor Andrews, Harry is not burning up with fever so how can you be so sure he is about to succumb to a congestion of the lungs?' She tried to shuffle sideways, increase the distance between them; his presence was already making her feel uncomfortable.

'I am a physician, Miss Carstairs. It is my job to know such things. His temperature will continue to rise and by the small hours he may well be fighting for his life. I recognize the signs.' He smiled warmly.

'But have no fear, I shall sit by your side all night, and you can be sure I shall devote all my expertise to his care.'

Charlotte was almost too tired to argue, but something prompted her to protest. 'Thank you, Dr Andrews, but I prefer to sit with my brother alone. If I have need of your assistance, I shall not hesitate to send for you.' For a moment she thought he would refuse to go – she could see his eyes narrow with annoyance – then he stepped back.

'Very well, Miss Carstairs. I shall not intrude where not wanted.' He walked towards the door. 'I fear you are making a dreadful error of judgement, but so be it. I shall pray that you are able to recognize the moment when Master Harry needs my medical skill and do not leave it too late.'

The door closed softly behind him. She brushed her palm for a second time across Harry's brow, it was no hotter than before. The doctor was scaremongering, using her brother's indisposition to insinuate himself. But a lingering doubt persisted: what if she was wrong and he sickened and died because of her actions?

She would call him back, apologize for her rudeness. She heard the door in the dressing-room opening. Rose appeared, bearing a tray with a tureen of chicken and vegetable broth and a plate covered by a cloth.

'Here you are, Miss Carstairs. Cook thought as you would prefer broth, nice and warming and ever so easy to eat.'

'Put it over there, on the small table, please. I shall come and eat in a moment.' She hesitated, should she involve the chambermaid in her problems? 'Rose, could you sit with me tonight? Master Harry is a little warm and he might develop a fever and need careful watching. But I am so fatigued I fear I might fall asleep.'

'Bless you, miss, of course I will. Mrs Baker said as you might need me. I'm a light sleeper so between us we'll not miss a thing.' The girl, having put the tray down, came over to join Charlotte by the bed. 'Can I touch him? I've nursed my little brothers and sisters and will recognize a dangerous fever right enough.'

'Please do, Rose. I should be glad of your opinion.' She did not mention that the doctor had already pronounced him to be in mortal danger.

155

The maid gently felt his face. 'Good heavens, miss, I don't reckon he's got a fever at all. Whatever gave you the notion that he's poorly?'

'His forehead is warm to the touch.'

'No warmer than it should be. He's a little lad, and they sleep hotter than us.' Rose stepped back. 'No, miss, I think you're worrying too much. But I'll be happy to sit up with you anyway, just to be on the safe side.'

Charlotte felt the knot in her stomach begin to unwind. 'No, Rose, thank you. I am over anxious. No doubt it is shock from the events we experienced today.'

'Of course it is, miss, and no wonder at it! But Lord Thurston will catch those villains. They'll not bother you a second time, I'll be bound.'

Charlotte felt it would be inappropriate to discuss the matter further with a servant but she wished she could tell this friendly girl that this was, in fact, the third attempt in as many weeks. 'I am sure you are correct, Rose. Will it be you who returns to collect my tray?'

'Yes, miss, it will. Mrs Baker says I am to attend to you personally whilst you are here. Beats dusting and polishing any day, I can tell you.'

Charlotte lifted the lid of the soup-tureen and inhaled the savoury smell. She wasn't hungry, but this was exactly what she needed. The clock was clearly visible in the light thrown by the four oil lamps. It was after eight o'clock. She rather thought she would ask Jack if they could change to oil lamps; they gave so much more illumination and less smoke and smell.

Using the ornate silver ladle she spooned out a generous bowlful and took it to eat beside the cheery fire. It was so delicious that she returned for a second helping but this time she remained at the table. She took a slice of the fresh bread and spread it thickly with butter, then added a slice of the game pie. The lemonade provided was a perfect complement to the meal.

She brushed off the crumbs and stood up, stacking the plates and utensils, before pushing in her chair. She checked that her brother was sleeping peacefully, reassured he was no hotter than before. Should she ask Rose to help her disrobe when she returned to collect the tray? She recalled how close the doctor had stood and his eagerness to sit up all night with her and decided against undressing.

She sincerely wished that Jack was with her. When he was there she felt safe, confident that nobody could harm her or take advantage. She grinned – that was not strictly accurate. She had, so far, been shot at twice and the only person who behaved improperly was Jack himself. She giggled – she was no better! When in his company all the years of instruction at her mother's side in what was, and what was not, accept-able behaviour for a young unmarried lady came to naught. Her common sense flew out of the window and she behaved as badly as he did. It was strange, when in Dr Andrews's company she had no diffi-culty behaving with absolute decorum – it was only with Jack she forgot herself.

It must be four hours since the men had left – what were they doing? Had he caught up with the attackers yet? Like Rose she had every faith in his ability to achieve his objective. He would be cold and wet and hungry, but he was a soldier, he would be able to function without comfort: he was trained to do so.

When Rose returned Charlotte had decided it would be safe for her to undress. 'Rose, is there a night-rail I can borrow? My brother is perfectly well and I intend to join him in the bed.'

'Yes, miss. I'll fetch it; it's been warming by the dressing-room fire.'

When Charlotte settled down beside her brother, the rain had ceased lashing the windows. She sent up a fervent prayer that Jack and his little band was safe and had found somewhere to shelter. She was woken by Annie, a few hours later, vigorously shaking her shoulder.

'Miss Carstairs, Miss Carstairs, you must come at once. Miss Beth's been taken right poorly. She's burning up with a fever.'

Charlotte scrambled out of bed. 'I do not have a robe; I cannot come out in this. Quickly, help me to pull on my dress over the top.'

Five minutes later she checked Harry was sleeping soundly and, with her bedside candle held aloft, she followed the nursemaid out into the silent passageway and into the adjoining chamber.

*

Jack led his band back to where the ambush had taken place. The two grooms carried lanterns but these were not lit, for there was still light enough to see, even with the rain.

Jack dismounted, pulling the reins over his stallion's ears. The horse was wild but, like all the warhorses he had ever owned, it knew to wait quietly if the reins were dropped in front. 'Bloody hell! Where are the cadavers?' Jack checked he had come to the correct place. Yes, there were broken branches where the body had fallen out into the lane, but the corpse itself had vanished.

He crouched down by the hedge and could see the pool of blood that indicated the man had indeed been dead. The heavy rain had begun to remove the sticky patch but it was still clearly visible. 'Jethro, is there a way through this hedge? A gate anywhere we can use?'

Jim, one of the grooms, answered. 'There is, my lord, a little further down. Do you wish us to go and investigate?'

'Do that. You are looking for a corpse, or failing that, evidence that someone has come back to remove it.'

'Light a lantern, Jethro, I wish to examine the lane more closely.'

Jethro, an expert in any weather conditions with his tinderbox, soon had a lantern illuminated and handed it to Lord Thurston. The pool of light showed clearly what the unaided eye had been unable to discern. 'Another carriage has been down here, the tracks are clear in the mud. Look, those are from the gig, these are from a far heavier vehicle.' He stood up and, lifting his beaver, brushed his dripping hair from his eyes then replaced his hat. 'Someone has collected the bodies, or at least this one.'

He could hear the sound of crashing on the far side of the lane. 'Are they there, lads?'

'No, my lord. But there have been several people here before us, and there's gore all over the place,' a disembodied voice called back. He heard the two men moving about obviously having a closer look.

'I've found some material and a couple of buttons snagged on a branch, I'll bring them back to you, my lord.'

'Good man,' Jack answered. He was deeply concerned. If the second body had also been removed it was not a casual passer-by who had taken them. Someone must have been following the gig and, when the ambush failed, they had stopped to take away the evidence.

But who? It made no sense; who was prepared to employ paid assassins, would risk so much in order to kill Charlotte and himself? It had to be connected to Thurston, to his title. There must be another heir, a man who had expected to inherit and was determined to do so even if it took murder to achieve his ends.

He hooked Lucifer's reins back and remounted. He would find nothing here. But perhaps he could follow the carriage tracks and they would lead him to the perpetrators? He waited until the two grooms had returned and handed him the scrap of cloth and buttons they had found. He recognized the material and the insignia; this had come from the jacket of an ex-soldier, a former member of the green-coats, the Rifle Brigade. He should have realized the shots came from rifles, not pistols.

'We need the other lantern, hold them down, close to the ground; I want to see if we can follow the carriage tracks.'

Jethro shook his head. 'In this rain, my lord, it will not be long before the tracks are gone. I doubt we'll have a trail to follow after a mile or so.'

'I know, but we have to try. Find the carriage and we find the paymasters.' He called across to the grooms from Renford Manor. 'I want one of you to ride to Ipswich and raise the militia.'

'I'll go, my lord. My mare, Bess, is not built for speed but she's got plenty of stamina. She can do the journey both ways, no trouble.' Jim volunteered.

'Excellent. Ask Captain Forsythe to meet me at Thurston Hall first thing tomorrow morning.'

The carriage tracks led them past Renford and on towards Hadleigh but there, as Jethro had predicted, they became impossible to distinguish in the quagmire the lane had become.

'Here, lads, hold the lantern out so I can see the time.' Jack pulled out his watch and flicked open the silver front. It was five o'clock, not late. He decided to go back to the lane and see if he could pick up the trail of the two men who had escaped. One was certainly wounded, and if the mysterious carriage had not found them, they were probably still abroad somewhere.

The rain eased then finally stopped making his task less onerous. He found an entrance into the wood that bordered the lane and led to where the men must have waited for them.

'Dismount here; tie your mounts to a branch.' He left his own horse's reins dangling as he had done before. Jethro and Tommy, the remaining groom, held the lantern in front of them.

It was almost pitch dark under the trees. Jack stood, head tilted as he considered which direction to go. 'They must have had horses here so I want you to look for where they tethered them. You will not find the place close to the lane; they would not have wanted to risk one of their mounts greeting our horses and alerting us to their presence.'

'How many do you think there were, my lord? You killed two, but there were others. I'm certain sure I heard them escaping,' Jethro said.

'There had to have been three men at least on this side of the lane, the first shot was fired by a decoy.'

The group separated. Jethro and Tommy searched together, whilst Jack took a lantern and set off on his own. The positioning of the men on either side of the road had been a clever ploy, the kind of thing a seasoned rifleman would do. It was a strategy he had used himself many times. Dealing with ex-soldiers made his task more difficult.

He knew many men had returned from their years of war to find the countryside in turmoil, no jobs to be had. It would have been simple to recruit such men, who would see it as easy money, not much different to killing for King and country. The thought saddened him that heroes should be reduced to such a pass.

The only sound in the wood was a distant dripping of water from the leaves and the occasional rustle of animals and birds in the trees and undergrowth. 'Jethro, Tommy, over here. I have found what we seek. The horses were tied up here,' he called. He hung his lantern on a convenient branch and crouched down to investigate more thoroughly.

In the soft leaf mould there were clear imprints of hoofs, but how many it was difficult to decide. He ran his finger round one – this horse had a lose shoe and its print was quite distinctive. Jethro and Tommy arrived at his side. 'Look at these you two, how many horses are tied up here, can you tell?'

Jethro seemed to barely glance at the churned up area before straightening. 'Four, my lord, there are four different sets of prints here.'

Jack slapped him on the back. 'Well done. That confirms what I thought. Now, can you tell me how many were ridden away and how many led?'

This was a more difficult task, but not beyond the two grooms. 'See over here, my lord, they left by a different route.'

He went over to where the path divided. 'Yes, I see, Jethro, and from the way the prints run, I would speculate that two were ridden, and two led. Am I correct?'

'You are, my lord. I can tell you something that you might not have spotted. There's blood on some of the lower branches, boot height I'd say, if the man was mounted.'

'I hit one of them in the leg; that was what I hoped to discover. Now I know what we are looking for. Two riflemen, one wounded, and leading horses, would not be a common sight in these parts, I should think. Riflemen are not renowned for their horsemanship, in fact only the officers ride.'

'In that case, my lord, they will not want to be out in the dark. Even a skilled rider thinks twice about travelling at night.'

'Then we should have no difficulty discovering their whereabouts for they will have been remarked upon if they were seen.'

'That's true, my lord, but folks will be abed by now, it's past eight o'clock. They won't answer our knock, not at this time of night.'

'Damnation! Then can we track these men, follow the trail?'

'Once they clear the trees and regain the lane their prints will be lost in the general mud, so I doubt it, my lord. We can try if you wish. I'm game, what about you, Tommy?'

The young man nodded. 'They might have holed-up at the inn. They must overnight somewhere. I reckon, my lord, if one is wounded he'll not want to be out all night in this weather, that's for sure.'

'You are correct, Tommy. And, as you are willing, we must give it a try. If we lose the trail we can visit the hostelry. Then if there's no luck to be had there, I shall stop the search for tonight and wait for Captain Forsythe and his troop to arrive tomorrow.'

Jethro elected to walk, he could see better that way, and the other groom led his mount for him. The four horses had left the wood and their prints had been remarkably easy to follow for a mile or so, but then they vanished, as if someone had spirited them away.

Jack dismounted to search. 'This is damned odd! Where the devil have they gone?' The road was much wider here, enough for two carriages to pass without incident. The hedges were lower and there were several gates that opened on to farm tracks. 'Tommy, stand in your stirrups – what can you see across this field, any lights or sign of movement?'

'Nothing, my lord, but I think there're some buildings, an old farm cottage and a barn, but no lights.'

Jack came to a decision. 'The tracks have vanished because they cut across this field. I would stake my title on the bastards being down there in that cottage.'

'What're you going to do, my lord? Are you going down there?' Jethro asked.

'No, but I would like you two to stand watch. I shall pay you handsomely for your trouble.'

'Happy to, my lord,' Tommy told him cheerfully.

'Keep out of sight. These are dangerous men who could kill you with one shot. If you see them trying to leave, one of you come to Thurston at a gallop, is that clear?'

'Yes, my lord.'

'Excellent! I am afraid you will be on short commons tonight, but I shall make it up to you tomorrow. I intend to return to Thurston Hall; I need to be there when the militia come.'

Jack gave his valet little assistance in the removal of his boots and wet clothes. He fell back on to his bed revelling in the warmth. Tomorrow he would have the answer to the puzzle, discover who was behind these attacks, but tonight he was too damn tired to worry about it.

He was sadly out of condition, had spent too much time drinking and not enough taking exercise. In the old days, with Nosy, he could have ridden all night, fought a battle, and then spent an hour or two in the local whorehouse. Thank God he would soon be a married man and would never have the need for such an establishment again. He fell asleep with a smile of contentment on his face at the thought of his approaching nuptials.

CHAPTER SIXTEEN

CHARLOTTE stretched out beside her sister but, tired as she was, she couldn't sleep. Her head was filled with wild imaginings. Jack should have returned by now. He could not have continued to search in the dark, so where was he? She tried to comfort herself with the knowledge that it was unlikely both grooms and Jethro had been so incapacitated that it had left them unable to return and raise the alarm.

What would she do if he was dead? How would she be able to carry on living without him? She brushed the tears away and bit her fist to hold back her sobs. It did not seem credible that she could love him so completely when she had known him for such a short time. Perhaps she was like her own mother who had told her that she had fallen in love with Papa at first sight. One glance was all it had taken; one brief meeting and they were destined to spend the rest of their lives together.

She sniffed quietly. Mama had disobeyed Grandfather and run away to marry even though it meant living without the luxury she had grown up with. She sighed. Jack could not be dead; she was certain that she would sense it if he was. But he could be grievously injured, or he might have been taken prisoner.

Charlotte abandoned any attempt to rest and slipped from the bed. Beth was sleeping, still a trifle warm, but nothing to fret over. She would go downstairs and see if any news had come in during the night. Maybe a message *had* arrived and she had been too busy with Beth to hear. Her hand was on the door when she remembered she was only partially dressed. She had her nightgown on under the hideous bombazine gown Mrs Baker had lent her. Annie was next door and could help her to adjust her appearance. Charlotte crept in and beckoned to her maid to join her in the dressing-room.

'Look at this, miss, your own gown back, pressed and ready to wear.'

'What a relief! It was very kind of the housekeeper to supply this dress, but it is most uncomfortable. Why any woman would wish to wear such a slippery material I cannot imagine.'

'It's one of her own, I reckon. That's why it's plain and serviceable so it won't show every mark like muslin or cambric.'

Charlotte smiled. 'I am being ungrateful, but I have seen too many matrons sailing down Romford High Street with gowns made from this.' She stepped out of the dress, glad to be rid of it. 'I shall go down the back stairs. I wish to go out to the stables and there is more likely to be someone up to let me out in the kitchen than anywhere else in the house.'

'Should I keep an eye on Miss Beth as well as Master Harry?'

'I was about to ask if you could do that. As soon as Rose is up she can take over.'

'I'll go along right now and sit with her for a bit. No doubt Master Harry will call out loud enough when he wakes.'

'Thank you. You are a godsend, Annie – I do not know what I should do if you decided to leave us.'

'No chance of that. I'm well past my prime; I'll finish my years with you, as long as you'll have me and glad to do so.' The middle-aged woman smiled. 'And I'm hoping that I'll have your babes to care for later on.'

Charlotte blushed. 'Annie, Lord Thurston and I are not yet married.'

Unabashed, her maid chuckled. 'But it's less than three weeks away. You could be presenting his lordship with an heir this time next year.'

'Annie, pray do not speak of such matters.'

'I apologize miss, I know it's not my place to comment.' Her chuckles followed Charlotte out of the door.

The stairs were dark and a single candlestick did not give sufficient light to make it possible to hurry. By the time she arrived at the bottom, in the servants' hall, her journey had served to reinforce her conclusion: she was glad she was not a chambermaid and obliged to carry buckets of hot water up, and brimming chamber-pots down, such a narrow winding staircase.

'Good morning, Miss Carstairs. Is there something I can do for you?'

Charlotte nearly dropped her candlestick in fright. 'Good heavens, Renshaw, you startled me. I did not expect to find anyone about so early.'

The butler bowed. 'I apologize for causing alarm, miss, and if you will forgive me for mentioning it, I was equally surprised by your sudden appearance from that particular door.'

She grinned. 'Of course you were. Did you think it was a ghost?'

His features relaxed. 'No, miss, I thought it was your Annie. I hope Miss Beth is not worse.'

'No, she is much better, thank you. Actually my intention is to go out to the stables and see if there has been any word from Lord Thurston in my absence.'

'I can answer that for you. I can assure you I would know if there had been. Neither of the two grooms who accompanied Lord Thurston has returned either.'

Her smiled faded. 'Oh dear! I had so hoped news might have arrived during the night.'

'Bad news, in my experience, always travels fast, Miss Carstairs. I am certain they will all return safely and that you are worrying needlessly.'

'I pray you are correct. Is Mrs Baker up? I should like a word if she is.'

'Yes, Miss Carstairs. She is in the kitchen talking to Cook.'

'Does everyone here get up so early?'

'Upper servants are expected to rise before the lower staff at Renford Manor. We use the quiet time to plan the day.'

Renshaw escorted Charlotte to the kitchen and ushered her in. She looked around in admiration. It was so different from Thurston Hall. A brand-new, shiny black cooking range stood in pride of place, almost filling one wall. The atmosphere was clean, no smoke or cinders from an open fire.

Mrs Baker hurried forward. 'Good morning, Miss Carstairs, how can I be of assistance?'

'Good morning, Mrs Baker. I should like to thank you for loaning Rose, she is an excellent substitute for my own abigail. I wish to ask if Rose could be spared to act as my personal maid, until my own can be sent for?'

'She can, Miss Carstairs. She will be down soon; would you like her to go straight up to you?'

'Yes, thank you. What time does Dr Andrews come down?'

'At seven o'clock, miss.'

Charlotte considered taking the backstairs but deciding against it walked through the servants' hall and up the stairs to the door that divided the staff from their masters. The spotless black-and-white tiled entrance hall was deserted, the front door still bolted. The handsome tall-case clock showed it was almost half past five. She had an hour and a half to wait.

She frowned as she recalled Jack's reaction to her last meeting with the doctor. Would he object to her being alone with her host? She believed things had improved between them since then, that they understood each other better now. She smiled. He had no need to be jealous. She was sure the man was a good physician but she thought of him as nothing else. There was no room in her life for anyone apart from her fiancé.

She paused outside Harry's door, but all was quiet. Re-entering Beth's room she was delighted to find Rose sitting quietly by the bed.

'Good morning, Miss Carstairs. Miss Beth woke and I have just given her a drink. She is dozing now.'

Annie left with Harry at eight o'clock, leaving Charlotte to pace the empty chamber, becoming more and more concerned about Jack's prolonged absence. Doctor Andrews had ridden out to visit a patient in the next village and Charlotte was relieved to see him go. He had been most conciliatory and helpful when they had spoken, but she felt uncomfortable in his company.

It might have been better for her not to have gone down and spoken to him herself. She had calculated Mary should be back with fresh clothes, and the necessities for her enforced stay by ten o'clock. She prayed there would be good news returning with the carriage.

'Beth, would you like some bread and butter?'

Her sister shook her head. 'No, I'm not hungry, Lottie. I think I shall sleep again.'

Charlotte smoothed out the coverlet and drew the bed hangings shutting out the morning sun. She wandered over to the window to stare out on the empty drive. It was almost nine o'clock and there had still been no word. She had eaten no breakfast; she had tried, but had found it impossible to swallow.

'Rose, it is Lord Thurston. He is coming down the drive with Jethro and two grooms. Thank God! Thank God! I have been so worried about him.'

'You go down, Miss Carstairs. Miss Beth's resting and I can attend to her.'

Charlotte didn't pause to check her appearance; she was desperate to discover what awful circumstances had kept him from her side for so long. Renshaw was in the hall when she descended.

'Lord Thurston is on his way, Renshaw. Please inform him I am waiting in the—'

'Yes, Miss Carstairs. Shall I conduct you to the drawing-room?'

She smiled. 'Thank you. I am making very free with Dr Andrews's home, am I not? But he is a kind gentleman and I am sure he will not object.'

The butler bowed. 'The room is this way, madam.' He led her to double doors on the far right to the hall. 'Shall I have refreshments sent in when Lord Thurston arrives?'

'Yes, I expect he will be hungry and thirsty after being out all night. I shall leave it up to you to decide what would be best.'

It is a further ten minutes before she heard the front door opening and the sound of Jack's footsteps approaching. Renshaw opened the door and announced him grandly.

'Lord Thurston to see you, Miss Carstairs.' Then he tactfully retired, closing the door firmly behind him.

Charlotte stared open-mouthed at her beloved. She was expecting a heroic but bedraggled figure, in mud-stained britches and dirty boots, his face grey with fatigue. He was none of those things. He was cleanly dressed and clearly well rested. 'You have changed your clothes,' she said, when finally she found her voice.

He smiled. 'Of course I have, sweetheart. I would hardly sleep in my filth. I have a man to take care of me now, remember?'

'You have spent the night in the safety of your own bed?' She was barely able to contain her fury.

Baffled by the frosty tone, he shook his head and began to walk towards her. Instantly she stepped back. 'Where else did you expect me to spend it, my love?'

Her anger erupted at his insensitivity, his callous disregard for her feelings. 'I expected you to have spent it outside, or under a hedge, or perhaps lying injured in a ditch. I have been beside myself with worry, whilst you, my lord, have spent a comfortable, untroubled night in your own bed, thinking of no one's comfort but your own.'

He understood. But he underestimated her anger and laughed. 'You should know me better than that, sweetheart, it takes more than a couple of murdering bas— murdering villains to stop me.'

'I am delighted to hear it, my lord. It might also amuse you to know that I spent the entire night nursing Beth who is very poorly still. No, do not approach me.' She held out her hand haughtily. 'I am disgusted by your behaviour. You sent no message to tell me you were well, or ask how we did. Is this how it is going to be, my lord? I am to stay at home worrying, whilst you gallivant around the countryside killing people?' Charlotte knew this was a silly thing to say, but she was so angry she did not care. Like a parent whose child has just narrowly escaped danger, she was overreacting.

He was no longer amused. He raked her from head to toe, his expression murderous.

'I shall tell you how it is going to be, Miss Carstairs. You are going to speak to me in future with respect, or I am going to be forced to teach you how to do so. Have I made myself quite clear on this point?'

She wilted. This was a man she knew it would be foolhardy to disobey. She had let her tongue run away with her once more and must now endure the consequences. She dropped her eyes.

'I apologize for speaking so intemperately, my lord. Pray excuse me; I must go upstairs to attend to Beth.' She didn't wait for his permission, but picked up her skirts and fled past him only to be stopped by the doors so thoughtfully closed by the butler. She flinched as a long arm reached past her.

'Allow me, Miss Carstairs.' He opened the doors and stepped aside, making no move to prevent her ignominious retreat.

She didn't go to Beth's room but back into the room recently vacated by Harry. She closed the door and leant, trembling, against it. She didn't know whether to cry, or scream with vexation. She had offended him by her childish outburst and still didn't know what had happened. Had he managed to capture the two men who had escaped yesterday, or were they out there waiting to renew their attacks?

She splashed her face with the cold water she found left in a jug in the dressing-room, then checked her eyes were not too red, before venturing downstairs. It was her intention to ask him to forgive her and to explain why she had been so upset. She was halfway downstairs when she saw him striding across the hall on his way out. She watched in despair as Renshaw opened the front door and bowed him on his way. She could not put things right today, but would tomorrow be too late to heal the breach in their relationship before it became permanent?

Lord Thurston stood at the head of the imposing marble steps that led down from Renford Manor, unsure whether to go back inside or return to Thurston. What was it about Charlotte that brought out the very worst in him? Made him revert to autocratic officer, treat her like a snivelling schoolboy? God, what a mull they made of it together. She, berating him like a shrew, and he, responding like the veriest nincompoop. He should have sent word to her, but was not yet used to having another care whether he was alive or dead.

He pushed himself away from the door just as Jethro rounded the corner with the carriage. 'Miss Carstairs and the children will not be up to returning this morning. Miss Beth is unwell. Take the carriage back, you can return to collect them tomorrow morning.' Jethro touched his cap and drove on. A stable-boy appeared with Phoenix, his second stallion, the horse's temperament as fierce as his coat.

Jack vaulted into the saddle and, ramming his boots home in the irons, clattered off down the drive. He had not told Charlotte what had happened overnight, how the militia had surrounded the cottage early this morning only to discover that one man had escaped under the cover of darkness, leaving his companion, the one with a bullet in the leg, behind to be captured.

The injured man was now at Thurston. Doctor Andrews had been found and was attending to him at this very moment. Perhaps the man was well enough to be interrogated, the quack had not been sanguine about the villain's chance of recovery. He had lost too much blood and fever had set in.

He was cantering out through the imposing iron gates, when he reined in abruptly. God's teeth! Beth! Charlotte had said she was too ill to come home, that she had sat up all night with the child and he had not even enquired how she did. He turned the huge horse, urging him back into a canter. It was no wonder she considered him insensitive; he could not believe he had ridden off in this way.

The same stable boy appeared on cue to take his horse, but he detected a certain reluctance. Dipping into his pocket he removed a silver coin. He tucked it into the boy's waistcoat pocket.

'Here, lad, take this. It should compensate for stamped toes and a lump or two out of your arm.'

The urchin grinned. 'Thank you, your lordship. He's a handful, this one, ain't he? But I'll see him right. Will you be wanting him again soon, my lord?'

Lord Thurston laughed. 'I have no idea; possibly.'

Renshaw, equally vigilant, opened the doors at the precise moment Jack arrived at the top step. 'Miss Carstairs is upstairs. Shall I send word that you have returned, my lord?'

'No, have someone conduct me to her.'

The butler snapped his fingers and a footman appeared. 'Take Lord

Thurston up to Miss Carstairs. I believe she is in the green room.'

The young man was about to knock on the door to the room but Jack waved him away. If he was to be sent packing he wanted no sniggering footman to witness his embarrassment.

Charlotte heard the knock on the door and ignored it. She had no wish to speak to Renshaw, and it could be no one else. Rose would come in through the servant's door as would the tray she had ordered. She rolled over and pulled the covers over her head. She had been so overcome she had not even paused to remove her dress before flinging herself on to the bed, hoping sleep would obliterate her misery.

She didn't hear the door open softly, or Jack's footsteps muffled by the thick carpet. The first she knew of his presence was when the bed dipped. She knew who it was and tried to wriggle away. She was not ready to receive a second scolding. But her escape was prevented by strong arms, one slipping under her shoulders, the other around her waist.

Held close, her tear-soaked face cradled in his hand, he rocked her gently. 'Sweetheart, I am so sorry. I am a brute. Come, please do not cry, little one. I cannot bear to see you so distraught.'

She couldn't answer, the sobs she had been doing her best to repress burst out. It was so long since anyone had held her, comforted her; it was normally she who had to do the comforting. He soothed her, stroking her back, letting her cry. Eventually she shuddered and raised her eyes.

'I am so sorry. I did not mean to shout at you, but I was worried and I had not slept.'

He mopped her face dry, his expression tender. 'It is I who must apologize to you, my love. I have no excuse to offer apart from the fact that—'

She reached out, stopping his lips with her fingers. 'Do not express regret to me. You do not have to. It is not your place to explain your actions; I promise I shall not question you like that again.'

She felt him tense and his lips opened, drawing her fingers into his mouth. Her breath stopped and a delicious heat pooled in her lower regions. Whilst his tongue caressed the tips of her fingers he pulled her close, crushing her breasts against his chest, and she knew whatever he wanted from her she would give it to him, willingly.

CHAPTER SEVENTEEN

Charlotte was melting, she no longer knew where her body ended and his began. She moved her head restlessly from side to side, not sure what it was she craved, but knew it had to be he who gave it to her. Her hand had fallen from his mouth and buried itself in his thick dark hair, loving the springy softness. His mouth seared its way along her collar-bone before finding her parted lips and covering them with his own.

She understood what he wanted her to do and widening her mouth allowed his intimate invasion to send spirals of pleasure around her body. Tentatively she tangled her tongue with his and his response showed she had pleased him. He swung his legs on to the bed bring-ing one across hers, intending to roll her under him. His boot caught her naked calf and she jerked back in pain.

Instantly he released her, realizing what he had done. 'God's teeth! What am I thinking of? I am sorry, sweetheart, my behaviour is unpar-donable.' As he spoke he removed his legs from the bed and sat up.

She felt abandoned, unsettled, did not understand. She only had the vaguest idea what actually occurred between a man and woman but knew it usually involved removing one's garments. She was fairly sure it was not normal for the gentleman to be wearing his boots and topcoat. But she knew Jack had no reason to apologize, apart from bruising her leg with his boots.

'It was your boots; they hurt my leg. Perhaps it would help if you removed them?'

He bent down, kissed her and stepped back. 'Do not tempt me, my love, I am finding it difficult enough.'

She giggled, stretching like a contented cat, unaware that her breasts strained enticingly within the confines of her rumpled bodice. 'I believe that I am beginning to enjoy this. . . .'

'Lovemaking?'

'Oh! Is that what it is called? How very appropriate.' She wriggled to the edge of the bed and tumbled off in a rush of arms and legs. 'Not only do you have your boots on, you still have on your topcoat.'

'I do, my love, and they must remain on for the present.' He reached out and tried ineffectually to straighten his neckcloth. Charlotte stepped up to do it for him but he warded her off. 'No, sweetheart, please do not touch me. I have not the willpower to prevent myself finishing what we started.'

'Your stock is ruined, whatever will people think?'

His rich, dark chuckle sent ripples of excitement down her spine. 'I expect they will draw their own conclusions and think that I am an unprincipled rogue.'

'And I am one too, for I was a willing partner in this . . . this love-making.' She attempted to shake the creases out of her gown. She feared that his arrival had destroyed any hope she might have had of being able to appear in public dressed as she was.

He strolled over to the *chaise-longue* and lounged back, crossing his legs. He pointed to a delicate walnut armchair with a padded seat. 'Sit there, my dear, we have to talk. Tell me, how is Beth? One of the reasons I returned was to discover how she does.'

'She is much improved this morning, I am glad to say. She has had bouts of fever before, and always responds to the cooling treatment Papa taught me.'

'And Harry? I am surprised he has not come bouncing in to see me.'

She raised her eyebrows. 'But he is at Thurston – he returned an hour ago with Annie and the animals.'

'I rode across the fields, not along the lane. I must have missed them, but I am glad he is well. How long will you be obliged to stay here?'

'I intend to return tomorrow, another day's rest is usually sufficient to restore Beth. I have sent for Mary and some fresh garments.' She grinned. 'I must look a sad romp, and this poor gown used to be my best.'

'You look enchanting, my love, as always. But I would suggest that you adjust your gown before going downstairs again.' His expression was innocent but his tone teasing.

She glanced down and flushed scarlet. 'How could you allow me to sit with you like this?' Hastily she pulled the bodice straight. 'I do not like your tendency to find fun at my expense, sir,' she said stiffly.

He yawned and stretched. 'Do you not, sweetheart? That is a great shame, as you are going to have to learn to live with it.'

She jumped up. 'There is no talking to you in this mood. I am going to see how Beth is.'

Ignoring her annoyance he said lazily, 'Very well, my dear, then I shall return to Thurston, my tale untold.'

She stopped. How silly of her – she did not know what had actually happened during the long night she had spent worrying herself sick. Crossly she returned to her seat and glared at him.

'Well, my lord, tell me.'

He straightened and began his story. When he had finished she had quite forgotten her bad humour. 'The injured man, do you think he will tell you who is behind these attacks?'

'I sincerely hope so, but, as I said, Andrews does not hold out much hope for his recovery.'

'And the other man, what of him?'

'Captain Forsythe and his troops are scouring the vicinity. He is also searching for the carriage which collected the two corpses; if we can find that we shall have the paymaster, the man behind all this, and the reasons for it.'

'I have been considering all the possibilities, and have come to the conclusion that it has to be linked to your inheritance. You must speak to the lawyers; they must have had a list of possible heirs to pursue when Grandfather died. I never asked you, how remote is your connection to me?'

He shrugged. 'I have no idea. When I discovered I had inherited, I did not question it. I was still recovering and was just glad I had somewhere to hide away.'

'We have not spoken of this before, but I must ask you, did a lady turn you away?'

'She did, and it damned near killed me. It was Sophia's image I had carried in my head when I fought, her love that kept me going in the most dangerous circumstances. Knowing I had her waiting for me, kept me alive, stopped me taking stupid risks.' He seemed lost in his thoughts and Charlotte did not like to intrude. 'It never occurred to me she would no longer wish to marry me. Maybe if I had been a lord then, she would have taken me and tried to ignore her revulsion.'

'I am sorry she treated you so badly. But she is the loser, not you.' His head stayed down so she got up and joined him on the day bed. 'Jack, your face is damaged but you are still a handsome man. You must know that it is what is on the inside that matters and you are brave, resourceful, kind and intelligent. Think, did you see anyone flinch away in horror in Ipswich the other day? Have you seen the maids and footmen here retreat in shock?'

Slowly he raised his head. 'I had not thought, but no, you are correct.' He ran his fingers over his scar. 'Do you know, I have not looked in a mirror since that day, is it possible things have improved?'

'Go and see for yourself, there is a looking-glass above the mantelshelf.'

He walked over and for the first time in over two years stared at his reflection. She held her breath. How would he react? She hardly noticed his injury now, and even when she had first seen him it was not that, that had repelled her, but his unkempt appearance, his brooding expression and his inebriation.

He straightened his cravat before turning back. 'I am not as hideous as I was, but I am still disfigured, have only one working eye. But obviously I no longer frighten old women and children by my freakish appearance.'

She laughed. 'It is your bad temper and drunkenness that frighten people, not your face.' For a moment she thought she'd gone too far, said too much, for he appeared to freeze.

He swung back to stare critically in the glass. He faced her, a strange expression on his countenance. 'How can someone so young and beautiful be so wise? It would seem I have been hiding myself away needlessly these past years and it took a girl, scarce out of the schoolroom, to show me.'

'I am not a schoolroom-miss, I am a woman grown – as you very well know.'

He chuckled. 'Indeed you are, sweetheart, but compared to a battle-scarred soldier of nine and twenty you are a babe in arms.'

'Jack, I thought you told me you are eight and twenty or did I miss-hear you?'

'Actually, I have anticipated the event by a few days. My name day is October the first, which I believe is next Monday.' He stood. 'Good God! Blower and Thomas; I had intended to go into Ipswich today to demand to see the originals of those documents. I ought to do so now. If their offices are still closed, I shall organize a warrant for their arrest and appoint a new firm to look into matters and I must find Captain Forsythe and speak to him before I leave.'

'I am not happy with the thought of you riding alone in the lanes. You have just told me there are still men at large who wish you harm.'

'I am not a noddy, my love. I shall take four militia-men to accompany me. I shall be perfectly safe.'

He stretched out and, placing a finger under her chin, raised her head to drop a gentle kiss on her parted lips, then strode out, calling back his farewells. She flopped back on the day bed. Being with him was like being tossed in a tempest: it left her emotions, as well as her appearance, in disarray.

She recalled his anguish when he had spoken of his rejection by someone named Sophia, a woman he had loved so much. What sort of person could break a hero's heart like that? She determined to do everything she could to make him forget. She understood now why he had reacted so badly when she had mentioned love. He had been so damaged by that woman he was no longer able to love another, but at least he held her in affection and respect. Did he not lard all his speech with endearments? She felt a rosy glow as she considered another aspect of their relationship. At least she could be confident that he desired her, that he wanted her in his bed.

The sound of a carriage turning on the gravel outside the window ended her solitude. She was pleased to see that it was Mary.

Charlotte had dined upstairs and had not spoken again with the doctor. However, he was waiting to say his farewells when they descended the next morning.

'I wish you God speed, Miss Carstairs and Miss Beth. Lord Thurston has sent some militia to escort you home so I am sure you will come to no harm today.'

'Thank you for your generous hospitality, Dr Andrews. When Lord Thurston and I are married you shall be the first person invited to dine with us. I hope we can count on you as a friend?'

He bowed. 'I am honoured. And I shall always be ready to offer my home and my skills if you or your family should have need of them.'

She curtsied and they left in a flurry of good wishes. Jethro handed them into the carriage and the four soldiers closed ranks. Charlotte was pleased to be on her way home where she did not have to ask permission to move from room to room. Beth was too tired from her bout of fever to do more than rest her head in her sister's lap.

'Good heavens, Mary, look at that. The gate has been re-hung and the weeds are gone from the drive.'

'Isn't it grand, Miss Carstairs? The men from the village are that glad of employment they are working all hours to please his lordship.'

Charlotte stared at the acres of parkland which a week ago had been a meadow. Things were certainly moving on apace. Jack was waiting on the steps, Harry dancing impatiently at his side, the new puppy clutched under his arm. He would have dashed forward before the carriage was quite stationary if Jack had not prevented him.

'Wait, Harry, do you wish to be trampled by the horses?'

Harry shook his head. 'No, and neither does Buttons.'

The stable-boy, smart in new britches and clean cotton shirt, ran round to open the door and let down the steps. Jack handed Charlotte down, then leant in and lifted Beth out.

'You are far too weak to walk, little one, so I shall carry you upstairs to your room, if you have no objection?'

'Thank you, Cousin Jack.'

Charlotte hugged Harry and kissed the overexcited puppy. 'How are you? Have you been a good boy for Annie?'

' 'Course I have, Lottie. But Buttons has been bad. He chewed a hole in the carpet.' He grinned up at Jack. 'But Cousin Jack wasn't cross; he laughed.'

She smiled. 'Well, you must be careful to see it does not happen again. Remember, your puppy has to learn his manners before he is allowed to remain inside.'

Upstairs, Charlotte could hardly credit the improvement. 'Jack, everywhere looks wonderful – even the gallery balustrade is shining.'

'Mrs Blake and her team have been working hard to get things in order for you. She has taken on a dozen village women to do the heavy work.'

'So many?'

'Do not frown, my love; I have sufficient flimsies to cover expenses, at least for the next few weeks. By then I should be in a position to start collecting rents and perhaps decide to sell one or two of the smaller properties.'

'Are you intending to visit the lawyers today, or did you find time to see them yesterday? Do you know who your heir is?'

'Good God! No, I do not. That is something I must discover. The estate is run down, and at the moment providing no revenue, but several hundred acres of Suffolk might, to someone, be worth killing me for.'

She saw that Beth was settled then began an exploration of the house. She was thrilled to find she now had a private parlour adjoining her bedchamber. The room had been scrubbed and the floors and panelled walls polished. A sideboard had been found and an octagonal marquetry table, two wooden armchairs and a *chaise-longue*. None was in the first stare of fashion, but a great improvement on nothing at all.

'Look, Harry, I have fresh curtains at the windows and a lovely blue carpet.' Harry was about to put Buttons down. 'No, not on my new rug, take him outside to play, please.'

Harry was about to argue, but hastily closed his mouth and trotted off as Jack appeared in the doorway.

'Well, do you like your boudoir?' She turned, ready to throw herself into his arms to show him just how much she liked it, but he restrained her. 'No, my love, I am determined to behave with propriety until we are wed. It will be the hardest thing I have ever done, but do it I shall.'

She dropped her arms in dismay. 'I cannot embrace you? I am not allowed to thank you for your kindness?'

'Do it from there, sweetheart; it is safer. I do not think you realize the powerful effect you have on me. When you are within my arm's reach I am consumed with a desire to make love to you, and I must not let that happen until we are married.'

Charlotte walked away as instructed. She stopped on the far side of the room, her back to the window. 'Am I far enough away? Can you manage to restrain yourself from there?'

'Baggage, come and sit down like a good girl. I need to talk to you before I go out.'

'What is it? Is there something wrong?'

'Nothing for you to fret about, but I admit it is a setback. You asked about my visit to Ipswich, I had to postpone it, as the man we have in custody took a turn for the worse. Unfortunately he turned up his toes before we had a chance to interrogate him.'

'Oh dear! What are you going to do?'

'I am going to Ipswich now to see those thieving lawyers.' He smiled as her brow creased in anxiety. 'Remember, I told you I am taking an escort so I shall be perfectly safe from whoever is seeking to harm us.'

'I shall worry until you return. I feel so much safer when you are here to protect me.'

He chuckled. 'I am flattered by your faith in me, my dear, but you are much better off with Captain Forsythe and his men. They are younger and fitter than I.'

'It was not Captain Forsythe who killed three men, or who tracked down the fourth.'

'The one who could have solved this conundrum has escaped, but I hope my visit to Ipswich will reveal something useful. The militia intend to remain at Thurston until this matter is settled one way or the other.'

'What will you do if the lawyers are gone, the office closed?'

'I shall break in, of course. They will be wanted men, their goods and chattels confiscated.'

'I hope it does not come to that, but the more I reflect the more concerned I become about their probity. There have been several worrying omissions in their handling of your affairs that point to dishonesty.'

'Let us hope I can recover what they stole. I am anticipating the contents of their office will be a revelation.' He stood, preparing to leave. At the door he turned back, the power of his smile made her knees tremble and she was glad she had remained seated.

'God speed, Jack.'

'I expect to be back before dark. If I am not, please do not imagine the worst. I might be obliged to overnight at the Crown to conclude my business.'

She smiled. 'As you have four soldiers with you, and will be in the middle of the town, I am sure you will be quite safe.' She preferred not to think about him travelling along the narrow lane where they had been ambushed two days before.

The day dawdled past, the children content to play with their pets and not requiring her intervention. Mrs Blake had the Hall running smoothly and had no need to consult with her about menus or other domestic trivia. Three girls were already occupied sewing her undergarments and making the necessary alterations to her new gowns. She had nothing with which to occupy her time.

She ended the afternoon curled up in front of a roaring fire in the drawing-room a book on her lap. She glanced at the bracket clock and saw it was four o'clock. It would be dark soon. She could feel the chill of winter in the air already. The unseasonable summery weather had gone and the outside men were fighting to keep up with the cascade of golden leaves pouring down on to the newly scythed lawns. She yawned. Life was flat without Jack there to spar with.

Jack's scarlet-coated escort turned several heads as they clattered into Ipswich. They halted in front of the building which housed the offices of Blower and Thomas. Jack scowled. His instinct had been correct – the place was still closed. It seemed as though his quarry had already flown. Thieving bastards! He threw his reins to the young lieutenant.

'Hold Lucifer, I am going to see if I can rouse anyone, but it looks as though the place is deserted.'

Several thunderous bangs received no response. Without hesitation Jack raised his boot and crashed it down against the lock. The door swung open. He strode in. These men had stolen his property; he had every right to search their premises for evidence.

The door opened into a vestibule in which was a high, clerk's desk and stool. Behind this was the main room and, if he remembered rightly from his brief visit earlier in the week, Blower's office was the room on the right. He pushed open the door and found a scene of chaos: the desk littered with papers, obviously a sign of a rapid departure.

Lieutenant Jarvis spoke from behind him. 'I am afraid it looks as though they have absconded with your money, my lord. You were right to be concerned. Shall I send for a warrant? I shall need their details, descriptions, and place of residence, if I do.'

'I have no inkling where they live, but I am hoping to discover something amongst these parchments that might give us the information you require.'

Although the office appeared to have been ransacked there were still boxes of papers untouched in the cupboards that lined the walls of both offices. Jack knew when to admit defeat.

'There is far too much here for me to wade through. I need to find another team of lawyers to make order from this confusion.'

Lieutenant Jarvis, armed with the sketchy information, departed, taking one trooper with him, to find the courthouse and obtain the necessary warrants for the arrest of the missing lawyers. Jack left a second soldier guarding the door and with the remaining two he went in search of new legal representation.

There were several firms in the vicinity and he selected the closest, one Desmond and Son It was dark before the four clerks and two soldiers had cleared the offices of Blower and Thomas. The many boxes, rolls of parchment and piles of letters were taken to be examined by Mr Desmond.

Mr Desmond being the son, the father having long since retired, was a youngish man, about Jack's own age. 'It is going to take me some time to sort through all these documents and remove any pertaining to yourself, my lord. But I can assure you, that as soon as I discover anything relating to you, I shall come to Thurston to inform you.'

'Good man; what I particularly want to know is who stands to inherit if I should die without issue and also any clues as to where Blower and Thomas might have hidden my money.'

'The injunction I have applied for will come into force immediately, which means that all their assets are now frozen. They can no longer withdraw funds from their bank account. However, until the bank reopens on Monday, I shall not be able to discover what has already been withdrawn. It is a great shame they have had four days' grace to move their funds.'

'Do your best, Mr Desmond. I am staying at the Crown this evening but shall be leaving early tomorrow. If you have need of me tonight you will know where to find me.'

The thought of Charlotte and the children alone at Thurston unsettled him. He knew Captain Forsythe was camped half a mile away with his troops, and that there would be an armed guard on duty all night around the Hall. He could have done no more; he had made every provision for their security. But despite all this he was tempted to cancel his room and ride back through the night. What was wrong with him, for God's sake? He was behaving like a greenhorn, not an experienced veteran of the Peninsula.

Breakfast was being served in the morning parlour when Jack thundered back down the drive, his escort at least two miles behind him. The stable-boy scarcely had time to drop his pitchfork and scamper around to the front of the house to take Lucifer's reins. The stallion was sweat stained and flecked with foam.

'Walk him for thirty minutes. He is too hot to stable.'

The boy touched his forelock. 'Yes, m'lord.'

Jack saw him view the horse with disfavour; no doubt the boy's toes had hardly recovered from the stamping they had received last time. 'He is too tired to give you any trouble, lad. I have been galloping hard this past hour.'

He was dishevelled, his boots mud splattered, his stock undone. He ran his fingers over his unshaven jaw; Robert would soon make him presentable. Grinning at the idea that he was worrying about his appearance – something he had not done for the past two years – he strode to the steps. What a difference the arrival of a delectable young lady made!

Meltham bowed him in. 'Is Miss Carstairs down yet?'

'Yes, my lord, she is in the breakfast parlour with the children.'

'Excellent! Tell her I am back and shall be joining her directly.'

Charlotte looked up as the butler entered. 'Lord Thurston has returned, Miss Carstairs. He has asked me to inform you that he will be joining you very soon.' Her radiance prompted an unexpected smile from Meltham.

'Could you ask Annie to come here, please?' Charlotte asked. He bowed and vanished back through the hidden door in the panelling. The nursemaid appeared moments later.

'Did you want me to take Master Harry, miss?'

'Yes, he prefers to play with his puppy in the yard and Beth and I are going to stroll down to the maze.' Harry dropped his spoon noisily and mumbled a request to leave the table. 'Yes, you may go, Harry. But remember, Cousin Jack does not want any of us to stray too far from the house at the moment.'

'Is he back then, Lottie?'

'He is. He is joining us here in a little while. Will you not stay to greet him?'

'I will. Perhaps he will let me talk to his big horses, if I ask him nicely.'

'What is it you wish to ask, lad?' Jack had come in and had heard the end of Harry's sentence.

The boy ran across and gazed up imploringly; he had to tilt his head right back to make eye contact. 'I'm going to the stable to play with Buttons, and I wanted to stroke your big horses. Jethro won't let me near them.'

Jack dropped to this haunches. 'Neither Lucifer nor Phoenix are suitable to pet, Harry. I am sorry, but they are more likely to bite you than anything else.'

'Then can I stroke the grey horses, are they safe?'

Jack ruffled his hair. 'You certainly can. I shall be along as soon as I have eaten and exchanged news with Charlotte. I shall be delighted to introduce you to my matching greys.'

Beth jumped up. 'Can I go too, please? I wish to play with Tiny and Silky.'

'Yes, of course. Shall I come and collect you later?' The girl nodded and ran out after her brother and his nursemaid.

'Harry obeys you instantly, Jack. I wish he was always so compliant.'

'It is because he is in sore need of a man's hand. No, do not poker up; we are to be wed in just over two weeks. It must fall to me to take responsibility for both Beth and Harry, and any children we might have together.'

Charlotte counted slowly to ten, a ploy her father had taught her, before answering. 'So I am to be redundant, to have no further part in their upbringing?'

'You are talking fustian, my dear, and you know it. I expect you to do as all wives do; take an interest in the children and organize their wardrobes. You will also act as hostess and run the house, but the all-important decisions must be left to me, which obviously includes disciplining any children.'

With commendable composure she folded her napkin and pushed back her chair. Her movements gave him no intimation of the bombshell she was about to drop upon his head.

'In that case, my lord, I have no wish to marry you. I have a competence; I am in a position to support my own household. What possible reason could there be for me to give up my freedom, and my brother and sister, in order to become the chattel of a man who does not love me?'

He thought she was jesting; then he saw her face. In that moment he knew he was no longer dealing with a half child-half woman. She had grown up. She watched him quizzically. 'Pray excuse me, Lord Thurston, I have promised to take Beth down to play in the maze.' She smiled politely and stepped round him, leaving him nonplussed by a woman for the first time in his life.

Charlotte was still smiling as she left the Hall in search of the children. She felt triumphant; she had finally emerged from a confrontation without losing her temper, bursting into tears or being frightened into obedience. She giggled – he had appeared stunned by her announcement.

She wondered what he would do to make amends. Last time he had provided her with a lovely private parlour, a drawing-room and half a dining-room. She sobered as she remembered exactly what she had said. Had she gone too far? Would he metamorphose into the formidable stranger and try and browbeat her into submission? She shrugged; no, he was not a bully, he was a soldier, and sometimes forgot she was not a recalcitrant recruit but his prospective bride.

Later that morning Jack caught up with her in the small drawing-room. He folded himself on to an adjacent chair. 'I have not told you what transpired in Ipswich yesterday, do you want to hear or am I still in bad odour?'

She blushed, realizing she had already forgiven him. 'Please tell me, do not tease.'

At the end of his account she frowned. 'So we are no nearer finding the answer? Discovering who is behind the attacks?'

'I am afraid not. However, with Captain Forsythe camped at Thurston, and an armed guard around the Hall, I am sure we are safe, for the moment, from further ambush.'

'How long will the militia stay? Will they not be wanted elsewhere?'

'They will stay until the culprits are apprehended. I had not fully understood my position in the county. I am Lord of the Manor, and attempts on my life are taken very seriously.'

'Then we can attend church on Sunday?'

He nodded. 'The path has been cleared so we are now able to walk there. I am assured that the building is clean and fresh chairs have been found for us.'

'I am so glad. I have not attended a service since we arrived and I do miss it. Do you realize that I have nobody to escort me down the aisle? I was wondering if I should ask Dr Andrews.' Seeing his sudden scowl she added hastily, 'He would not be my first choice, obviously, but he has been kind and offered to assist us in any way he could.' Jack looked unconvinced. 'And he is the nearest gentleman. Remember, Renford Manor borders your land. He is your neighbour. You are going to have to learn to deal amicably with him.'

'If there is no one else, then I shall ask him for you. If you are quite sure it is what you want?'

'It is not what I would like, but we have no alternative, unless I am to progress down the church by myself.'

'Then the matter is settled.'

A discreet tap on the door interrupted their conversation. It was the butler asking if trays should be sent up to the schoolroom for luncheon, or if the children would be coming down. She looked at him.

'The children are to eat in the nursery. But Miss Carstairs and I will eat in the parlour right away, thank you, Meltham.'

The butler bowed and backed out. Her stomach rumbled loudly and they both laughed.

'I do not believe that either of us had the opportunity to eat much this morning, and I am famished.' He stood up, offering his hand to her. She stood, a hand's breadth from him, and could feel his heat pulsing towards her, knew he wanted to embrace her, but he remained true to his word and merely folded her hand into his arm and guided her out. She had no idea the effort such restraint required, how close to breaking he was.

CHAPTER EIGHTEEN

A T fifteen minutes past ten on Sunday morning the Carstairs were assembled in the hall, ready for the short walk to church. They were all dressed in the garments that had been purchased in Ipswich earlier in the week. Beth twirled, sending her ruby red skirts flying out around her calves.

'This is the best gown I've ever owned, Lottie. And I have a spencer and bonnet to match; I feel I'm a real lady of fashion.'

'Indeed you are,' Charlotte replied, 'but please stop spinning like that, you are making me dizzy.'

Harry in his navy velveteen britches and matching jacket was not as sanguine. He tugged at his stiff collar and neatly tied cravat. 'This is too tight, it's strangling me.' He pretended to choke, clutching his neck and staggering around the hall sending both of his sisters into peals of laughter.

'I had not realized attending morning service was a time for merriment. I rather believed it to be a time for reflection and contemplation,' Jack said as he joined in, resplendent in buff pantaloons, spotless Hessians and a square cut, navy- blue topcoat.

'We shall have more than enough time for quiet reflection during the sermon,' Charlotte answered, 'so do not be so curmudgeonly.'

He chuckled and the children relaxed, they had not realized he was jesting. 'My, we do look fine this morning. I am afraid Harry, that you and I will have to slowly strangle to death in order to be smart enough to accompany these lovely ladies.' He gestured to his high jacket collar, stiff shirt points and exquisitely folded cravat.

Harry giggled and flung himself into Jack's arms. 'Will the service be very long? I usually fall asleep halfway through and Lottie gets cross with me.'

'I promise to poke you in the ribs if you should happen to nod off, if you will do the same for me.'

'I will. Can I sit next to Cousin Jack, just this once?'

'If he has no objection, of course you may.' Charlotte smoothed down her moss-green satin pelisse and adjusted her green and cream-striped scarf. She was delighted with the outfit she had purchased and was certain she appeared to advantage.

He stepped away, tipping his head to one side, the better to admire the ensemble. 'That particular shade of green is perfect for you, my love, and the cream skirt with the little folds along the bottom is delightful . . .'

'But?'

He smiled. 'But I have sincere reservations about the bonnet. It is strongly reminiscent of a coal scuttle and I can hardly see your face inside it.'

Beth and Harry collapsed in fresh fits of giggles at his outrageous comment and even Charlotte smiled. 'I did wonder about the length of the brim, but it is the height of modernity, you know.'

'That is as may be; I prefer your little straw confections, with narrow edges and the long silk ribbons that match your gown.'

She was surprised he had noticed so feminine a detail. 'But you must admire my boots?' She held out one shod in a dark-green kid half boot. He pretended to consider his answer, shaking his head and drop-ping to his knees to hold the proffered foot. Beth and Harry believed he was playacting for their benefit – Charlotte knew he was using the opportunity to his advantage. As his long supple fingers caressed her ankle she felt the all-too-familiar heat and the accompanying throb in her lower regions.

'Let me go. I am about to lose my balance. Standing like a heron has never been a skill I have mastered.'

He sprang up and, taking her neatly gloved hand, threaded it through his arm. 'Let us depart; the Reverend Peterson awaits.'

Charlotte attempted to ignore the militiamen shadowing them on either side of the track. She wanted the day to be perfect, with no unpleasant reminders intruding and spoiling it. She watched Beth and Harry skipping happily, the danger forgotten in the pleasure of the moment and wished she could be like them. But she felt an ever present sense of foreboding, as if something catastrophic was about to happen; some evil stalked them, she was certain of it.

'What is it, sweetheart?' He had felt her fingers tighten on his arm.

'Nothing, I am quite well, thank you.' She did not wish him to think her fainthearted; she was a soldier's daughter after all, not a gently bred debutante.

She tried to enjoy the fifteen-minute walk; the late September sun was shining warmly, the brambles that bordered their way were a spectacular show of red, crimson and gold, and she was on the arm of the man she loved. What more could she want? She felt her happiness shrivelling. She wanted him to love her, for without this she faced a long and empty future. Sharing passion was not the same as sharing love, for what would be left when desire waned?

She was surprised to find the tiny stone church packed with worshippers. The rear of the building was full of standing villagers who touched their forelocks, or curtsied, as they passed. On the chairs were families of well-to-do farmers and even a squire or two. Her face was stiff from smiling by the time they reached their designated place.

Thurston staff had been given leave to attend the service and Harry had spotted both Annie and Betty sitting at the rear of the church. 'Can I go and sit with Annie? There are children at the back,' Harry whispered, for once remembering to lower his voice.

Lord Thurston answered. 'No, your place is here, at the front, with me. Sit down and be silent.'

The child subsided instantly. Charlotte slid into her place, Beth followed and Lord Thurston took the seat nearest to the aisle. There were still fifteen minutes before the service, so the murmur of voices continued, giving Charlotte the opportunity to speak without fear of being overheard.

'I did not expect so many in the congregation. Do you recognize any

191

of the seated families?'

He shook his head. 'Word that we would be attending must have spread through the neighbourhood. I expect people are curious to catch a glimpse of the reclusive Lord Thurston and his intended bride.'

'That is what I thought. But I am finding it uncomfortable to be the centre of attention like this.' She straightened, to face the front, glad there was no one either side, that everyone was seated behind them. It was gratifying, however, to know they were all looking their best. She had not spotted a single lady dressed more fashionably than herself. Her satisfied smile faded as she realized where she was: the Lord's house was not the place for vanity.

She bent down and groping under her chair, found the horsehair cushion, then knelt to say her prayers, starting with one asking for forgiveness. She had regained her seat when she heard a stir at the rear and the vicar hurried in, his face pink, his cassock flying wildly round his ankles. It had obviously taken him longer to travel the few miles from his earlier service to join them at Thurston church.

The congregation stood and the service began. Charlotte waited impatiently for the banns to be read after the first lesson. A shiver of anticipation went down her spine, only one more Sunday and she would be Lady Thurston, the tall man standing next to her would be her husband.

An hour and a half later he led her down the aisle to say their farewells to Reverend Peterson. The rest of the congregation waited politely for them to pass but Charlotte was aware of curious eyes boring into her back.

'Thank you for the service, Reverend Peterson. Your sermon was most uplifting,' she said politely. Jack merely nodded. She felt him gently pull her arm and she was moved on, allowing the next worshippers to speak to the vicar. As they had left first they were able to make good their escape without being obliged to speak to anyone else.

He finally slowed down when they were out of sight of the church. 'Excellent! I find I am not yet ready for social chitchat; perhaps in a few weeks I shall feel more comfortable in a crowd of strangers.'

'That was very long, do I have to go every week?' Harry asked.

'You do, Harry; we all do, it is expected of us.'

'We go for other reasons as well, Harry. It is the time to commune with God in peaceful surroundings.'

Beth slipped her hand into Charlotte's. 'I loved it, Lottie. It is so long since we have been able to attend.'

Jack and Harry drifted ahead, seeking nuts and other interesting things on the path. She watched them and knew she was doing the right thing, whatever her personal reservations. He loved her brother and sister; he would take care of them, give them a position in society they could never have if she attempted to raise them on her own.

'You can run on if you wish, Beth, I am quite content to stroll on my own.'

Beth grinned. 'If you're sure, then I'll catch them up.'

The soldiers had followed Lord Thurston, obviously considering him their priority, leaving her to walk on unprotected. Without their escort the path became less attractive, the hedges too close, the over-hanging branches claustrophobic. She glanced around nervously. She had a distinct feeling she was being watched and not by anyone friendly. She increased her pace but was aware that corresponding noises behind the bushes were keeping up with her. She picked up her skirt and ran, bursting round the corner to find Jack crouched on the ground buttoning Beth's boot. He leapt up and she stumbled into his arms.

'Charlotte, what is it?'

She struggled to catch her breath, unable to answer for a moment. She did not see him gesture with his hand to a couple of the soldiers to go back and search the fields that bordered the path. Eventually she pushed herself away. 'There was someone following me, I am certain of it. I heard them moving in the bushes on the other side of the hedge.'

'You are safe now, sweetheart. But we must go back to Thurston, if you are recovered enough to walk with me?'

She forced a smile. She did not wish the children to be more fright-ened than they already were. 'I am. I was being very silly. I have an over-active imagination. Mama was always telling me so.' She felt Harry's cold hand clutch hers. Instinctively she pulled him closer.

'There is nothing to be worry about. I must have heard a deer in the fields and panicked. Was I not a silly goose?'

'Lottie is a silly goose, Beth. I wasn't scared cos I'm a big boy.'

'We had Cousin Jack with us and the soldiers, but Lottie had no one.' Beth moved in beside her sister, preventing Jack from offering his arm. They were all relieved to reach the safety of the park without further mishap.

'Annie and Mary are not back from church so we shall have to manage. Shall we go up and change out of this finery? By the time we are ready luncheon should be served.'

'Me first, me first,' Harry chanted. 'Then I can go down and see Buttons, he will be wondering where I am.'

'You cannot go down without Annie or myself, Harry, so it makes no difference in what order we disrobe.'

It was late afternoon before Charlotte and Jack had time to talk about the morning's incident. He sought her out, finding her in her usual seat, curled up in front of the fire in the drawing-room.

'Charlotte, you were right to be concerned. We found evidence to confirm your suspicions.'

'I had hoped I was mistaken. Does that mean whoever it is has recruited more men to do his murderous work?'

He sat down beside her. 'I fear so. We have to be extra vigilant. These are no amateurs; they are ex-soldiers, expert in stalking their prey. We are in danger every time we leave the house. Riflemen can hit a target from a quarter of a mile away.'

'Are you saying that we have to stay inside from now on?'

'For the moment, yes. Captain Forsythe is sweeping the grounds again. When that is done we should be safe for a while. But it is far too easy for a determined man to infiltrate the park. It would take a regiment to ensure no one got through. And these men, although willing, are not real soldiers and they have never fought a battle. They are up against veterans with nothing to lose.'

'I wish we would hear something from Ipswich. Not knowing who, or why we are being targeted makes it so much worse.' Ignoring his previous strictures to keep her distance, she slid closer to him and snuggled into his arms. His stroked her hair, running his hand back and forth across her rigid shoulders until finally the tension ebbed. With a sigh, she sat back.

'I cannot wait for Monday week, then you can be beside me all night and I shall be able to sleep without fear.'

He chuckled. 'Darling girl – I am counting the very minutes to that time – but I rather think it is for a different reason to your own.'

'Jack!' She sat back with feigned outrage. 'You must not say such things.'

'But I promised never to lie to you, my dear.' He cupped her face and scanned her features as if imprinting them on his memory. 'You are so incredibly lovely. I do not deserve you.' He kissed her, hard, and stood up. 'But you are mine – I shall kill anyone who tries to harm you, or take you away from me.' His tone was light but Charlotte knew he meant every word.

'You are the man I want to marry. We are a perfect match for we understand each other.'

He bent down to whisper in her ear, his breath on her neck sending waves of heat around her body. 'I promise, that eight days from now you will understand a great deal more about me, my sweet.' Then he straightened, striding off to assist Captain Forsythe with the search.

Since Charlotte had discovered today was Jack's name day she had been trying to conjure up an idea for a gift that he would really appreciate. She had already planned a special anniversary dinner. She was interrupted by a footman.

'Miss Carstairs, there's a village woman here wishing to see you. She says as it's urgent.'

Intrigued, she agreed to see her. 'Show her in, please.'

The woman who came in was unknown to Charlotte. 'Begging your pardon, miss, but there's something what I think you need to know.'

'Of course, what is it you want to tell me?'

'Well, miss, it's like this. My Ben, he's a good lad, but he was over Ravenscroft way last night and he noticed some smoke from the chimney.' Charlotte nodded, waiting to hear why this was significant. 'It was empty up to then, you see, Miss Carstairs. It was sold a while back but no one came to live there. Ben went to have a look but apart from the smoke there was no light, and no sign of anyone living there.'

This was news indeed. 'Thank you, I shall tell Lord Thurston right away.' The villager dropped a curtsy and departed. Charlotte understood why the woman had not wished to tell him herself, as her son Ben had obviously been poaching in the woods of Ravenscroft. She would inform Jack as soon as he returned.

Charlotte was forced to wait until dark before passing on her information. He understood immediately the significance. 'We have them. They must think they are safe three miles from us, but they are not. I shall find Captain Forsythe and send him over right away.'

'You will not go with them tonight?'

He slipped his arm around her waist. 'No, my love, tonight is for us. I shall have to trust Forsythe and his men to deal with things initially, without my assistance. All they have to do is surround the building and wait until I arrive to take command.'

'Then you are going to go?'

'I have no choice. But I shall stay for dinner. I promise I shall not leave until you retire.'

Upstairs, Mary had her evening gown ready. It was in the newest fashion, the skirt falling from directly under her bosom and it required no corsets or stays to improve its appearance. She stepped out of her promenade dress and raised her arms for the silk and sarsenet creation to drop softly over her head.

The *décolletage* was square-cut, and edged with delicate pale-green lace. Mary tied the sash, in a darker shade of emerald green, and handed Charlotte the ribbon that held up the demi-train.

'There, miss, you look like a princess, what with your lovely red hair and all.'

Charlotte turned slowly, admiring herself from every angle in the long glass that had arrived in her room that very day. 'I was not quite sure about the colour. Emerald green is not considered suitable for someone my age, but it is the exact shade of my eyes, and I could not resist it.'

She stroked the sarsenet overdress, loving the way it glittered and reflected the candlelight. The small cap sleeves, also finished with the green lace, made her arms seem longer. Sadly she eyed the matching silk gloves, but Jack had asked her not to wear them. He had said he found the practice of wearing gloves in the house quite ridiculous.

CHAPTER NINETEEN

MELTHAM ushered her formally into the drawing-room. Charlotte felt her cheeks flush under the power of Jack's gaze.

'It is my grandest gown. I must admit it does make me feel like someone out of a fairy-tale.'

Magnificent in black evening dress he moved to her side, taking her left hand. 'I have something here for you, sweetheart, that will perfectly complement your *ensemble*. I, too, wanted tonight to be memorable.' From his waistcoat pocket he withdrew a small velvet casket and flicked it open.

She stared in awe. 'This is so beautiful. Is it an emerald?'

He removed the ring and pushed it over her knuckle. 'It is the same colour as your eyes. I know it was extravagant, but once I had seen it, nothing else would do.'

'It is stunning.' She held out her hand, turning it so the stone reflected the candlelight. 'It is exactly what I would have chosen for myself. I love it, thank you.'

He captured her hand and took it to his lips, kissing her palm lightly. 'It is a beautiful ring for a beautiful lady.'

'My lord, Miss Carstairs, dinner is served.'

Jack bowed politely and offered his arm. Together they progressed through the house like royalty. The dining-room, freshly painted, was lit from end to end with candles. The sideboard was laden with several covered dishes and the huge table sparkled with shining silver cutlery and polished wood. Tonight the butler had chosen not to cover the walnut surface with a damask cloth.

'This is splendid, Meltham, thank you,' Charlotte said.

The butler's eyes gleamed with pleasure.

The footman held out a chair for her. Charlotte had arranged for dinner to be served *à la française*, all dishes placed in the centre of the table. When she finally left Jack to his port she was bubbling with excitement. She had decided what his gift was to be.

She believed the evening had been the most enjoyable of her life, even the dinner she and Jack had shared a week ago did not compare. She smiled sleepily, perhaps it was the sherry wine and two glasses of claret she had consumed during the meal that had made everything about the occasion seem magical. She fell into her favourite armchair, forgetting to lift the back of her skirt as she did so. The material bunched under her bottom pulling the bodice unpleasantly tight.

'Botheration!' Her exclamation echoed round the enormous room, as she attempted to extricate her trapped skirts.

'Allow me to assist you, sweetheart,' a deep voice purred from beside her and before she could protest, Jack's hands cupped her posterior lifting her free of the entanglement. Her intention had been to use her hands merely to steady herself, but as soon as they came into contact with his chest everything changed. They found their way around the strong column of his neck and, without conscious thought, she began to pull his face down to hers. She felt his fingers curl into her buttocks and she swayed her hips in response to his caress.

'Please, darling, desist that; I am barely in control as it is.' His voice sounded different, deeper, almost as if he was in pain. She stilled, but continued to explore his features with her lips. His hand slid upwards, lifting her clear of the chair, until she was crushed against him. Then his hot mouth found hers, and his kiss melted her insides. She was burning from his touch, not just on her lips but everywhere. Slowly she withdrew her mouth and stared up into his face. Now was the time to tell him of his gift.

'I wish to be your wife tonight, not wait another eight days.' She felt him tense.

'If you are quite certain, my darling. You will have no regrets tomorrow?'

'It is my birthday gift to you. I am quite sure.'

He did not need telling a third time. He swept her up into his arms and strode out of the drawing-room, taking the stairs two at a time. He carried her past her bedchamber and along to the far end of the corridor to his own. He paused outside the door.

'Do you wish to come in with me? It is not too late to change your mind, but once you are inside I know I shall not be able to pull back. I have thought of nothing else since I first set eyes on you outside the Crown a month ago. I burn for you, my love. I am consumed by a fire that only you can put out.'

'I am sure. I want to make love with you, to discover what it means to be a woman.'

He expertly unlatched the door with his knee and carried her in. The room was dark, but she could see the faint outline of a massive tester bed in the moonlight that shone through the unshuttered windows.

Jack needed no candles to light him to his destination. He covered the distance in two long strides and once beside the bed allowed Charlotte to slither down his body, deliberately letting her feel the extent of his arousal. Her knees buckled with anticipation and she clutched his evening coat for support.

'Sit here, darling.' Tenderly he placed her on the bed. 'Do you wish me to light some candles?'

'No, I can see well enough without.' She would much prefer to disrobe in the dark. He understood her fears and did not insist. She could see his silhouette as he began to remove his garments, throwing his clothes haphazardly across the room in his eagerness. The sight of his naked chest made her want to reach out and touch. He was broad; even in the almost darkness, she could see his muscles rippling.

She felt she ought to close her eyes as he kicked off his slippers and undid the front of his trousers. But she was riveted, could not take her eyes away. Unexpectedly he paused, raising his head, seeming to sense her avid gaze. His smile liquefied her limbs.

'It is your turn now, my love.' He moved closer and she almost swooned with desire as his bare arms brushed along her own.

She stood up and her smile was as knowing as a courtesan. 'Help me, please. I am not used to undressing myself.'

She heard his breath hiss between his teeth. 'How precious is this gown?'

'It is my best. It was expensive.' Charlotte was finding it difficult to speak, his proximity was making coherent thought impossible.

'Pity – then I must remove it in one piece.' Reaching down, he grasped the hem and began to raise it.

'No, you must untie the sash first, undo the buttons at the back of the bodice.'

He appeared to growl, then reluctantly dropped her skirt and did as she bid. By the time the emerald silk puddled around her feet she could feel his hands shaking. He did not stop to enquire as to the value of her undergarments. She felt his fingers grip on either side of the central seam and then he tore the chemise and petticoats in half, leaving her naked in front of him.

She shivered as the cold air licked along her overheated limbs and raised her hands to cover herself.

'No, let me look, you are incredibly beautiful.'

He ran his thumbs across her nipples and they hardened under his touch. Gently he pushed her and she toppled willingly on to the bed. And in seconds he was beside her, his arms gathering her close.

An hour or so later Jack propped himself on one elbow and gazed down lovingly. 'I am sorry for hurting you the first time, darling. I did try to be as gentle as I could.'

She could feel a slight throbbing between her legs, but there had been only the one flash of real pain as he made her his. 'You did not hurt me, not really, and it was worth the small pain for the bliss of after-wards.' Lazily, she stroked his chest, revelling in the sensation of rough hair and soft skin beneath her questing fingers. 'I did not know how things worked between a man and a woman until tonight.' She giggled. 'In fact, if my mother had told me, I should not have believed her.'

His free hand smoothed back her unbound hair, lying like a red cloud on the pillow. He smiled. 'Did you never see animals mating?'

'I did, but I always averted my eyes and never thought too deeply about the ... er ... ins and outs of it all.'

He chuckled, delighted by her answer. 'And do you fully understand how things work, or would you like another demonstration?'

'I believe that I have not quite mastered it yet, so further practice would be most helpful, my lord.'

The house was silent when Jack, spent, lay back, Charlotte held close. 'It must be after midnight. I shall have to go, sweetheart. I must ride to Ravenscroft; Captain Forsythe will wonder what is keeping me.'

She laughed. 'I hope you do not tell him the truth.'

He sat up. 'It is a full moon tonight. I shall not need a candle. Remain here, my darling, I hope to be back before you rise. I shall have to rouse Meltham to lock up after me, but it cannot be helped.'

She ran her hand down his spine and felt his reaction. 'I am still a pupil in this matter, and shall require a deal more instruction before I have the mastered the art.'

'You are insatiable, darling; let me be – I promise I shall return as speedily as I can.'

Charlotte watched him walk proudly naked across to his closet and emerge a few minutes later in his riding clothes. Her eyes widened as she saw he had his sabre in one hand, his boots in the other. He came to sit beside her to put them on. As instructed she didn't touch him again, knowing his mind was elsewhere, focusing on the battle to come.

'Jack, take care. I . . .' She almost spoke the words, but swallowed them back in time. She would not embarrass him with her love; he did not need it. He had what he wanted, and she had enjoyed the experience as much as he. 'Godspeed – and come back soon.'

He stood up. 'Tonight shall see an end to this. One way or another it will be over.' He stepped away, then, unexpectedly, turned to lean over the bed. He kissed her one last time, imprinting his possession on her lips. Then, his sword and scabbard in his hand he vanished out into the corridor, leaving her bereft.

She lay wakeful for some time before finally deciding it would be better to return to her own chamber. She did not relish being found in

Jack's bed by his valet, and there were the children to think of also.

She gathered up her scattered garments, including the ruined chemise and petticoats, and wrapped in the comforter, she crept like a thief from the room. She tiptoed down the corridor and was about to unlatch her door when she thought she heard something downstairs in the hall. Who could be up at this time? Had the butler decided to wait up?

Hastily she slipped into her room and dropped her clothes on the floor. She found her nightgown, pulling it on over her head, then added her wrapper. She discovered her slippers and hastily pushed in her feet. Now she was ready to investigate.

Whatever she thought she had heard a few moments earlier, there was no noise now. Emboldened, she hurried to the gallery, the light from the hall making her passage easy. Light? There should be no lights, unless Jack or Meltham were around. She inched her way forward, keeping to the edge of the gallery, in the deep shadow. Cautiously she peered over. Yes, there was a flicker of light from the corridor leading to the study.

For some reason Jack was still here; it had to be him, for who else would wish to visit the study at this time of night? She was about to run down to ask him when she heard voices. She froze, her hand on the banister, her foot on the top stair. It was not a voice she recognized. It was a rough, untutored voice, not that of a gentleman. Not Jack's, not the butler's.

Terrified, she backed away and had reached the welcome darkness of the gallery when two men emerged into the hall. They were strangers and carrying rifles. She clutched the balustrade for support. These were the men Jack had just gone out to capture. How could they be inside the house? The shadowy figures halted at the foot of the stairs. Could they see her? She felt her bowels loosening and feared she might disgrace herself.

'What was that bastard doing up and about at this time of night?' the nearest figure said, in a harsh whisper.

'Buggered if I know. Reckon he thought he would join that idiot and his toy soldiers at Ravenscroft.'

Charlotte strained to catch the rest of their whispered conversation. They were talking about Jack, they had to be.

'Well, his lordship will not bother us again. That's one done for. Now for the bitch and the brats.'

She could not digest this information. Jack was dead. They had killed him and now they were coming to do the same to her and the children. From somewhere she found the strength to rally, to push away the knowledge that she had lost her lover, and force her limbs to obey.

Beth and Harry, she had to save them. It was her duty; there was no one else to do it for her. Almost blinded by tears, she backed down the passage and into Beth's chamber. 'Beth, get up, now. Quickly. Come with me, your life depends on it.'

The child sat up and half asleep tumbled from her bed. Charlotte handed her a robe, but there was no time to search for slippers. 'Beth, the bad men are in the house. They are coming upstairs, we have to get Harry and hide before it is too late.'

The door between the rooms creaked loudly and both of them froze, expecting angry armed men to burst in brandishing guns at any moment. Nothing happened. Charlotte ran across to Harry.

'Beth, get his robe. I shall carry him, and with luck he will stay asleep.' She knew her brother was a heavy sleeper. She prayed it would be the same tonight.

She reached out and grabbed him, pulling him towards her. He did not stir as she lifted him, just threaded his arms around her neck. 'We will go out through the servants' door. There's no time to light a candle, so hold on to my belt. If we go slowly we shall manage in the dark.'

Reaching the dressing-room was easy, for there was enough filtered moonlight to guide them. Once inside it was different. There were no windows in here. 'The door is between the closets, Beth. You find it for us, darling. Close your eyes and use your hands. Do not try and see; it will confuse you.'

Obediently Beth groped forward, arms outstretched. She knew the room well and by visualizing its layout she was able to discover the exit easily. 'Over here, Lottie. I've found it and I have a lamp and tinderbox. I can use them when we are through the door.'

She followed Beth's voice and they slipped silently into the narrow passageway. She sank back against the wall to steady her breathing. Harry was becoming heavier by the minute.

She heard her sister kneeling on the boards and the tinkle as the glass mantle was removed from the lamp. 'Hurry up, I am not sure how far behind us they are.'

'I'm having to do this by touch, Lottie. Wait, I have the tinderbox. I shall try and strike it now.'

Charlotte saw flicker of light then somehow Beth managed to transfer the spark to the wick of the lamp. A welcome yellow glow filled the space. 'Oh, Beth, you are amazing. Well done. It will be so much quicker with a light.'

'Shall I go first, Lottie, lead the way?' Beth stood up, the lamp in her hand. She stared up and down the passageway. 'Which way do we go? Downstairs or up?'

Charlotte's instincts were telling her to flee outside, but her sister's words made her reconsider. There might be more than two men. She swallowed convulsively, pushing away the image of Jack lying dead. They could be downstairs waiting, so it would be foolish to go that way.

'Upstairs, Beth, to the servants' rooms. We can rouse the men, and they can protect us.' Even as she said it, she knew three footmen and a valet were no match for the evil that sought to dispose of them. They had already managed to kill Jack. She gulped. She would not give way, not now, not when the children were still in danger. She had to get them to Annie, she could hide them somewhere, then she would send for Captain Forsythe. All they had to do was stay hidden until then. In such an old house that should not be too difficult.

They crept along the corridor and up the steep flight of stairs. Charlotte had never visited these rooms, but Beth seemed confident she was taking them in the correct direction. She stopped outside a door.

'This is the one, Lottie. Shall I knock?'

'No, go in, quickly. We can explain when we are safe.'

Inside the room were two single beds, an armchair, a wardrobe, a commode and little else. Annie, who occupied the bed nearest to the door, woke up instantly.

'Good grief, Miss Carstairs, what is amiss?'

The nursemaid was out of bed and took the sleeping Harry from Charlotte's arms just in time. 'He can go in here, miss, into my bed.' Annie pulled the covers over the sleeping child. Betty was now awake and had taken charge of the shivering, barefoot Beth.

'Hop in here, lovey. There, pull over the covers, and get warm.'

Charlotte drew Annie to one side; she could hardly speak through her chattering teeth. 'Lord Thurston is dead, Annie, they have killed him. Now they are looking to do the same to us.'

'Sit down for a minute, miss, before you fall.' The nursemaid guided Charlotte to the bentwood chair and pushed her down. She asked no questions, she was too wise for that. She waited until her mistress was able to continue.

'Lord Thurston went down an hour ago, intending to join Captain Forsythe. Somehow these men got inside and ambushed him. He told me we were safe inside this house, for the doors all locked on the inside and the windows are too stout to break open. I cannot understand how they got in.' She clenched her fists, her nails biting into her palms. The pain steadied her a little and helped her to concentrate. 'This place is like a rabbit warren, thank God. It will take them hours to find us. With God's help, Robert, or one of the other men, can ride and fetch Captain Forsythe before that time is up.'

Betty, night-cap fluttering, voluminous flannel nightdress ballooning around her, began to pull cloaks and mufflers from the closet. Beth had snuggled down and fallen into a fitful doze. Annie checked she was asleep before speaking.

'There is a far easier way for them to murder you, Miss Carstairs.'

Charlotte started shaking, hardly able to whisper her response. 'What? Annie, tell me, what could they do?'

'They could burn this blooming building to the ground. It's that full of old dry timber it would go up in a flash. Then none of us would get out alive.'

CHAPTER TWENTY

'FIRE? Are you suggesting they will set fire to the Hall and burn us out?'

'I am, Miss Carstairs, it's what I'd do in their shoes.'

Charlotte's stomach revolted and she placed a hand over her mouth, looking around desperately for a suitable receptacle. Annie held out a china bowl and Charlotte cast up her accounts. The noise of her retching woke both children.

Harry sat up. 'Lottie's being sick, Beth,' he announced, then seconds later, 'I'm being sick too.' And he was. Annie had no time to offer him a bowl, her bed was covered with the noxious mess.

'Never mind, my love. Here, come out of that. Stand there, like a good boy, and I'll clean you up.' The smell of vomit in the room was almost too much for Beth and she too began to gag.

Charlotte, her stomach empty, felt better and took command. 'You are not sick, Beth, it is the smell. Harry is the one who throws up in sympathy, not you.' She put the bowl down under her chair and picked up the little oil lamp. 'Beth, darling, do you know where all the girls sleep, or just Annie and Betty?'

'Everyone – Mary is two doors away, she shares with Jenny—'

'I do not need to know who is where. I need you to go and wake them, tell them to put on their cloaks and shoes over their night clothes – there is no time to get dressed – and start to make their way downstairs. Don't tell them why, just tell them it is urgent.'

'I'll go with her, miss, it's no job for a child,' Betty said.

Charlotte took off her own slippers. 'Put these on, Beth, now off you go with Betty. Do not come back here either of you. I shall meet you in the servants' hall.'

Betty pushed open the door and, holding Beth's hand, she vanished. Annie had completed her task and Harry was now clean. 'Lucky I had some garments of his here, miss.'

Harry did not understand what was happening but was happy to join in the excitement. Even being sick was something of an event in his life.

'Do you have any spare slippers, Annie? I have given mine to Beth.'

'Wear my clogs, miss, they're in the wardrobe.'

Two minutes later they were ready to go. Charlotte did not really believe Annie's preposterous prediction, but could not take the chance she might be right. She could hear the small sounds of others shuffling along the passageways towards the back stairs. Good, Beth had done her job well.

'Annie, can you take Harry, I must check everyone is awake.'

'Mary will have done that, she's courting young Robert, and she'll not want him to be left behind.'

Charlotte headed the silent group of women as they crept downstairs. She still thought they were in more danger going down than staying put. Then the unmistakable smell of smoke wafted around the corner. She stiffened and stopped.

'I can smell smoke, Miss Carstairs. Is the house on fire? Is that why we're going out?' Jenny asked from behind Charlotte's shoulder.

'It is worse than that, Jenny. There are at least two armed men loose inside and it is they who have set the fire. I hope someone will have woken Mr Meltham and Mrs Blake.'

'Mary was going to tell Mrs Blake on her way to wake Robert and he will rouse Mr Meltham and the other men. They will be on their way down the other stairs by now, don't you fret,' Jenny told her.

'We have to be very quiet. I do not know where the intruders might be.'

Annie spoke from behind Jenny. 'I reckon they will have set the fires and got out whichever way they got in, miss. From the smell, the blaze is well alight, and they will be long gone.'

Charlotte coughed; the smoke was denser here on the first floor where she and the children had slept. She could hear the sound of crackling, of flames taking hold on the other side of the wall. She was glad the house had thick panelled walls which gave the fire something to burn through before it could reach them.

It was becoming much hotter and she knew they must not linger. 'Quickly, downstairs. Do not touch the walls they are far too hot. With luck the fire was set on the ground floor and will be burning up the stairwells and corridors, and the servants' hall will not yet be aflame.'

The two flights of stairs met in the lower passageway and Charlotte was relieved to see the men emerging as her party arrived. The air was becoming thick, the heat stifling, and most of them were coughing, their eyes streaming, but none complained or cried; they stood waiting for Charlotte to tell them what to do next. She knew it might be a matter of minutes before the stairs behind them became too hot and smoke-filled for safety. She had to risk a confrontation with the rifle-men and their paymaster or else they would all die, trapped inside the house.

Holding her hand over her nose, she plunged forward and out into the servants' hall. It was fresher here but not by much. 'Hurry, we shall exit through the boot-room door. Robert, go ahead and unbolt the door. Annie, you take Harry and Beth first. Girls follow and then the men. Be as quiet as you can.'

Asking them not to cough was like asking the sun not to shine, but they did their best. She waited until the last person was out and away down the corridor, before she followed. As she moved she heard a horrible groan, like a giant in pain, then the ceiling a few yards behind her, collapsed, spewing flames and searing heat in her direction.

She fled down the corridor remembering, with horror, that as soon as the back door was opened the inferno would follow them. When she had been a small child in Spain she had witnessed this phenomenon. A family, trapped in their house, opened a window only to be consumed by flames which suddenly engulfed the room. The fire appeared to wish to escape, like the occupants, through the opening. The poor family had all perished in the conflagration. It was an image she had kept buried deep until now.

'Do not open the door!' she screamed down the corridor.

The butler, at the rear of the group, heard her and shouted, 'Robert, don't open the door. Do you hear me, lad?'

Robert did. He removed his hands from the bolts as if they were red-hot already. Charlotte raced up to Meltham. 'We need to create a barrier between the fire and ourselves before we open the door or we shall all be burnt to a cinder.'

The butler did not question but pointed to the walls of the boot-room. 'Quickly, lads, pull this lot down, the shelves will make a fire break.'

All six men ripped at the wooden racks and boxes, throwing every-thing into a heap a few feet behind the terrified group waiting to get out into the safety of the night. The barrier, Charlotte hoped, would give them the extra seconds' protection from the approaching fire that they needed. In the confined space, the heat was becoming unbearable and the smoke-filled air as dangerous as the fire. With streaming eyes the butler stepped back.

'We can do no more, miss, it will have to do. We have to get out or we shall choke to death.'

Charlotte eyed the flimsy wall – it almost reached the ceiling – but would it be enough? She prayed that it would. 'Ready, Robert, when I shout, open the door and everyone run for your life – we have given ourselves a half-minute's grace, no longer.'

There was a chorus of coughing from which a few assents could be distinguished. She had positioned the children at the front with Annie and Betty; she had to be sure they got out safely. She intended to leave last, but the butler and Mary had other ideas. Before she could protest they bundled her forward. And the press of coughing people passed her along, flattening themselves willingly to the wall as she passed.

'Open the door, Robert,' Meltham yelled, and Charlotte was ejected behind her brother and sister.

'Run, keep running, to the shelter of the barn,' she called, as she pounded along, her bare feet slipping in and out of her borrowed clogs. Mary's arm came round her, holding her upright when she was in danger of falling.

They stumbled into the empty barn. Charlotte's chest burned, her throat felt raw, as if she was suffering from a severe head cold, otherwise her physical state was unimpaired.

'Is everyone here? Mrs Blake, check your girls; Meltham, do the same for the men.'

The headcount established all were present none the worse for their experience. The two footmen at the rear had been forced to remove their cloaks, and were busily stamping out the embers.

One of them told her cheerfully, 'It's a good thing you said to put these on, Miss Carstairs, or one of us might have suffered a lot worse than a few holes.'

'I am relieved that everyone is safe. We can . . .' Her voice faded as she remembered that not everyone had got out alive. Jack was gone – killed by the monsters who had set fire to her home. How was she to live without him? First her father, then mother, and now him – it was too much. She could not endure the pain.

Strangely, her hands stopped shaking and her mind cleared. She knew what she had to do. She turned to Annie. 'You will take care of Beth and Harry for me?'

'Of course I will, miss, that's my job.'

'Thank you, Annie. I knew I could rely on you.'

She walked, trancelike, from the barn, seeing nothing, hearing his voice calling to her. She went steadily back towards the blaze. She would join Jack: Thurston Hall could be their funeral pyre.

The stable hands, led by Jethro, were occupied fighting to calm the horses and lead them away from the smoking stables to the safety of the meadows behind the barn. It seemed that no one saw the tall, slim figure, dressed in clogs and night apparel walk ever closer to the conflagration.

Charlotte could feel the heat of the massive flames and welcomed the warmth. The fiercer the blaze the sooner it would be over. She could endure any agony, but the one of losing Jack. To be with him, she would walk through fire.

Flying embers settled on her hair and she flinched, hearing it fizzle. Her wrapper, floating round her ankles, started to burn at the hem. She could feel her ankles blistering, her face burning, still she walked on.

'For God's sake, Miss Carstairs, what are you doing?' Strong arms grabbed her preventing her from continuing. These were not Jack's arms. She struggled, her madness magnifying her strength. Doctor Andrews knew he could not hold her, if she slipped from his grasp she would throw herself into the fire and die. He would not let that happen. He raised his fist and punched her on the temple.

She collapsed like a stringless puppet and he threw her over his shoulder and raced away. Robert and Mary had seen Charlotte leave but had been too far away to stop her. Now they were here and beating out the flames on her garments with their bare hands.

'Is she dead? Please God, not her as well,' Mary whispered, as she held Charlotte's limp hand.

The doctor placed his finger against her neck, under her chin. 'No, she's breathing steadily. But I fear she has suffered considerable burns. I must get her back to Renford Manor and attend to her immediately.'

She remained semi-conscious throughout the carriage journey, her mind adrift in a sea of pain and despair. Doctor Andrews carried her inside. He had roused his entire staff before galloping across to Thurston, alerted, as were many in the vicinity, by the tell-tale orange glow in the sky. He had also had the foresight to order his carriage to follow, and now it held Annie, Betty, the children and Charlotte. He rode alongside, his face grim.

He could scarcely credit that he had seen Miss Carstairs about to cast herself into the flames for the sake of her dead love. He was glad he had saved her, but feared for her sanity. She had suffered too much loss over the past two years. He wondered if she was strong enough to recover from this latest and most devastating of blows.

*

The smell of the fire acted like a burning feather waved under a swooning debutante and Jack twitched. He lay immobile, fully alert, listening before he moved. Too often he had seen a man recover his senses and sit up, glad to be alive, only to be skewered by a passing enemy soldier. Keeping still was the answer until you knew it was safe to move. His caution saved his life.

The sound of booted feet approaching at the double made him freeze and he prayed the smoke would not make him cough, revealing he was conscious. The boots passed and he opened his eye, and seeing the butt of a rifle, realized these were the men he sought. How had the bastards got into the house, been able to ambush him? He remembered strolling unconcerned down the stairs, candlestick aloft, intending to ring the bell for the butler on his descent, when a crushing blow to the head had sent him plunging into blackness.

He saw the men enter the study and knew it was safe to rise. He sprang upright and raced to the hall to be forced back by the heat as the wooden stairs and gallery burned fiercely. There was no way of getting to Charlotte and the children – the whole of their corridor was ablaze.

He collapsed in an agony of grief. He wanted to throw himself into the blaze, to join his beloved there. Then a killing rage worse than he had never experienced, even in the bloodbath of Waterloo, consumed him and he turned and ran back down the corridor. He stooped to collect his sword and belt, buckling it on as he ran. He had done this so often he could do it without conscious thought.

The passage ahead was a solid wall of fire and the men had not come out of the study. He had them trapped – if he could kill them both he would not care what happened to him. He stopped, but it did matter, he could not give in until the paymaster was dead as well. Revenge would keep him alive a little longer.

He pushed open the study door, his sword in his hand, ready to kill at the slightest movement. God damn it to hell! The room was empty, the ceiling smouldering from the heat of the flames above, but definitely empty. Where were they? The two men had not come out, he would have met them, and the other way was blocked by fire. Think – damn it – think! He urged his formidable brain into action and the answer came. There had to be a secret passage and it led from this room. The red glow from the fire shone in brightly through the leaded panes making it easy for him to see. He had no need for a candlestick.

Where could it be? He scanned the room and his eyes were drawn to the fireplace where there were two raised wooden roses, one on either side. He had always thought them out of place on the austerity of the panels. It had to be one of those. He grabbed the first, it burned his hand, but did not shift whichever way he pressed or turned. He abandoned it and attacked the second.

Yes! Yes, it was turning, he twisted a further half inch and a section of wall slid open in front of him. A blast of welcome fresh air greeted him to be instantly followed by the horrific sight of the walls on either side glowing red. He threw himself through the space and slammed the panel behind him. He heard the explosion as the windows blew in.

He stretched out his fingers until they touched either side of the narrow corridor and began to jog. He was confident he could find his way out; all he had to do was follow his nose. The heat lessened and he became aware of a cold, dank smell and the walls beneath his fingers crumbled. He was out of the house and in a tunnel. He stared ahead and was sure he could see a glimmer of moonlight, which meant he was nearing the end of the passage.

He slowed his pace; he wanted to surprise the murderers, not the other way round. He paused at the end, sniffing the air like a wolf. They were close, but not dangerously so. He had emerged some distance from the burning building but the air was full of smoke making visibility difficult. He noticed that the exit was concealed inside a spinney of hornbeam near to the tradesmen's track that led round to the stables.

Silently he withdrew his sabre and moved stealthily towards his quarry. He could hear voices just ahead and the chink of a bit as a horse threw its head up, worried by the smoke. Using the trees as cover, and keeping windward of the horses, for they might not hear his approach but they would certainly smell him, he drew nearer.

He stopped. What were they doing, why hadn't they galloped off to safety? Then white hot rage obliterated his calm as he heard their conversation.

'Old houses burn a treat, don't they, Billy? I like to watch a good fire.'

The one called Billy answered, chuckling loudly. 'And a grand pile of roast meat to be had inside, my friend, if your taste runs that way.'

He forgot caution and burst from the bushes like an avenging demon. Billy's head left his shoulders in mid-sentence to land in gory silence at the feet of his stupefied companion. The second man saw death staring at him and then saw no more as he was decapitated with a second sweep of Jack's sabre.

Casually he wiped his dripping blade on the body of the first man and calmly restored it to its scabbard. One horse had bolted as the headless body had fallen beneath its hoofs the other, more securely tethered, skittered – wild eyed – hating the smell of fresh blood.

He stroked its sweating neck. 'Gently, old fellow, nothing to worry about. Come along now, we must follow your stable mate, for I am certain he will lead me to the man I seek.'

He vaulted into the saddle and rode away from Thurston Hall believing he left his heart incinerated in the building along with his beloved. He sat straight in the saddle; he would not allow his pain to destroy his willpower until his task was complete. He knew what he felt now was far worse than the sabre cut that had ruined his face. How could he ever have thought he loved Sophia? He had felt anger, humiliation, betrayal at her rejection and had mistaken this for a broken heart. He had not felt the agony he was now suffering. Why had he not told Lottie that he loved her whilst he had had the chance? Now she was gone, never knowing how he felt. His life, like his home, had been reduced to a heap of ash.

The loose horse increased its stride to a canter. He held back, not wishing to be seen. In the light of the full moon he could distinguish the outline of the carriage. Surely he had seen it somewhere before?

Then he heard men talking quietly- so it would appear that he had more than one man to kill. No matter – one or ten – they would all die tonight.

He urged his horse close enough to be able to recognize the voices. He leant forward in order to hear more clearly. God in his heaven! It was Blower and Thomas in the carriage. Then he saw their coachman, blunderbuss at the ready, sitting on the box and realized it was not the right time to attack.

Finally he knew who was behind all the attempts. These two seemingly benign old gentlemen had killed his lovely girl, and the children, but still he could not understand why they had been prepared to murder so many innocents for a paltry thousand or two. He shrugged. People were killed for sixpence in the backstreets of London.

He decided not to storm the coach, the odds were not in his favour, but he would follow them, and break in and dispatch them in their home. The arrival of the riderless horse caused panic in the carriage. Immediately the coachman dropped his gun and whipped up the horses. The carriage rattled away down the narrow lane with Jack keeping pace in the darkness behind.

He followed them until dawn. They bypassed Ipswich and did not stop until they reached the entrance to a prosperous estate. The name emblazoned on the high brick wall was Goodly Hall. He watched the gateman fling open the wrought-iron gates and wave the carriage through. His shoulders drooped, inexplicably his desire to pursue them, his white-hot rage evaporated and all he had left was a crushing weight on his chest and a black hole where his happiness used to be.

He would ride into Ipswich and inform the magistrates; they could take it from there. The two men would face trial, be convicted, stripped of their assets and strung up. He no longer cared how they died, as long as they did. He wanted no more to do with killing. Too many good people had died that night. He unbuckled his sword and tossed it into the hedge. He would never use it again.

His death wish had gone along with his desire to kill for he had accepted that he had responsibilities. His people had suffered enough. His staff, if any had survived, needed him to provide for them. His borrowed horse was exhausted by the time he reached Ipswich; it could carry him no further. He left it at the Crown and hired a jobbing hack from the ostler there, it was a sturdy mare, well up to his weight, and could take him back to Thurston when he was ready.

He had no appetite but forced himself to consume a plate of ham and eggs and drink a mug of porter before he set out to find the magistrate. It was midmorning before he was satisfied things were arranged correctly, certain the murdering pair would be arrested that day.

In misery he headed back to Thurston. He saw nothing on his journey; his vision was blurred by tears.

CHAPTER TWENTY-ONE

CHARLOTTE could hear muted whispers and knew that someone had come in to check her progress. She wanted none of them. She wanted to be left alone to grieve. She didn't want broth or fresh lemonade, she wanted nothing.

'Lottie, it's me, Beth. I have come to read to you. You don't have to answer, or take any notice, but you always read to me when I'm poorly and it makes me feel much better, so I'm hoping it will do the same for you.'

Charlotte hadn't the energy to tell Beth to go away, to leave her in peace. At least if she was listening it might stop her thinking for a while. She was unsure how long she had been at Renford Manor, perhaps one night, no longer.

Her sister started reading from *The Mysteries of Udolfo* and did it surprisingly well. Charlotte listened, trying to blot out her misery, knowing she had to make an effort, the children needed her more than ever. The pain from the burns she had sustained was not enough to drown out the agony of her loss. That was far worse, it was all consuming.

She let the words drift over her head, losing interest in the story. With Jack gone she had to provide a house for them, but where? She recalled that Mr Blower had said there was a house in Ipswich and an annuity from her grandfather; would that be sufficient to keep them from poverty? But the lawyers were thieves, liars; it was possible there was no money or even a house in Ipswich, and what then? Would it be the poor house for them all?

She heard Beth sigh and close the book but she had no words of comfort. The children had not yet been told of Jack's death; they thought she was shocked from the fire and the loss of all her possessions. She bit her knuckles to stop a groan escaping. How was she going to cope on her own? She must pull herself together, explain to the children what had happened, but not now, she was too tired, she needed to sleep.

Jack plodded down the drive on his rented nag and couldn't bring himself to look at the smoking ruins of his home. He had yet to discover how many had died in the fire, but he must ensure that any survivors were taken care of properly, and he had decided that he would offer financial help to the bereaved families.

He had ridden in along the tradesmen's track he had left by the previous night. Idly he wondered if Captain Forsythe had found the remains of the two rifleman. He took the path that led round to the stables, glad to see that they, at least, were still standing. He could hear voices in the barn next door; the militia must be here.

Where was everyone? Why did no stable-boy or groom come to take his weary mount? He led the mare through the archway. Jethro was talking to the captain; both glanced up to see who the intruder was. He watched Jethro turn deathly pale and stagger backwards. Captain Forsythe did not look much better.

Then the young man leaped forward and Jack found himself being pummelled on the back. 'My God! My God! We thought you dead in the fire – we all did. Miss Carstairs is beside herself with grief.'

'Dead? Good God – it did not occur to me that anyone might think that. When you found the bodies I assumed you would guess who had despatched them. There was a—' He choked. 'Christ in His Heaven, did you say Miss Carstairs? Is she alive? She was not trapped in the fire?'

Captain Forsythe was crying with joy. 'No, my lord, she led the staff to safety. No one was hurt. They all got out through the boot-room in the nick of time.'

Jack felt his head spin and for a moment thought he would faint. Then his world spun back into focus, a world in which his beloved Lottie was still living. 'Everyone was saved, you say?'

'All safe and well and accommodated at Renford.'

He had to get to Charlotte, hold her in his arms and be sure she was a living breathing woman and not a cinder in the house. He needed a fresh horse; Captain Forsythe's mare was standing beside him. Without a second's thought he snatched the reins and sprang on to it. 'I need this horse, I shall return it to you later.'

Seconds later he was galloping flat-out down the drive. He covered the distance to Renford Manor in a dangerously short time, fatigue forgotten, as he hurtled down the drive.

Harry was kneeling on a window seat in his sister's room, Annie beside him, but she had her back to the window, listening to Beth reading. Harry recognized the rider.

'It's Cousin Jack, Annie, I knew he would come. Lottie will get better now.'

His nursemaid had seen nothing and when she turned back Jack had already dismounted and was on his way to the front door. 'Master Harry, if you dare to say such a thing to Miss Carstairs I shall be forced to punish you severely. Your poor sister does not need to be told such lies.'

Harry's eyes filled. 'I did see him, I promise, Annie. I would not lie to Lottie.'

His protest had alerted Beth who dropped her book and ran over to her brother. 'Who did you see, Harry? Tell me.'

He sniffed. 'Cousin Jack. She says I'm telling Banbury tales, and I'm not.'

Charlotte had heard this exchange. She rolled over and pushed herself upright. It was not Harry's fault. She should have told them the truth. 'Harry, darling, you could not have seen Cousin Jack, for he is dead. He was killed last night by the intruders.' Her face was haggard, her voice cracked from crying.

Harry shook his head. 'No, Lottie, I promise he's not dead and in

Heaven like Mama and Papa. I saw him on a different horse, a big grey one like Captain Forsythe rides.'

Annie rarely got angry with her charge, but this time she did. She was about to snatch him up and take him away for his spanking when the bedchamber door flew open. Harry screamed in delight.

'I told you, I told you! Cousin Jack, you're not dead at all!' He threw himself across the room and Jack scooped him up, swinging him round as he kissed his upturned face.

'No, young man, I am here. It has all been a horrible misunderstanding.' He bent down and included Beth in his embrace. 'Little one, I am so glad to see you, you will never know just how glad.'

Annie, tears streaming down her face, was unable to do more than nod and curtsy simultaneously.

Jack's gaze was fixed on Charlotte, staring at her in a way that only she could understand. He had worn the very same expression ever since he realized the woman he loved more than life itself was still alive. Without tearing his eyes from her he spoke to the nursemaid.

'Take the children somewhere, anywhere. I need to be alone with Lottie.'

Annie bundled them out of the room, but neither of them was aware of their leaving.

'I thought they killed you, I heard them say they had done so. Then the fire. I knew you could not have escaped from that.'

He flung himself on to the bed, tears streaming down his cheeks, and pulled her, unresisting, into his arms. 'Sweetheart, Lottie, my little love, when I thought you trapped in the fire I wanted to throw myself in, to die with you there. Darling girl, I should have told you last night how much I love you. I cannot believe I have been given a second chance and can tell you now.'

He was punctuating his words with kisses of such sweetness, such tenderness, she was incandescent with happiness. 'I love you, my darling, I love you. You are my life. I am going to make you the best husband any woman could have.'

'And I love you; I have longed to be able to tell you and thought I never could.'

Many kisses later he sat back. 'We have no home and not sufficient money to rebuild, but we have each other; we shall manage somehow.'

'I do not care about possessions. I have lived in small rented houses most of my life and will be content to do so now, as long as you and the children are in there with me.' She frowned. 'Do you realize you have nothing to change into and I have no clothes of any sort? I am dreading the imminent arrival of Mrs Baker's bombazine gown.'

'I shall have to go into Ipswich and purchase what we need, but before we talk of clothes there are other things I need to tell you.'

He omitted the details of the death of the riflemen and she was content just knowing that they were dead. But when he explained who was behind the past four weeks of terror she was as shocked as he.

'Your lawyers? I can hardly believe it. To wish to kill us for a few thousand pounds! Why did they not just flee with what they had stolen? It makes no sense. It is quite extraordinary.'

'It is; by now they will be in jail and their property forfeit. My new lawyers will be applying to search their premises and with luck we shall recover the value of the silver and paintings they stole. It will not be enough to rebuild Thurston Hall; however, I think there is a small property near Diss. We can move there, and take as many of the staff as we can with us.'

'I have just thought.' She struggled to remove herself from his embrace. 'I have nothing to wear and it is only four days until we are married.'

Reluctantly he rolled off the bed; he knew what women were like when it came to clothes. 'I shall see if I can have a bath and borrow some of Andrews's clothes and then I must ride back into town and organize the replacement of essentials. If I take Annie and the children they can help me choose.' He stopped. 'Why are you laughing, Lottie?'

'You cannot wear Dr Andrews's clothes, my love. He is half your size.'

He grinned. 'Well, perhaps not, but I refuse to wear these any longer. They stink of smoke and are beyond repair.'

Charlotte rather thought some of the darker stains might be blood, but did not wish to enquire too closely. 'My goodness, what about

Buttons and the kittens? Did the stable burn?'

'No, thank God. The roof was a little damaged from flying cinders but nothing that can't be patched. Which reminds me, I stole Captain Forsythe's horse. I must return it and collect the gig.' He walked over to the window. 'There is a closed carriage coming up the drive, followed by Captain Forsythe and his troops. I hope they have not come to arrest me for a horse thief!' He heard her laughing and then cry out in pain. He spun round and his face paled as he saw the bandages on her ankles and feet.

'What have you done, my darling? I had no idea you had been injured.' Forgetting the visitors he rushed to her side. 'Tell me, Lottie, are you badly burnt?'

'Doctor Andrews says my ankles might be scarred, but the burns are not too deep. My skirt caught fire.' She hesitated, not sure if she should tell him, then decided it was something he had to know. 'I was trying to walk into the house, to join you there.' The shocking words struck a chord with him.

'Thank God you did not do so. What stopped you? For me, it was my determination for revenge.'

'Doctor Andrews stopped me, but he had to knock me unconscious to do so. Then Robert, Mary, and he put out the flames with their bare hands. They were so brave; we owe them so much.'

Jack felt sick. To think they had both so nearly thrown their lives away needlessly. He thanked God for his intervention, for he knew what had happened was nothing short of miraculous.

A loud knock on the door startled them both. He chuckled. 'I expect they do not wish to find us occupied in unseemly behaviour and are giving us due warning.' He helped her settle back under the covers before answering.

'Enter.'

The door opened and Renshaw hovered at the door. 'My lord, if you could spare a few minutes, Captain Forsythe and your legal man are downstairs and wish to speak with you. Both say it is on matters of utmost urgency.'

'Thank you, I shall be down directly.'

'Come straight back and tell me what they wanted.'

'I shall, darling. But only when I have had a bath.'

'You may have it here. I shall organize it in your absence.' He did not reply, but blew her a kiss as he shot out of the door. Charlotte reached out and rang the small brass bell. Rose appeared from the dressing-room.

'I should like something to eat. I do not care what it is. And could you have a bath prepared? Lord Thurston requires one when he returns.'

Rose almost choked with shock. 'Yes, Miss Carstairs. But I believe that—'

'Rose, Lord Thurston and I are to be wed in four days' time. Until an hour ago we thought each other dead. I am afraid this household will just have to accept our outrageous behaviour.'

The girl smiled. 'Of course, miss, but the notion did give me quite a turn. You're as good as wed anyway and it's no one's business but your own.'

'Exactly!'

Charlotte wished she could share a bath with him, but her burns were to be kept clean and dry, at least until the blisters healed. But even the thought of doing so sent her pulse racing. The maid had returned with a tray. Lottie had spoken to the children and the bath was ready, before she heard the footsteps she was waiting for.

'Jack, you have been so long. What is it? You look so odd. It is not more bad news, I hope.'

He carefully closed the door. 'No, my love, it is quite the reverse. It appears that your grandfather's fleet did not go down in the tropics. They berthed safely. The lawyers stole, not thousands, but millions of pounds. We are wealthy, sweetheart. Now we can rebuild Thurston Hall. You can have a new gown for every day of the week, if that is what you want.'

She smiled. 'I want only one thing, my love, for you to join me here, in bed.' He returned to the door and turned the key. His bath was stone cold by the time he finally stepped into it.